Sonata

Cassandra Frew

I0597975

This is dedicated to my family. My parents Barbara, and Roy (who we sadly lost in 2012), my brother Andrew, and my nephew, Lachlan. A supportive family, just like the Standish's - our blood is our bond. And, as always, my late husband Chris. Without your love and support, this series of books would never have eventuated.

Commenced 7 April 2010

Completed 1 June 2010

 ISBN: *978-0-6488635-8-8*

TABLE OF CONTENTS

PREFACE

I WAS AT the dining room table, going over some finances and trying to finalise some decisions when Elijah came through the door. A now five year old Mercy ran and flung herself at him, narrowly missing his groin by a few precious inches. "Hi Daddy!"

"Whoa, slow down Honey," he laughed, and swung her into his arms, planting kisses over her cheeks and forehead, making her giggle. I watched their little interaction with a smile, so glad that she had such a wonderful man as a surrogate father, nearly as good as the real thing.

One decision I'd been stewing over was did I go back to work? Now that Mercy would be at 'big' school, there was no reason not to; I would work the same hours she was in class. However, Lorien had made a lot of money with his music compositions before his death, which had set us up financially, so I didn't really *need* to work. The school was waiting on me though, to extend my leave without pay, or resign.

Mum picked up Mercy whilst Elijah was in the shower, and now we were going to be alone, I intended to broach the other subject I had been putting off. It was time we were out on our own and let Elijah have his life back. He hadn't really dated, let alone had a girlfriend since Lorien died. Between Mercy, work and me he didn't have time. I did not intend to move far away. If I were to return to Sommersett High School as the Music teacher, it would be ludicrous to move from the town, and I would never dream of taking Mercy from Elijah or him from her. I was happy to have Elijah buy us out of our share of the house or to keep it as a future investment. Whatever he wanted would be fine with me.

SUMMER

Christmas

"WHY ASH? Why do you want to move out?" Elijah asked, flumping down at the dining room table opposite me, the two beers he'd grabbed from the fridge sitting in front of us unopened. I hadn't raised this subject with the clarity I had hoped and should have spent a little time building my case rhetorically before opening the floodgates. "Jesus Ash, where is this even coming from?" He ran his fingers through his wet hair in apparent frustration. It was a little longer than he had ever worn it, as was the goatee he now sported.

"It's not for any specific reason Elijah, I've just been going through some finances, working out whether to go back to work now Merce will be starting school in January... Wondering where the next step in life is going to take me..."

"What's wrong with where you are right now? Aren't you happy here Babe?"

"Very happy Honey, but we can't all live here as we are forever, can we?"

"Why not? It's working well for us at the moment. If it's a question of money...?"

"No Elijah, it's not about money. I need to decide what I want to do about work. My leave without pay runs out at the beginning of the new school year and I have to make a decision."

"Do you want to go back to work?"

"I think so. It's been eighteen months and I'm ready to face the world again. It was a much-needed break at the time to let me get my head around things and to raise our girl." He smiled when I referred to Mercy as 'our girl'. He knew this was a fact and he was the only thing she knew as a father now. Regardless of what my future brought to the table, Elijah would always be Mercy's father, along with any step that may evolve.

"So, go back to work. It's right across the road from here, why would you want to move?"

"It comes down to you, Elijah."

"Me?" he asked, frowning a little.

"Yes you. We've captured your life, without your consent even, and for the past eighteen months. It's time you had your own space. We can't expect you to always be here for us."

"But it's where I want to be Ash. I want to look after you and Mercy. You're my only family with Mum and Dad being so far away. I wouldn't feel complete without you here with me."

"Don't you get lonely?"

"Don't you?"

"I asked you first," I said and smiled.

"I deal with it when there's a need."

"On a physical level…?"

"That's all I have time for –," I cut him off.

"Exactly, if you had the place to yourself, you'd have more time to chase women." He laughed.

"I'm nearing thirty Ash, 'chasing women' as you so eloquently put it is a little behind me. Anyway, the only two women I want to chase are living right here in this house." He grinned at me, thinking his point so entertaining.

"*Romancing* women then, and you won't be thirty for another twenty-six months." He went to say something but stopped. Maybe he was finally seeing my point.

"Ash, it's Christmas Eve. Can't we talk about this in a few days? I'd like to have a little joy tonight with my two girls and leave the normality alone for the holidays."

"That's not going to happen," I said. "Mercy is already at Mum and Dad's. They're waiting on you getting out of the shower so I can let them know if we'll be there tonight or in the morning."

"What do you want to do?"

"I'm happy to go tomorrow if that's OK with you."

"That's OK with me," he said, knocking the lid off a beer and handing it to me. "Here's to a night off." He opened his own and clinked the bottle against mine, smiling widely before he drank from it. His dimpled smile was hard to resist, and I smiled back, letting this go for the moment, for a few days. It would still need to be discussed when the festive season was over. "What are we doing New Years?"

"We're still on for Michael's unless you have other plans."

"Nope, sounds great."

"Mercy can't wait to get to Uncle Michael's, the pool calls to her she said." Elijah laughed.

"What a little drama queen."

"She gets that from her Uncle Michael, not to mention her father."

"Yes, he was rather dramatic at times. I miss him so much. He's never far from my thoughts."

"Tell me about it," I said and smiled weakly.

He got up and came around to my side of the table, and I stood so he could hug me. Without each other, I don't know how we would have made it through to the other side of our grief. I had lost my beloved husband and he, his twin, someone who was joined to us eternally in such different ways. Learning to live with grief was harder than the actual loss, I think. Knowing for the rest of your life that you'll never see them again can make it a long life, a half-life.

And Lorien's parting thoughts... If only it was possible, my Darling. Even on his deathbed, with his brother by his side, he was thinking so selflessly of me. I still wished I had a chance to say goodbye, but he knew how much I loved him. We were truly soul mates, not needing anyone or anything until the love of our daughter came along to prove otherwise. "Babe?" he said, drawing back to look at me. "Are you OK?"

"Yes Honey, I'm fine," I answered, then added, "You're still wet though." I moved away, looking down at his near-nakedness, concealed only by the towel swathed around his hips. He had not dressed since his shower. He simply smiled at me as his response, and I returned it.

"Let's go out for dinner tonight," was his eventual reply.

"It's Christmas Eve Elijah, nothing will be open."

"The Chinese restaurant might be. Let me ring and find out." It turned out he was right.

The restaurant was empty; it was a great idea to come here, we had the place to ourselves. The wait-staff were attentive, and our meals came quickly. We also took our time eating; we were in no rush. A few people came and went getting take-away, which I found a little weird.

Why weren't they with their families? "Not everyone has a family Ash, and even those who do aren't always with them, like us." He smiled at me and called for another bottle of wine. I was feeling a little tipsy. "That's another reason I don't want you to move out. I don't want to be a lonely old bachelor on Christmas Eve or any other day of the year."

"Elijah, they'll be forming a line for you."

"Is that right? And where exactly is that line Babe?" He looked around, noting no females climbing over the top of each other to get to him.

"When there isn't a five and twenty-eight year old hanging around..."

"Ash, please, I really want you to reconsider this, especially if you *are* only doing it for me. It would be to my detriment, not my benefit, if that's how you *are* contemplating this."

Maybe he was right. I certainly didn't need to be thinking about this immediately; perhaps I'd let fate work its magic for a while longer. It had done quite well on our behalves so far, with exception of taking my Lorien from us all.

He knew he had me, prompting even further, "It can be my Christmas present..."

"I've already bought you one."

"Can I have it when we get home?" I laughed.

"You're a man-child Elijah."

"Is it a grown-up present then?"

"Yes, one in particular is very much so."

"Excellent," he said and rubbed his hands together, eyeing me bawdily. I shook my head and smiled at him.

"You'll like your gifts this year. Bump and I put a lot of thought into them."

"Can I have them when we get home?"

"You've already asked that."

"But you didn't answer me."

"Well, there's one I should give to you privately, it's not one Mercy should see." He tilted his head to the side and raised his eyebrows. "I'm not giving you any hints; you'll have to wait until we get home." He smiled and as the waiter brought the fortune cookies, Elijah asked for the bill.

He handed me a cookie and broke his open. "There'd better not be any allusions to arse licking," I said, reminding him of the cookies Lorien and I had bought from the sex shop many years ago.

"I washed it extra specially Babe!" I clipped him across the shoulder, and he grimaced, rubbing at the spot enthusiastically.

"Give me a break. That would have been like a mozzie bite."

"With big teeth," he grinned, with his big teeth.

We fell silent as we read. "A secret admirer will soon send you a sign of affection. Hmmm, that could mean anything, and where the hell are they? What's yours say?" he asked.

"Love is like wildflowers; it is often found in the most unlikely places." I pulled a face at him, saying, "Like the clover in our backyard."

"Are you having a shot at me about mowing Babe?"

"Of course not Elijah, but when I found Mercy out there yesterday in her great white hunter helmet wrassling with an ornery grizzly, I got a little scared."

"You are one funny lady Ash." I laughed and crumpled my fortune and threw it onto the table, which Elijah picked up and slipped into his pocket with his own.

He was at me the moment we walked in the door. "Present time!"

"You're only getting one tonight, Mercy will want to see you open the others tomorrow."

"OK, I can live with one. Do you want one tonight too?" he asked mischievously.

"That depends on what you're talking about." I said and laughed.

We had such an easy relationship with each other, flirtatious at times, which was to be expected, as we didn't socialise with too many other adults of the opposite sex, other than our friends. We were best friends and very comfortable, which is why I'd bought him what I had.

It was a sexy nurse's uniform, something I thought he could get his next conquest to model for him. It was a tight, white cotton, zip down dress, the wide lapels ending under the bust leaving lots of room for cleavage, with a built-in red belt and Red Cross badges on the two small front pockets. It was very short, just below the thigh and a cheeky pair of red suspenders hung from it, attaching to a set of white stockings with a Red Cross trim. It also had a matching nurse's cap, a stethoscope and a name badge – 'Nurse Naughty'. He would love it. "Ash, you're still standing there empty-handed girl, go get it!"

I handed it to him, and he handed me mine. "You first," he said, and I tore off the wrapping, not believing what was contained within it.

"Elijah, what have you done?"

"That's from me. You get the ones from Mercy and me tomorrow."

"Oh Honey! I love it!" I went to him and hugged him fiercely, turning so he could do the clasp up for me. "This must have cost you a fortune!" I ran into the bathroom for a closer look. The diamonds and rubies shone in the light like a thousand stars, twinkling and bursting into flame.

"You like it?" he asked, cuddling into me from behind.

"I've never owned anything like it, thank you so much."

It was true; I had never owned anything like it. Lorien had bought me jewellery before, a lot of it, but nothing as ornate as this. The choker necklace was a twisted rope of diamonds, inset with a dozen equally spaced rubies, each one the size of my little fingernail. This *must* have cost him a fortune, assuming it was real. I had no reason to believe it wasn't, the Standish's were nothing if not extravagant. As if reading my mind as I fingered the strand, he said, "It's real and it's insured so you can wear it outside the house too. Not much point in having it if you're too afraid to wear it."

"I don't know what to say Elijah. It's just so... beautiful."

"I know what you can say," he said.

"What?"

"Here's *your* present Eli." I laughed and he smacked me lightly on the bum to get me moving back out into the lounge room. I couldn't keep my hands away from my throat. "Want some more wine Babe?"

"Sure," I muttered, still a little befuddled over my elaborate gift. He smiled at me warmly as he handed me a glass and my return smile reflected my happiness. We were having a wonderful Christmas Eve. "Your turn," I said and passed him the gaily wrapped gift. A big part of Christmas for me was plenty of ribbons and bows on brightly coloured paper. Mum and Dad had always been a little remiss when it came to wrapping Christmas presents in comparison to what you saw on Yule-themed TV shows and movies. I wanted all the gifts I gave out to be reminiscent of a Hollywood Christmas.

Elijah watched me as he removed the wrappings, a slight look of confusion on his face when presented with what lay inside. The confusion turned into an open-mouthed gape as he pulled the dress and accessories from the package. "I've been a good boy this year Santa, yes I have!" He flicked the dress out over the table and ran his hand across it slowly, then looked up at me, grinning. "Put it on," he said and threw it to me, "and these..." He tossed the rest of the ensemble in front of me.

"You put it on," I said laughing, pushing the pile back toward him.

"It won't fit, and didn't you buy it *for* me?"

"Yes, but it was never my intention to wear it. It's for your next lover." He looked at me thoughtfully for a moment then his face dropped. "What?"

"You're taking Christmas away from me Babe, it's not fair that I don't get to see it on someone," he said lightly.

"You can play that card all you want Doctor Standish, there is no *way* I'm wearing that outfit."

"Scrooge."

"Taunting me won't change anything."

"Are you my secret admirer?" he asked, sidling over to me.

"Not that I'm aware of."

"The fortune cookies don't lie." He picked up my foot and started to thread the nylon over my toes and up my calf slowly, his eyes glinting devilishly, not leaving my gaze.

"Elijah…"

"Babe…" he retorted. "Come on Ash, please?" I almost relented… almost. Then I realised he was teasing.

"No, you're making fun."

"I'm not."

"You are! And I'm going to bed. It's going to be a long day tomorrow." He smiled ruefully, letting it go.

I woke at 7.30 am and Elijah was standing in the doorway, smiling down at me. "I was just about to wake you. Merry Christmas Ash."

"Merry Christmas Elijah, thanks," I said, taking the mug from him. I squidged over as he sat on the bed.

"You slept in it," he said and laughed. Was he talking about my pyjamas? "The necklace," he added when he caught my baffled expression.

"Oh, I forgot I had it on." He leant forward and lightly ran his fingers across the strand. "It's so beautiful Elijah, thanks again."

"It looks beautiful on you Babe," he said, "and I know how you can thank me."

"How?" I asked playfully.

"By getting out of bed. Come on Ash, Bump will be driving your folks crazy by now." She would, no doubt.

She met us at the door when we arrived, flinging her arms around me, and then wanting to be picked up by Elijah. "Merry Christmas Mum and Dad," she exclaimed, and Elijah brought her closer to me so she could hug us both.

"Did Santa come?" I asked and she nodded excitedly. I was hoping we'd get another year of 'Santa' before the bubble popped for her.

I knew once she was at school it was only a matter of time before the playground whispers put an end to that myth. My best friend Christine had told me at the age of seven that the Easter Bunny and Santa were our parents, although the tooth fairy was real. Kids!

We got the formalities of Christmas hugs and kisses out of the way before Mercy was tugging at my hand, taking us over to the Christmas tree to start on the unwrapping. It had always been Dad's job to hand out the gifts, but this year he allowed the pleasure to be taken on by his granddaughter. I assumed she had memorised the lay of each present last night, handing them out with the skill and speed of a blackjack dealer. We all soon had a pile in front of us.

Mercy and Elijah had bought me the matching ring and earrings for my necklace, and I looked at Elijah and smiled. He winked back and I put them on. I also had a range of scented bath accessories, a gorgeous satin floor length nightgown in light blue with a matching chiffon robe, and my favourite Lindt - dark chocolate and orange. The final present held the new Stephen King book from Mum and Dad. I still liked a hard copy.

I smiled at our girl as she wrenched the Patrick from Spongebob Squarepants slippers onto her feet and she shuffled over to me to help her put on her 'Mercy' necklace. "It's not as nice as yours Mum," she said and checked out what was circling my neck.

"I think it is Sweetie," I said.

"Did Daddy give that to you?"

"Yes, and you and Daddy gave me these," I said and showed her the ring and earrings.

"You look very pretty."

"Thank you Merce." With that, she schlepped her way back to her mound of gifts including a beading kit, skates, a jewellery box, a Trendy doll - I swear she had the entire Trendy family now, and an e-learning system. She also had a pile of books, clothes, colouring pencils and crayons to add to her collection.

Elijah had been quiet for some time and I went over to him, sitting on the sofa. "Do you like them Honey?"

"They're wonderful Ash." He was currently admiring the cufflinks we'd bought him, complete with the Wand of Hermes medical insignia.

"You're hard to buy for, being the only doctor who doesn't play golf." He laughed and picked up the antique medical instrument replicas.

"I know what these would have cost, you shouldn't have, Ash."

"You're worth every cent." I leant over and kissed him lightly on the cheek.

"What's your favourite Daddy?" Mercy asked.

"It would have to be this one Pumpkin," he told her and held up the doctor caricature of himself. We'd also bought him a game for his Sony game system, some new undies and socks, and a box of Quality Street chocolates – his favourite.

"Can you help her get some of this stuff out of the boxes, I'm going to give Mum a hand."

Mum eyed off my new jewellery when I approached her in the kitchen, and I smiled at her like a loon. "You've been good this year Ashlyn."

"Very good, I'd say," Dad interjected.

"Yes, I have," I said and smiled at them. "Has she found the trampoline yet?"

"No, we didn't let her out the back yesterday," Mum said, and then to Mercy, "Come with me and Grandpa, we have one more present for you in the backyard." She leapt to her feet, thrusting the instruction manual for the e-learning system at Elijah before trotting out the door behind Mum and Dad.

"Need any help?" he asked, joining me in the kitchen.

"You can drink this," I said and passed him a coffee. He put it on the bench and hugged me to him.

"So, you like your gifts?"

"Love them," I said and smiled up at him.

"Are you going to put on your new nightgown for me?"

"Maybe later stud," I laughed and hugged him again. "Are you going to model yours for us?"

"Maybe later stud," he answered. I'd bought him some sexy undies this year as well as his much-loved Calvins. One pair he would look very hot in were a pair of sheer low-rise camo shorts and another being a zebra print G-String. "Got a preference?"

"These," I said, handing him the black fishnet shorts. He pulled them over my head and kissed me on the forehead, letting me go only when Dad came through the door.

"Lovely hat Ashlyn," Dad grinned at me. "Mercy wants you both to come and watch her."

The rest of Christmas day went past as Christmas days do. We all ate too much, drank too much and complained about eating and drinking too much. Dad and Elijah fell asleep in front of the TV after lunch, a well-practiced tradition in the Mercy and Standish households, and I joined Mum in the kitchen to start the clean-up. "Don't make too much noise Mercy or you'll wake Daddy and Grandpa," I warned as I left the lounge room.

"I won't Mum," she promised in her best 'I've been a good girl all year waiting on Santa, I think I can hold it in for another day' voice.

I rinsed all the plates, glasses and cutlery before putting them in the dishwasher as Mum started on the pots in the sink, and me. "How much longer is this 'Daddy' phase going to last Ashlyn?"

"Forever I suppose Mum," I replied, a little acidly. Mum and Dad loved Elijah and I couldn't see why it was now such a big problem.

"Do you think it's good for her?"

"Do you think she'd be better off being completely fatherless? Elijah and Mercy love each other like father and daughter, and I see no harm in letting this continue."

"What about when you settle down again one day; find another man to live the rest of your life with? How do you think he'll react to all this?"

"That, I can't predict. However, I assume any man I choose to spend the rest of my life with will understand our little arrangement. I don't think it has a negative impact on her Mum, I think it's quite the opposite."

"And what about Elijah."

"What about Elijah?"

"How does he feel about all this?"

"He's taking it one day at a time, the same as me."

"Do you see a future with him Ashlyn? I mean a relationship, not just living together as 'mates' for the rest of your lives."

"It's not like that Mum," I tsked.

"Are you sure about that? It's a pretty expensive jewellery set he gave you today. My guess would be upward of the forty thousand mark." I gulped. I had no idea what the cost would have been. That certainly *was* a lot of money. Mum stopped her scrubbing and set the pot down, taking note of my lengthy silence.

"I'm pretty sure about it Mum. Don't you think he would have said something by now if it was an issue?"

"No, I don't. He's a man and they just don't do things the way we women do. He could be in love with you for the rest of his life and never tell you. I can't imagine your background with him would make it easy to admit Ashlyn."

"Well then, there's not much I can do about it, is there?"

"I just don't think it's healthy for him either."

"How about you let us worry about that? Relax Mum, everything's fine."

"Do you still miss Lorien?"

"I will miss him until the day *I* die Mum. He was my soul mate." She smiled at me and nodded sadly. They missed him too.

"I just don't want you trying to replace him with Elijah."

"That won't happen Mum. I wouldn't do it to Lorien *or* Elijah. Stop worrying, everything's OK." She nodded and resumed work on the pot. It was sweet that she had my best interests at heart, I couldn't be upset with her for that, but it didn't mean she had permission to air my personal life as she so willed. At least it was only to me.

I glanced into the lounge room; the two men were still asleep. Mercy had one eye on the TV and the other on her Trendy doll, working the clothing off. My little family was at peace.

No one really wanted dinner that night, still full from the lunch feast. Regardless, Mum and I made sandwiches out of the leftover ham and turkey, adding a little cranberry sauce, a dab of hot mustard, a roll of Quickeze... Out of habit, we all sat at the table and each managed to pick our way through one sandwich at least.

At 8.00 pm, just as the sun was setting, I went out the back and hunted Mercy from the trampoline. "Time for a bath Bump."

"Aw Mum!"

"Come on Merce, you've been on that thing nearly all day. It'll still be there tomorrow." She sighed dramatically and climbed off.

"Where am I sleeping tonight?"

"In your usual room."

"Where are you sleeping tonight?"

"In with you."

"Why aren't you sleeping in the spare room with Daddy?"

"Daddy and I don't share a bed at home, why would we share one here?" Her question threw me a little.

"Because I want the bed to myself."

"Well too bad Mercy, you can sleep with me, or with Daddy, but it's one or the other." I gave her bum a little pat and got her moving into the house.

I woke with Mercy lying across the bed horizontally, her feet digging into my thighs. I tried to manoeuvre her around into a better position, but she was having none of that. I glanced at the clock - it was only 12.15 am, way too early for me to get up. I crept into the spare room.

Elijah was lying star-fished across the bed on his back, and I pondered how to move him over to make room for me. I took his hand lightly, to drape it over his chest and he sat up with a start. "Shit!" we both said.

"Ash? Christ girl, you know how to scare a guy."

"Sorry Honey, I didn't want to wake you. I was just trying to move you over. Mercy has ransacked my sleeping quarters."

"Little bed hog, hey?" he asked, and slid over to let me into the bed.

"She gets that from you apparently." He laughed and rolled onto his side to face me.

"Sexy nightgown Babe." He grinned at me lewdly.

"It feels great, so soft..." He ran his hand over my thigh briefly, agreeing with me. "Do you have yours on?"

"I sleep in the buff." My eyes grew wide, not sure whether he was having a go at me or not. He took my hand and lowered it slowly. What the hell was going on? When my fingers touched the netting on his thigh, I realised he'd been teasing, and I clipped his shoulder playfully. "The look on your face was worth it Ash," he said and laughed quietly. We were silent for several minutes before Elijah wished me a goodnight and rolled onto his other side.

"Good night Elijah," I answered and rolled away from him.

I woke with him nestled into me, I on my back and him laying over me. The warmth of his waist baked into my hand, its smoothness and texture a caress of soft silk. He had me captured. One leg was thrown across me and his free arm draped over my stomach, his cheek nestled into the sweet spot near my ear. I desperately needed to pee. "Elijah," I whispered, trying to ease out from under him. The deep breathing became a murmured groan. "Elijah..." I tried again. He strengthened his grip on me and his hand sidled up to run lightly over my breast. A small chuckle and then a sigh could be heard. I counted to three and yanked myself out from under him. He mumbled something and moved his head to face the other way, sinking back into the bed on his stomach.

He still had a sexy and hard body. I eyed the black fishnet shorts, working my view up and over his back, then down his thighs. He had a magnificent bum. My stomach rolled lazily, and I backed out of the room, feeling guilty.

Mercy had formed herself into a ball by this stage, so I re-joined her in our bed once I had used the bathroom. I was back asleep almost immediately.

Realisation

THE DAY AFTER BOXING DAY, Elijah went for a run and Mercy and I sat on the back verandah, working with her beading kit. "I'm going to make you a mat for when your pots are hot and you want to put them on the table Mum," she told me.

"That would be lovely, Merce," I said and took the instructions from her briefly, not believing these beads would be heat resistant. Surprisingly, a particular set of them were for this very purpose. Mother's all over Australia would no doubt be receiving a beautiful pot mat of their own, post-Christmas.

I was helping her separate the beads when Elijah came running through the back yard. "That was quick," I said and went to get his water bottle as he bent and laid his hands over his knees, re-catching his breath.

"It's too hot," he said, and I smiled before going into the kitchen. I could have told him that.

He was sitting listening to Mercy chatter and I handed him the bottle. He skulled most of it before pulling off his tank, pouring the remainder over his head. "Daddy! You're wetting me!" she cried.

"Sorry Pumpkin," he laughed and shook his head at her like a dog, flicking more water at her.

"Daddy!" she admonished and moved herself and the precious beads further away from him. He smiled at me and I laughed.

"Are you going to have a shower?" I asked.

"No, I'm going to mow the lawn whilst I'm all sweaty, I can take a hint." I thought back to our conversation on Christmas Eve and smiled, happy that he *could* take a hint.

"Are you OK with the pattern Bump?" I asked.

"Yep." She was already threading the beads onto the metal twine. The pattern was a complicated one, but she seemed confident, and I was sure she would be able to follow it without too much trouble. Our girl was a craft lover and had completed many varying projects over the years. I went inside to get my new novel.

Absorbed in the world of Mister King's latest horror tale, I was drawn from its pages by a few softly muttered choice phrases. "Problem?" I asked Elijah, setting the book on my knee.

"Damn thing won't start." He said and proceeded to check it out.

I had never been much of a perve in my youth with exception to taking in the sultry lines of the man I was involved with, namely Lorien. However, I found my eyes raking over Elijah. He'd always had a gorgeous frame, not as lithe as Lorien, but captivating and sexy under his own merit. Where Lorien was hairless, Elijah was not and the sweat on his body trickled through the hair on his chest, pooling just above his navel.

He turned slightly and I was now faced with his broad back, brown and hard. The muscles in his arms and upper back bunched and worked in an enticing dance as he grappled with the lawn mower. My eyes were drawn lower to his narrow waist and hips, and finally the firmness of his perfectly rounded glutes.

His shorts had the high splits at the sides to allow better movement when running and I could see where his muscular thigh met with his bum. I wondered how it would feel to run my finger across the lineage. I shook myself and came out of the trance, feeling a little shameful. This was my brother-in-law for God's sake. Since I had been with Lorien, I'd not once ever been attracted to Elijah; solely encompassed by his twin was I. I always appreciated Elijah's good looks and strong body though, but it was like living with any other person. He was no one I'd even had second thoughts about.

I was having them now however... My eyes kept returning to him unbidden. *Oh, what the hell*, I accepted, and allowed myself the pleasure of the sight before me. Not many girls would have this delightful eye candy opportunity, and I feasted on him. Whew, it certainly was getting hot out here.

Our relationship, especially since Lorien died, was always close. We would cuddle and kiss each other, not on the lips, but cheeks and foreheads were more than acceptable. It had always made me feel loved and special, not alone in the world after all. I assumed he got the same reflection from our actions too. But neither of us had ever taken it for more than what it was - playful banter.

I sat forward on the lounge, seeking his quality with a more refined eye. As the book slid off my lap onto the verandah, Elijah looked up at the sound. "What are you smirking at Madam?" he asked.

"Your white thighs," was the first thing that popped out. He looked down, noting where the tan line stopped. He threw me a dazzling smile and yanked the shorts down partially over his bum, showing me other patches of his white skin. He needed to stop this now or I was going to disgrace myself in front of my daughter. I blushed.

"I can always turn the peaches and cream complexion into watermelon hey Ash?" I pulled a face at him and reached for the book, going back to my reading. Within ten seconds, I was watching him again.

He tried the mower, and it started this time. He turned and gave me the thumbs up over the noise, starting in on the ever-decreasing cycle of his mowing.

I knew right then and there that my feelings for Elijah had changed in a heartbeat. My body felt flushed, and I separated my legs a little, stopping myself from pressing my thighs together as the wanton thoughts of a full-on lawn-romp passed through my head. *What was this*? I asked myself, realising I wanted this man and in the most carnal of ways. *When did this happen? Just now Ashlyn, right this very moment*. I put some reasoning skills into play, trying to work out where this had come from, why now. Was I simply horny and this mouth-watering body before me awoke my sexual appetite?

Unfortunately, there was little point. Elijah obviously had no further feelings for me since we broke up either, and I was not about to throw myself at him, ruining the relationship we had. It would be the end of it, and life as I knew it would change instantly. Christ though, he looked good enough to eat. *What the hell are you doing Ashlyn!* I chastised myself. *Enough!* I chose to ignore my sane reasoning and fell into a little daydream. It wasn't about sex though; it was a simple kiss. His arms wrapped around me, kissing me softly at first and then with more intent. It was a kiss to turn me inside out and upside down and I snapped myself out of it with a shake of my head. And just in time too, he was motioning to me, wanting some water.

I grabbed his bottle and went inside to fill it, laughing nervously at my own thoughts. They were self-destructive and dangerous, and I had to pull myself together. What had happened to me in the last fifteen minutes? Why did it have to happen at all?

I touched him lightly on the shoulder and he stopped and turned to me, taking the bottle. I let my hand fall down over him in the pretence of his motion verses mine, a simple interchange of our individual movements causing my hand to have slipped down over his back in the act. He didn't seem to notice, but I certainly did. "Are you OK?" he asked, a concerned look on his face.

"Fine! Do you want lunch when you're finished?" I called over the noise of the mower. He nodded and smiled. I was glad to have something to do inside so I couldn't watch him any longer.

I smiled a little to myself when I realised I was making his favourite – beetroot and cheese sandwiches. Not a personal favourite of mine, but Mercy loved them too. She had disappeared and I went in search of her, finding her in her room. She looked up as I entered. "Nearly ready for some lunch Bump?"

"What are we having?" she asked, all-but finished her latest project.

"Cheese and beetroot." She smiled and made a 'yummy' face at me. "Five minutes Merce."

"OK Mum."

When I got back downstairs the yard was silent; I could hear the shower running in the back bathroom. *Need a hand in there big boy? Want me to wash your back? Do you want to take me standing up in the recess? How about I get on my knees for you?* "Ash!" he called out, "I need a towel!" I grabbed one from the linen cupboard and opened the door bravely. He stood there, full frontal nudity with the water dripping from him as he turned off the taps. "Are you going to take a picture there Babe?" he asked cheekily, his hand outstretched for the towel. I threw it to him and smiled, backing out the door hastily.

Mercy was making her way down the stairs and I poured two glasses of milk and pulled a Gatorade from the fridge for Elijah. "Here Mum," she said and passed me the table protector.

"It's beautiful Honey, I love it. I think we'll keep it on the table as a decoration so it's there when we need it." She plonked it at the centre, and I put the plate of cut sandwiches on it. Elijah came into the dining room, the towel still swathed around his hips.

"Just in time hey girls?" He planted a kiss on Mercy's head, already tucking into her first half. "And my favourite Mummy, thanks," he added, planting one on me too. Great...

"Since we're all sitting here together, I want to talk about our holiday this year."

"Shoot, Mummy," Elijah interrupted.

"Without interruption please!" I chastised playfully.

"Sorry Mummy," he added, causing Mercy to giggle. Elijah joined her.

"You two..." I sighed and laughed with them.

"What did you want to go over, Ash?" Elijah eventually asked, bringing us back to my initial point.

"We're booked in for two nights and we're leaving the day after tomorrow. Has anyone started pulling out what you want to take? I don't want to be rushing around the house last thing Tuesday morning."

"Will it make you happy if I pack today Babe?" he asked.

"It will make me ecstatic Honey, thank you. And, don't forget we'll be back on New Year's Eve and pretty much going straight to Michael's. Make sure you're ready to get home, drop off and get going again."

"Ma'am, yes Ma'am!" Elijah said and saluted me, causing Mercy to splutter out her laughter again.

"OK, enough." I said and smiled. "Mercy, is there anything in particular you want to take? I'll pack for you, but you need to work out what toys you want."

"OK Mum, I'll pack today too." I smiled at our sweet girl. "Why aren't we staying longer?"

"I thought you wanted to go to Uncle Michael's for New Year?"

"I do."

"Then we can only stay two nights Merce."

"We could have left after New Year," Elijah said and I drew my eyebrows in, frowning at him. We had already spoken about this and we'd agreed on a short holiday this year. There was plenty that needed doing around the house and if we didn't tackle it these holidays, it would have to wait until Easter.

Mercy had a pile of things she wanted to take which would fill the boot and the back seat alone. "Bump, you don't need all this for three days. Can you have another go at it please?" I sat on the bed and watched her sift through the pile, separating it into a large pile and a smaller one. I feared the larger of the two was *still* what she wanted to take away.

I pulled her pyjamas, swimmers, four changes of underpants, shorts and T-shirts from her cupboard, and a set of warm clothes, just in case. Either we'd be eating at the hotel or in semi-formal restaurants at best, so there was no need for dresses and court shoes. One pair of sneakers and her sandals completed the clothing for Mercy. "Right, let's see what you've picked out to take Merce." Of course, she pointed to the large pile. Elijah came in behind me.

"Trouble?"

"Do you want to have a go?"

"Sure, my stuff's on the bed if you want to add yours and Mercy's to it. I think we'll get away with one bag this year." I smiled, glad the formalities of packing were well underway.

The dreams I wrangled with that night were for once not tragic to me when I woke. Many, many times I'd woken from previous such dreams, always about Lorien. Waking from those dreams left me feeling helpless and lost, mourning again for my lost love and lover. However, when I woke the next morning, I realised I'd dreamt about Elijah. And what a dream...

Our lovemaking had been primal, clothes-ripping and lustful. He brought me to orgasm so many times, as I did for him, but he never lost his erection, continuing to carry me away in a primitive aching of desire and need.

It was hard, for want of a better word, to meet his eye over breakfast. "Are you OK Babe?" he asked at one stage.

"I'm great, in fact if I were any better..."

"You'd be dangerous?" he laughed. He had no idea of how close to the mark he had struck. He was sitting opposite me in his silk boxers, exactly the same kind of sleepwear he had worn since I'd known him. I felt stupid, but still moved around to the head of the table so he was now positioned adjacent to me. "Are you sure you're OK Ash?" he asked again a few minutes later. All I could do was grin at him and nod. He gave me a slightly puzzled look and went back to reading the paper.

I dropped my face into one palm, arm propped up on my elbow on the table. I toyed with the remainder of my cereal and watched him through my sheaf of hair that had fallen between us. If I could still see him through it, could he see me?

I watched his muscles flex as he turned the pages and at one stage, he leant back, eyes still on the paper, and rubbed his hands over his chest and down onto his stomach. I shuddered slightly and realised he had me hypnotised. I also mentally smacked myself. *What the hell are you doing*? I chastised. *You are nearly thirty and are the mother of a five year old. Grow up Ashlyn!* I knew I'd been acting like some form of demented teenager. This did not deter me though and I smiled to myself, acknowledging the wonderful feelings I had just experienced. I welcomed them in. "Did you check on Merce when you came down?" he asked, snapping me from my reverie.

"Yes, she was still asleep, but I think I'll go and wake her. It's nearly 9.00 am." He nodded and left me to it.

We were a family of sleeper-inners and Mercy was no exception. She grumbled at me when I woke her, wanting to stay in bed for a while longer. She was on holidays, so I didn't see the harm, backing out of the room and closing the door behind me. As much as I loved our girl, life was lovely and quiet whilst she slept. There was plenty of time left in the day for roughhousing, laughter and playing. And, we were leaving tomorrow for Forster.

I found I didn't know what to do with myself and got dressed, then went in search of Elijah. He wasn't downstairs and I couldn't hear the water running so he could only be in his room. I knocked softly at his door. "Hang on one sec," he called out. "OK, come in." When he saw it was me, he smiled. "Sorry Ash, I didn't know if it was you or Merce. I was getting dressed."

"Nothing I haven't seen before," I said and laughed. He smirked and raised one eyebrow.

"What can I do for you?"

"I'm bored."

"What do you want me to do about it?" he laughed.

"Un-bore me!" I said and sat on the edge of his bed.

"Now that's a request I haven't had before. What do you feel like doing?"

"I don't know, that's why I'm bored. What are you going to do today?"

"Not much, I was thinking of getting into the gardens maybe, clean them up a little." I pulled a face. This wasn't something I wanted to do to make the day more exciting. "That doesn't take your fancy I'm guessing," he said. I knew what I wanted to do, knew what *would* take my fancy. In fact, realised I was possibly going to seek him out all the time now this understanding had sunk in, if only for a perve. It was hard to close a door when your own foot was still jammed in it, keeping it open.

We were still sitting there discussing the options for our day when Mercy trundled in, wrapped in her robe. She flumped on the bed between us, face down. I loved my little drama queen. "Are you actually awake

Bump?" I asked, smiling at Elijah. She mumbled something, but stayed on her stomach.

"I think she said she needs a good tickling," Elijah offered. She mumbled again.

"Sounds like a yes," I agreed, and we grabbed her.

"No!" she sat up screaming.

"Well, what did you say then?" Elijah asked, his fingers still working into her sides.

"That I wasn't awake yet!" she yell-laughed, not able to escape him. "Daddy! Stop!" she finally cried.

"Honey, stop, you'll make her wet herself."

"So?" he asked and smiled down at a scowling Mercy.

"Fair enough, it's your bed." He stopped.

Mercy and I decided to make some cupcakes to fill in the time. After all the ingredients were in the bowl, she lost interest. "Hey, I thought you wanted to make cupcakes?" I called to her as she headed for the stairs.

"You can do it," she said, and kept going.

"Thanks Merce," I called.

Of course once they were cooked and ready to be iced, her interest was recaptured. "What's Daddy doing upstairs?" I asked.

"He's on the computer. What are we going to put on the top Mum?"

"What do you want to put on them Bump?" She went to the cupboard and pulled the green and pink food colouring, then going back and grabbing the silver balls, hundreds and thousands and the bag of smarties. "Got enough?" I asked. She nodded, not thinking my question to be a joke.

I iced the pink ones, and she iced the green ones. Six each. We both then settled into decorating our six. I was happy to just run the frosted edges around in hundreds and thousands, but each of Mercy's were elaborate, fully decorated tops complete with smarties, silver balls and hundreds and thousands. The green icing was now merely acting as the glue to hold it all on. "Aren't you going to make yours more interesting?" she asked.

"Should I?"

"Yes," she said and handed me the silver balls. I created a small heart outline in the centre of each of my six and told her that was enough. I wanted to be able to eat some of these without getting sick from the influx of lollies. Thank God the gummy bears had been used up in our last baking session.

"Hmmm, what smells good ladies?" Elijah asked, coming down the stairs.

"Look what Mum and I made, Dad!" she called and ran over to pull him by the hand to the island bench. "Have one," she offered, and Elijah took one of mine. He was no fool either.

"Hmmm, someone made these full of love, just for me!" he said.

"And for me too," she reminded him, licking the top off one of her green ones. When it was bare, she put it down and reached for another.

"You know better than that Merce," I scolded her. "You eat the whole thing, not just the icing and lollies."

"But they're *my* cupcakes!" she whined.

"That doesn't matter, you don't waste food." She rolled her eyes at me and commenced to pull apart the soggy mess of the cupcake. Elijah smiled at me, mouthing *Meany!*

School Holidays

WE HEADED OFF at 9.30 am on Tuesday and arrived right on noon. We'd expected some bad traffic and were surprised at the breezy run we'd had. After we checked in, Mercy dressed in her swimmers and grabbed a towel. "Merce, you need to put your clothes and sandals on, we're having lunch first." She pulled a face at me but went back into the bag to retrieve the clothing. Elijah, already in the bag, passed her some clothes and then pulled his boardies out.

"Do you want these Babe?" he asked, handing me my swimmers.

"And my sarong too please." I went into the bathroom to change. My family was ready when I came out and we headed off to the local coffee shop for a quick bite.

Mercy and Elijah played in the wave-wash for most of the afternoon whilst I sat and read on the shore. She came running up to me to show off the assorted finds in her bucket from time to time, as did Elijah seek me out every now and then, but usually to shake himself off near me or tease me in some other annoying way.

At 5.30 pm I'd had enough and ordered everyone out of the water. "Fun police," Elijah said and smiled, drying himself off on a mostly saturated towel.

"You can stay here with her if you like," I told him, "but I've had enough."

"Come on Merce," he called, "time to pack up."

"Not going to do this on your own, Daddy?"

"If you've had enough, then so have I," he grinned at me.

I got Mercy into the bath when back at the hotel and I grimaced when I realised I should have had a quick shower first. There was little I could do now until she was out, and I sat uncomfortably on one of the chairs on the balcony. "Isn't a problem when you're a guy," Elijah teased, wrapping a towel around his waist and stripping off his boardies from beneath. He gave them a shake and the amount of sand that fell from them was unbelievable. He dragged the towel around in a way to wipe most of the sand off his still damp lower body; the towel remained between him and me. Unfortunately for him, he was standing with his back angled toward the glass sliding door of the balcony and I copped a face full of the back end of him. White and tight....

"Ah Honey," I said and gestured toward the door with my chin.

"Having a perve, are we?" he asked, and plonked himself down on my knee, towel draped over his lap.

"Get your bare arse off me!" I said and laughed, sliding my arm around his waist and pulling his chest to my cheek.

"You'll have to let me go first, lady." He finished this statement with a kiss to my forehead. I smiled up at him.

"Finished!" Mercy called out from the bathroom and I realised I hadn't given her any clean clothes to put on.

"Do you want to help her or shall I?" I asked Elijah.

"I'll go," he said and stood again, his back facing away from me as he reshielded himself in the towel.

We had room service sent up that night, none of us felt like going out again. After dinner, Mercy lay next to me on our double bed and Elijah flumped onto the single bed that he'd be sleeping in tonight. And then the fight started. Of course, Mercy didn't want to sleep with me in the double bed; she wanted the single all to herself. "But I want the special bed Mum!" she complained.

"You can sleep with me or Daddy, but you can't have the single bed Mercy," I explained.

"But it's just my size, like Goldilocks in Baby Bear's bed." Elijah laughed and climbed off.

"Get in Merce; I'll sleep with Mum tonight." If only that were true. Elijah simply shrugged and climbed in. "It's not like it's the first time we've shared a bed."

"The circumstances were a little different, eleven years ago," I reminded him. He chuckled and rolled onto his side away from me, his intention to make me at ease. He wasn't aware of what I'd like to have happen in this bed, or what *did* happen late Christmas night...

It was hard to get to sleep, knowing he was so close but yet so far. I had to get over this and soon. It would be nothing more than a detrimental course for me, as I could *never* tell him how I felt. If he rejected me, where would that leave all three of us? It would be a totally uncomfortable situation that couldn't be rectified, or ignored. I eventually fell into a fitful slumber.

I woke with Elijah curled in behind me, hips writhing gently and so very hard. My eyes flashed open. *Was he asleep? If he was asleep, should I wake him? If I wake him, how will he react?* My panicked thoughts didn't ease as he slowly ran his hand over my arm and down my thigh. He moved in even closer and whispered my name, nuzzling lightly at my nape with his lips, his fingers flitting under the edging of my pyjama shorts. What was I going to do?

My daughter solved the problem, taking this exact moment to dive onto the bed, hugging me. "Morning Mum!"

"Morning precious." I rolled onto my back so she could snuggle between us and I looked down at Elijah, his eyes now open, whether or not they were before. "Did she wake you?" I asked. He sat up, rubbing his hand over his face before answering,

"Ahhh, yeah..." Mercy went to clamber on top of him and Elijah stopped her immediately. "It's not time for cuddles yet Sweetie, Daddy needs to pee first, and you'll hurt me if you climb on me now."

"OK Dad," she said and burrowed back in between us. It took him a few minutes before he got out of bed to use the bathroom. He had my mind spinning and I knew my wild thoughts were now cemented. I was in love with him.

We spent an uncomfortable breakfast together in the dining room of the hotel. Elijah and I never seemed to be together for more than a few minutes at a time. We'd refill our coffee, or assist Mercy with a second helping of fruit and such. It was only at the end of the meal that the three of us sat for a period of more than five minutes. Elijah looked away from the window he'd been staring out of for most of that time and I caught his eye. Actually, his caught mine, as I'd been attempting *not* to be noticing him looking out of the window. He smiled and I smiled back.

On the waterfront, I once again left him and Mercy to their play. I just couldn't get it out of my head though - he'd been saying my name. Saying *my name*. There were no other Ashlyn's he knew, not even from a book or movie. The closest was the male lead out of 'The Evil Dead' and I doubted that he would have woken with me in his arms, calling out for that Ash. He had to be referring to me, and considering what he'd been doing at the time led me to believe that he *wanted* to do that to me. I certainly wanted him to do that to me.

I watched them over the top of my sunnies; the book in front of me could have been upside down for all I knew. Point one of my view was the beautiful interaction he had with our girl in the water. He was completely besotted with her and she with him. The love I felt for him included the relationship he had with Mercy, regardless of how the two of us could fit together. Point two was the twitch in my groin he was causing as I watched his brown, hard back flexing in the movement of swinging Mercy around and dumping her into the water. At times, his boardies would sneak down the curves of his rear, showing off the sultry lines of his plumber's crack. Not a usually an attractive thing on most men, but on this man...

They were trying something new today. Elijah had Mercy stand on his hands with her holding onto his shoulders. I didn't know what to expect when the countdown reached one, and he threw her backwards into the water headfirst. She came up spluttering and laughing. "Again Daddy!" This time she arched her back further and I could see she was attempting to do a backward somersault. I clapped loudly when she came up for air. "Did you see, Mum?" she called. I nodded my head and smiled at her and she then went back for thirds.

Elijah seemed to be his usual self again once they exited the water, both starving for their lunch. He dragged Mercy onto his lap and wrapped a towel around them both, laying back with her over his chest, catching their breath. "Did you have a sleep Ash?" he asked, his hand held at an odd angle, keeping the sun from his eyes.

"No, I read, watched the waves, watched you two clowns..." He smiled at me warmly and Mercy interjected.

"I'm not a clown Mum!"

"You are sometimes Bump," I said, and we all had a laugh. "What do you two want for lunch?"

"How about we check out the club? I hear they have a great smorgasbord."

"I'm game."

"Let's go change then," he said to Mercy and took her by the hand. She pulled back and waited on me to grab my bag, taking my other hand. I smiled at Elijah over the top of her head, which he returned.

We went through the same scenario with Mercy that evening; she wanted the single bed to herself. Maybe it wasn't such a great idea putting her into a double, straight out of the cot. Elijah and I lay as far apart as the bed would allow, which was not a great deal as Elijah was a big boy. We were watching a pay-per-view movie, Mercy sitting up in her bed, humming away and colouring, not really paying all that much attention to the drone of the TV. I didn't think that either of us were paying a great deal of attention either; we were more focussed on ensuring we kept to ourselves under the covers, not even allowing a slight pressing against each other. I knew why I was being so adamant but was unsure as to Elijah's concern. He obviously didn't want me getting the wrong idea.

Eventually, I heard him mutter, "This is ridiculous..." I looked over at him and he smiled, raising his arm and moving into the middle of the bed. "Come and have a cuddle Babe," he said, and I moved against him immediately, smiling up at him like a Cheshire cat. I was finally able to pay attention to the movie.

When Mercy fell asleep, I took the book and pencils from her hands and put them back into the toy bag. We'd be leaving after breakfast tomorrow so she wouldn't need them again. I also pulled out her clothes and found her sandals to speed up the departure. "May as well get our stuff out too Ash," Elijah said from behind me, and it did make sense. Three full sets of clothes later we decided whether to check out in the morning and head back to the beach, or just go straight home. I then remembered New Year's at Michael's. We'd be lucky to get home by 12.30 pm, maybe even later, so deemed right after breakfast to be the most suitable time for departure. That settled, we crawled back into bed. "Are you OK about this morning?" he asked, cradling me back into his arms. He didn't explain but I understood his reference.

"Of course Honey, these things happen."

"Not usually with us though Babe."

"You don't remember Christmas night?" He looked at me with a confused expression, finally answering,

"You slept in my bed but were gone when I woke."

"I won't enlighten you any further then," I said and smiled up at him.

"You can't do that to me Ash, you'll have to explain now."

"It's embarrassing."

"Was it like what happened this morning?" he asked.

"What happened this morning Elijah? Were you awake or asleep?" I wanted him to dig himself into a hole, tell me that he was conscious and that indeed his actions were made as a conscious decision.

"Not until Mercy landed on us, but I was aware that I had you in my arms and we didn't go to sleep like that."

"Well, that's pretty much how I woke up in the wee hours of Boxing Day. But you were nestled into me and I had you in my arms."

"Merry Christmas Eli," he said and laughed.

"It was more like Merry Christmas Ashlyn!' I corrected him.

"In what way?"

"You copped a pretty good feel before I managed to wrangle out from under you."

"Sorry about that Babe." He didn't look, nor sound, very sincere. I made a face at him and pulled in tighter.

"I think we should sleep like this, so it won't matter if we wake up together in the morning."

"Sounds like good advice. There's no need to be uncomfortable," he agreed.

"It's not like it won't be the *third* time it's happened either, hey?" I laughed.

"No," he said and raised his eyebrows at me. I was glad that we'd re-found our comfort level with each other. The last thing I wanted was for him to be avoiding contact with me. I sought out the contact and wanted it to be there, always...

We got to Michael's by 2.30 pm and they were just about to eat. "Don't wait for us; we ate when we got home as we didn't know what you had planned for this early in the day."

"Ever heard of ringing or texting?" Michael asked with a smile.

"Ever heard of having to deal with a five and a twenty-seven year old?" I threw back. He then got his chance to deal with that five year old as she threw herself at him and he scooped her up in his arms.

"Hiya Merce!"

"Hiya Uncle Michael," she called and laid a wet one on his cheek. "I had a dream last night..."

"And what was this dream about?"

"Your pool!"

"I thought it may have been about your *boyfriend*," he teased.

"I don't have a boyfriend!" she exclaimed, wriggling free and standing in front of him, hands defiantly on hips. "You're the one with a boyfriend!"

"Where is Glen?" I asked, pulling Mercy in front of me and leaning down to speak quietly to her. "And you don't speak to anyone like that young lady. Now you apologise to Uncle Michael." Her face fell, not having meant to be rude to him.

"I'm sorry Uncle Michael," she called and leapt back into his arms.

"It's OK Mercy, and Glen is in the pool." He delivered this last comment to me, but faced Mercy to let her know *someone* was already in the pool. She wriggled free again and went in search of him. Seconds later, there was a splash, a giggle and man's laughter.

"Come on Glen!" Michael called. "We're eating!"

"I can't get out now, Mercy wants a swim."

"Mercy, get out of the pool" I called, "Uncle Glen wants his lunch!"

"Leave them Ash, there's plenty here." I followed Michael out to the patio, Elijah behind me.

"Where's Simon and Bree?"

"They're over at her Mum and Dad's; they'll be back before dinner." He offered me the plate of steak and I shook my head. Elijah however, took one and turned it into a steak sandwich, adding onions, salad and sauce.

"Thanks mate." He sat down and took a massive bite and I smiled and rolled my eyes at him. "What?" he mumbled, mouth full.

"You're a bottomless pit." He smirked back.

When he'd finished eating, I followed Elijah into the garage to get three of the single mattresses. With Bree and Simon home tonight, we decided to sleep downstairs, all together. It offered more space than cramming into the spare room. This would make Mercy happy all over again, getting another night in a single bed. As we came back through the grounds with them on our shoulders, Michael took over for me and helped Elijah carry them into the lounge room. I sat with Glen who was getting Mercy a snack. "We've got some fun games for later," he said and laughed when he saw my expression.

"Of course you do! It wouldn't be a visit to your place without them."

"Are they ones I can play too?" Mercy asked.

"Most definitely Merce," he said and winked at me. "Some we'll leave for later though."

When Michael and Elijah came back out, I stood, about to make the beds for us. "No need Babe, they're done."

"Thanks Honey," I said and sat back down, but Elijah took my hand and pulled me into a standing position.

"Come for a swim with me."

"I didn't bring my swimmers."

"I packed them for you," he said with a wide grin. "Now go get changed."

I couldn't help but notice the bedding formation he'd created when I walked into the lounge room in search of our bag. He had a single all set up, and in the corner, two of the single mattresses had been made into one double bed. Were we going to be sleeping in the same bed from now on? It was a bittersweet sleeping arrangement for me. On one hand I got to sleep in his arms, on the other, I wanted to ravish him before falling asleep in those arms. I sighed, knowing this predicament was only going to get worse for me. I chose not to make a big deal out of the configuration though.

My careful entry into the pool via the steps was interrupted by Elijah grabbing me around the waist and dragging me in on top of him. "Why do you always have to do that?" I gasped, catching my breath.

"It's been years Babe, I thought you were due!" I raised one eyebrow at him, not agreeing. "This seems familiar," he said and smiled, and I noted I was on his hip, like so many years before.

"Planning on relieving some memories Doctor Standish?" My light suggestion was heavy with innuendo.

"I'd love to go through the midnight swim scenario again with you Ash," he winked.

"I'm sure you would." He laughed and hugged me to him, then let me go completely. That wasn't my intention from the last remark...

Bree and Simon got home around 5.00 pm and Mercy went straight to them for her hug. What Mercy didn't know was there was another Christmas present here for her from the four of them. We hadn't seen them since before Christmas day, and when Michael brought the large box downstairs, she nearly had a conniption. She was so excited when the wrapping was off, and Glen and Simon helped her set up her new Barbie Townhouse, complete with an internal elevator. This would keep her busy for a while.

I had brought one of her dolls with me but didn't need to; this was another gift they'd bought. She was settled in for the evening it seemed.

On a night like this in the past, pre-Mercy, we normally wouldn't eat dinner until around 8.00 pm, but as this was Mercy's bedtime, Michael threw the lasagne into the oven shortly after Bree and Simon got home. Bree and I joined him in the kitchen. "Got your New Year resolutions ready gals?" Michael asked. I certainly did, but had no intention of telling them what it was. This was acceptable though, as neither Bree nor Michael were keen to reveal theirs either.

"What are you doing Standish?" we heard Simon say to Elijah. All three of us dropped our salad-making utensils and peered around the corner for a closer inspection. Elijah had Barbie's clothes off and was sizing her up.

"I was just seeing if she's more anatomically correct these days."

"And is she?" Simon asked.

"Nope," Elijah said and they both laughed.

"Daddy, give me Barbie!" Mercy said and took her from his hands, taking the pink gown she had come dressed in from the floor where Elijah had left it.

"Sorry Pumpkin, I thought Barbie may have had a fever. I was just checking her out." Simon guffawed at this and told him he was in desperate need of a woman. Elijah glanced toward the kitchen, not realising we three were watching their little scene. His face went red when he saw me standing there, as if he had been terribly busted. I laughed, not realising he'd care all that much that we saw him undressing Barbie, for whatever weird reason it may have been.

After dinner, Twister was brought out of the cupboard and I passed, letting the adult children play it with Mercy. "You only get to pass on one game Ash, and this will be it for the night if you choose this one."

"I will accept that Michael, but I still warn you..." I pointed my finger at him and frowned.

"I have something special for you this evening, something we haven't played in a long time." He was currently looking at me upside down and between his own arms. He was bent over in a horseshoe, hands and feet on opposite corners of the mat. My flexible little girl had one foot in the air and her arms worked in under Uncle Michael's; between them, they nearly formed a knot. Not wanting to hurt her, people got hurt in the game of Twister when the pile eventually fell in a heap of twisted limbs, Simon, Glen and Elijah were calling encouragement from the sidelines. Bree and I opted to go out onto the patio, and grabbed our beers on the way.

"What's that look for?" she asked, and I hadn't realised I'd been grinning at her.

"Nothing specific, I'm just happy."

"Well good for you Ash," she said, knowing it had been a long time since I had any such joy. They'd all been so wonderful helping me get through the Lorien aftermath. "You have a lovely little family thing going on there hey?" I wasn't sure exactly what she was getting at, but nodded anyway.

"And when will it be your turn Bree? Are you and Simon planning on having kids?"

"One day," was her elusive and wistful answer. I didn't press her for more.

Elijah came out to get me eventually, asking if Mercy could have another swim before her bath. "You're her parent too Elijah, you don't have to ask my permission."

"I just wanted to make sure you were OK with it. It's getting pretty late." I looked at my watch. It was 7.40 pm and she *should* have had her bath already. But, it was New Year's and a later than usual night wouldn't hurt her.

"That's fine Honey, but you can get her out of the pool. That's an argument I don't want to get involved in."

"No problem," he said and led Mercy outside, already in her swimmers. I smiled and shook my head at him, and he laughed.

They swum until just after 8.00 pm and Elijah took her up the back stairs through the spare room to deposit her in the bath, coming down several minutes later with a freshly scrubbed, pyjama-wearing little imp. She made her round of good nights to us all and Michael switched the TV and DVD on, letting her select a movie to watch whilst falling asleep.

At each of our houses you would still find at least one DVD player and many DVDs. None of us considered it 'old school' and we enjoyed having the tangible movie selections we owned, and not just the 'rental' of streaming airspace. "Night Bump, I love you!" I said when she came to me last, on her round of good-night kisses. She wanted to be picked up and carried to her bed, and I blew a few raspberries on her cheek on the way through. "I'll be back in a second," I said. Elijah followed me inside.

We tucked her in and adjusted the volume on the TV, giving her a final kiss each and wishing her a Happy New Year. She snuggled down in her bed and I knew she'd be asleep in minutes. "Excellent!" Michael said and clapped his hands together when we returned to the patio.

"What?" I asked suspiciously.

"Time for the adult games."

"Which are?"

"Just for New Year, we thought we'd bring out old reliable, and you can't say no, Ashlyn!"

"No Ashlyn," I said and laughed.

"You had better be in a good mood, because we're playing Truth or Dare." We hadn't played this since we were in high school, and the last time I had to perform a rather embarrassing act on Elijah. Since they were all couples here, other than Elijah and me, I was worried instantly at what Michael had in store. Surely it wouldn't be too hideous, he knew we weren't together. Mind you, when had Michael ever let me off the hook? I waited for the worst.

"Who's first?" Michael asked.

"Not you!" I protested.

"Fine then, it can be you."

"Not me either!"

"OK, Elijah, truth or dare?" he asked.

"I meant that it wasn't your turn to pick someone."

"Ashlyn Diane Mercy Standish... it is *always* my turn to pick someone..." Yes, it usually was. "Elijah, truth or dare?" he asked again.

"Gimme a dare Michael," he taunted.

"Dare it is - you have to give Ash the frigid test." Elijah looked at him in confusion. He hadn't started at Sommersett High when 'the frigid test' was all the rage in the lower forms, but I knew what it was.

"How old are you Michael?" I asked.

"Twenty-eight and it has nothing to do with it."

"Can't you pick on Bree or Simon?"

"I'll get around to it, don't you worry." No doubt he would.

"Ahhh, I don't have a problem with it Michael, but I have no idea what it is," Elijah confessed.

"Get up Ash," Michael told me, and he proceeded to perform 'the frigid test' on me.

"You just proved that I'm not frigid," I said and sat back down.

"I believe the dare was mine?" Elijah countered. I frowned at him, and he laughed. He could have stopped this.

"Up Ash," Simon, Bree and Glen agreed. Elijah held his hand out for me, grinning from ear to ear.

"When did you become such a Michael-pawn?" I goaded.

"Since today," he answered, "now get up." He helped me to my feet, and I stood in front of him. For once, this didn't actually bother me. But, I couldn't appear *too* eager!

"Go twin!" Michael laughed and Elijah placed his open palm on my forehead. He smiled at me before starting the trek down my body.

"Space those fingers out!" Simon called as he traced his hand down between my breasts. He chuckled and opened the span of his hand, his pinkie and thumb running lightly over my nipples.

"Lower, slower, lower, slower!" They started to chant.

"Shut up or you'll wake Mercy!" I chastised them.

"*Lower, slower, lower, slower*," they now whispered, and I laughed.

Finally, I was standing there with Elijah's palm firmly cupped between my thighs. "Are you done?" I asked, unable to prevent the smile breaking onto my face.

"Yes, thanks," he said and gave a slight squeeze before letting me go.

"We don't get the fabulous blushes that we were so used to anymore Ash," Michael complained. When I looked up however, he realised how wrong his statement had been.

"My turn and I pick Michael!" I said.

"Truth," he said.

"Oh, come on! You have to be able to take it as well as give it."

"Truth," he reiterated, and I pulled a face at him.

"Fine then, is it true you fancied both Lorien *and* Elijah when they started at Sommersett?" I expected to be met with a slight hesitation to this one. I *knew* Michael thought they were both hot.

"Yes, and I still wouldn't kick this one out of bed," he finished, gesturing to Elijah. The room roared in laughter, all except Glen.

"Oh really?" he asked Michael.

"Well look at him, he's still fucking gorgeous!" We all laughed again, including Glen. I glanced at Elijah to see how he was taking it, and in true Standish form, he was taking it in his stride. He even dropped Michael a wink and he blew Elijah a kiss.

We played until Bree noticed the time - it was nearly midnight. Michael turned up the stereo in time to catch the final ten-second countdown. "Looks like I'm kissing you," Elijah said from behind me. The others were in their coupled embraces, waiting on the last second.

"Looks like it," I said and turned to face him.

"One!" they all cried, and Elijah's lips were on mine. It was a pulse-racing kiss, no tongues but still opened mouthed, and I wanted him to drag his mouth down my body, once again proving I wasn't frigid.

"Wow!" I said as the kiss ended.

"Happy New year Babe," he whispered into my ear as he drew me back against him. "Let's hope it's a year full of wonderment and surprises for us both."

"I'll drink to that," I laughed, and he kissed me again lightly. No one seemed concerned with our coupled arrangement. After all, we had to kiss *someone* at New Year.

We were all ready for bed by 1.30 am, and I knew Mercy would be the first one up. We whispered our good nights as the crowd made their way upstairs and Elijah and I climbed into bed together. "This is a rather intimate arrangement you've set up here Honey," I said, rolling onto my side to face him.

"I knew Merce wouldn't want to sleep with either of us."

"We could have had three single mattresses though."

"I never thought of that," he said and draped an arm over me. "Roll over Babe." He spooned in behind me and played his fingers lightly over my hair. "Is this OK?" he asked. It was wonderful; words could not express exactly how wonderful this was. *I think I love you Elijah,* I wanted to whisper to him, but of course, I didn't, especially since I *know* I love you, was a more accurate point. I wriggled into him as close as I could and reached down to take his hand in mine, securing him to me. It was going to be difficult going back to our own rooms on our return home tomorrow.

He Said

Journal Entry – Friday 25 December: 6.45 am

MERRY CHRISTMAS JOURNAL, we've nearly made it to the end of another year although I haven't written in you since I was at University, and for that I do apologise. Life has changed a lot me for me since I last wrote, and all things will be revealed in due course. However, you need to be aware of a few essential facts before I get to the everyday life.

Lorien died eighteen months ago, breaking not only Ashlyn's heart, but mine as well. They had a little girl, Mercy Cara-Anne who just turned five. She and her mother are the light of my life. I don't know what I would have done without them when Lori died; don't know if I could have gone on. He was hit by a car whilst crossing the road, and I know that nothing else in life will ever compare to this focal incident in my life. How could it?

It had been impossible for me when Lorien died in my arms at the hospital, something that no one could ever understand. The only thing harder had been to write the note from him to give to Ashlyn, and then read it to her. I knew what he had dictated to me. He wanted me to look after her, to love her for the rest of our lives, knowing it was something he could no longer do, and he wanted her to be happy. He thought I could provide this happiness when he was not around anymore. I wanted to give the love to her that would make Lorien happy, not that she had taken up the offer.

I struggled Journal, don't you worry, about whether to give it to Ashlyn on my return home that afternoon. It was the last thing she would be worried about, but did I carry out his last wishes or did I spare her his final request? 'Eli loves you' he'd said, and although I argued the point with him at the time, he wanted me to write exactly what he was saying. I gave her the note. And I did love her. I knew if he'd never died that what I wanted now with her would never have eventuated; I'd had my go such a long time ago... Fate was a weird mistress at times, but I would give it all back to have my twin beside me again.

I had been conscious of my reborn feelings for Ashlyn since she was pregnant, although I'd never acted on them; even after Lorien died, even on his request. I never held any hope of her wanting me in return, but was happy in my own knowledge of how I felt. Maybe one day things would change, and she would be able to think of me in that way again. I was a surrogate father to Mercy and not only Ash's best friend but also her sounding-board and she mine, when either of us needed it.

For five long years I'd managed to keep my feelings in check, but have now decided that next year was to be *the* year. I was going to see where my love for her could take me, take us. I planned to interpret her body language, putting myself out there a little more to see what reaction I got back, pushing the boundaries ever so slightly. If nothing came of it, at least I'd know I had tried. I would then give up the fight and focus more on my career, on my life without her. Not that my life would ever be without Ash and Mercy. They would always be my family, if nothing else.

I knew it was only a matter of time before some guy came along and swept Ash off her feet. Eighteen months had elapsed since Lorien passed away and I didn't expect her to stay single forever. It was unbelievable that she had for this long, but I knew how much she loved him, how much a part of each other's world they were so totally encompassed.

It was only the past six months that she'd reverted to the old Ashlyn again, finding a bounce in her step and laughter in her eyes. I took pride in having kept her going for this long, being her emotional and physical support when she needed me. I liked it when she needed me. I needed her just as much, and not only in the emotional sense. I wanted her...

I'm going to start with as recently as last night now Journal, the rest will fall into place as time goes by. They say the best laid plans of mice and men and all that, me being the mouse, me being the man; and here I was, realising what we had was all about to fall apart around me. I had taken too long, and she was now talking about moving out. As the words tumbled from her mouth I stopped, frozen, two beers in my hands just taken from the fridge. I sat with her at the dining room table, expecting the worst. However, I wasn't going to accept this without a fight. The obvious reasons first jumped to mind: was she unhappy, was it about money, work, someone else? Unbelievably it turned out to be about me. Totally out of left field.

I almost laughed when she felt guilty about kidnapping my life away from under me, leaving me without female companionship, alone, lonely... I let her know, in as much of a courteous way as possible, that I took care of those issues when the need arose. She claimed that without her and Mercy living here I would have more time to chase women. *Chase women...* Was she kidding? I was no kid anymore.

It was Christmas Eve and all I wanted to do was to enjoy the festive season. We were going to Anna and Dom's tomorrow for lunch, and it was not the time to be considering the gestation of bad news. I needed some more time to think about it, chew it over and come up with a reasonable argument to dissuade her. She seemed happy to put this conversation on hold for the time being and told me Mercy was already at her Grandparents'. They were in fact waiting to hear whether we were joining them tonight or tomorrow. I wanted it to be tomorrow. Ash was OK with this too and I finally relaxed, returning the conversation to a lighter mood.

We chatted about New Year; we were still on for Michael's, and our girl was eager to get there too it seemed - the pool called to her. She was such a little drama queen, Journal, and it made me laugh at the thought. Ashlyn made mention of this quality coming from her Uncle Michael and also from her father, my twin. We both missed him so much and she understood my loss as I did hers. She was the only person I could speak to about Lori's death, speak to openly and without barriers.

I didn't mean to upset her or to make her melancholy at a time of the year we all loved so very much. I hugged her in an honest act of affection; no underlying inferences were included when it came to soothing and caring for one another. It was always a sincere display of genuine love, being there solely for each other.

I suggested going out for dinner, which she seemed to think was ludicrous. I knew that there'd be an option if we wanted one though, and sure enough, the Chinese restaurant was open for business.

We walked, as it was so close. I was surprised to find it empty however, with exception of the occasional person coming in for take-away. When Ash commented on them not being with their families on Christmas Eve it gave me what I hoped would be the final move in our chess game.

I would have her cornered with nowhere to turn. It was only with the slightest feeling of guilt that I reminded her, this could be me in the future, if she and Mercy were to move out.

She was under the impression I would be in high demand once I was free of them. Where she got these ideas from amazed me, and I realised how *she* saw me was with a little more affection than those who didn't know me. I knew damn well there would be no queue forming for me, regardless of what she considered as my handsome looks and excellent career. The fact I didn't want anyone else but her was something I couldn't explain though.

We talked about Christmas over dinner and when I found out one gift was too adult for me to open in front of Mercy, of course I wanted it the second we got home. I couldn't wait to see it. She'd love what I'd bought for her; a ruby and diamond jewellery set which had cost nearly fifty thousand dollars in total. It consisted of a necklace, ring and earrings and I hoped she would interpret my obvious statement the right way. The rubies, although her birthstone, captured the love and warmth I had for her in my heart, and the diamonds would shine and dazzle her, as she had done to me.

When we finished our meal, I asked for the cheque, wanting to get back to our place to play a little more, banter over giving at least one gift each tonight. Whilst waiting, I passed her a fortune cookie and broke one open too. I smiled to myself at their possible psychic fortune-telling; mine being about having a secret admirer waiting in the wings and hers referring to love being where you least expected it. She crumpled hers up and threw it onto the table. I wanted to keep these prophecies, and I took it, placing it in my pocket with my own.

We flirted a little when we got home, about 'getting one each' tonight. We had an easy relationship, which allowed this kind of behaviour without it being taken the wrong way. I wished I hadn't allowed all of our kisses and cuddles and downright flirtations to become harmless, comforting fun. I wanted her to feel the heat I felt when I played such verbal games with her, wanted her to know that I spoke the truth. It was something I had to work on.

We handed over our one gift each, and I insisted she open hers first. I'd given her the necklace last night. Today she'd get the matching ring and earrings from Mercy and me. It was the right decision; she loved it. I did the clasp up for her, then wanted to run my hands down over her back and around through to her stomach, to hold her against me. The vision of then grazing one hand north and the other south was enough for me to take a step away from her, letting her turn to show it off to me. I followed her into the bathroom so she could get a better look. Under the incandescent lights, the gemstones shone in a radiant brilliance that matched her eyes and ignited the fire in my own heart.

I sat at the table after pouring some wine and she passed me my gift. Ash's wrapping of any present was always a wonderful aperitif to the bounty that lay inside. Tasteful paper, wrappings and bows were a big part of making a simple present into a gift. I kept my eyes on hers as I removed the paper, wishing it was wrapped around her instead, that *she* was my gift, a gift I would treasure for eternity.

She'd bought me a sexy nurse's uniform, obviously not in my size, and I didn't understand why she'd bought it at all. It gave me hope though that maybe she was thinking about me in the way I wanted her to. Had she bought it to wear for me? No, apparently not, because she turned down my request, telling me it was for my next conquest. I caught her eye, wanting her to be exactly that, but not knowing how to voice it. I still couldn't fathom why she'd buy something like this to use with someone else. And then I fathomed it, she obviously wasn't interested in me at all. This knowledge of someone else wearing it didn't cause any jealousy in her, and I had to accept that. For now...

I woke early this morning and checked on Ashlyn before I started my scribe here with you, Journal. She had slept in her necklace and I melted a little, knowing she loved it so much. It was a good gift choice and she'd be delighted when the rest of it was revealed. I am just about to wake her Journal and get this Christmas Day underway.

Journal Entry – Saturday 26 December: 11.30 pm

Christmas Day was wonderful, and we spent it in the usual family fashion. Mercy greeted us both at the door of Anna and Dom's with hugs and kisses which warmed my heart. I loved that little girl so much. These two girls were the centre of my life and I would be a fallen man if they were ever taken from me, simply by moving into another house.

Merce distributed the gifts this year and I was nearly in tears at the choices they'd made for me; that Ashlyn had made for me. Everything was so intrinsic to whom I was, and I knew that she'd spent a lot of time looking for and finding the medical instruments, not to mention the cufflinks. What had taken me a little by surprise was the sexy underwear she'd bought. Did she want to see me in them? I was happy to show them off to her Journal! Of that, there was no question.

Mercy had another surprise in the back yard and Anna and Dom took her out to find it. I stayed with Ash in the kitchen, and we had a soft embrace. I teased her about wearing the new nightgown I'd bought for her, the intention of seeing it on her eventually, even if that only meant her swanning through the lounge room at home with it on. I was then teased about wearing my new undies. I asked her what ones were her favourites. She passed me a black pair of fishnet shorts which I dragged over her head. She looked up into my eyes and my heart started to race; her warm smile drawing me in to kiss her, only angling up toward her forehead at the last moment. I stood there with her in my arms, lips pressed into her smooth skin, until Dom came through the door.

I fell asleep on the lounge room floor at some stage after lunch, having eaten excessively. They say it's the tryptophan in the poultry, but I believe it has more to do with the accompanying alcohol that throws the final punch.

I showered, shaved and washed my hair before going to bed that night, putting on the black fishnet shorts. I knew it was in vain, knew she wasn't going to see me decked out in her favourite pair, but it was a nice daydream. Lying in bed she was all I could think about and I spread myself over the mattress and allowed the vision to take me.

The softness of her lips caressed mine as I reached to cup her breasts, teasing her into breathy moans. Her fingers played through my chest hair before gliding down to stroke me into hardness and I found my own hand emulating hers. I wasn't actually masturbating at this stage, more gripping myself, but I knew I would be eventually. I imagined working my hand down her frame, delving under the silk of her sleepwear and finally coming to rest at her heat, heat I'd stirred within her. Then I felt a hand on my extended free arm; I sat up in alarm.

I'd scared her apparently, but the instant ripping from my daydream was nearly painful for me. Mercy was hogging her bed and I moved over willingly to let her into mine. I told her the new nightgown was sexy and she loved it, being so soft and all. This sounded like an invitation to me, so I ran my hand over her thigh, agreeing with her.

She wanted to know if I had my new shorts on and I told her I slept naked. Her eyes grew wide, growing wider still when I took her hand and started to lower it slowly. I wanted to direct it to my still raging hard-on, but drew her hand to my fishnet-clad thigh instead. She had assumed I was naked and what I *wanted* to do with her hand was what I was actually doing with it. She clipped me over the shoulder when she found I didn't sleep in the nude after all, nor ended up with my cock in her hand, but the look on her face had been worth it.

I wished her a goodnight and rolled onto my side. When I woke, she was gone.

Journal Entry – Monday 28 December: 2.30 pm

If anything, I can take a hint. I went for a run yesterday morning with the intention of mowing the lawn when I got back. She'd teased me about my lack of home maintenance on Christmas Eve and, if anything, I *can* take a hint!

It was a stifling hot day. All I concentrated on was the beat and rhythm of my runners on the concrete - Ashlyn Standish Ashlyn Standish Ashlyn Standish; they counted my pace. Christ, she already had my name. Would I have allowed my feelings for her to continue this long if not for my twin's last words? Would the guilt be there if he hadn't asked me to take care of her and Mercy, to love them as my own family? I knew he meant to truly love her, as I wanted to do, but would my morals have allowed it without his permission? I knew it was stupid to be even asking myself these pointless soul-searching questions because 1: he *had* given his permission, but, 2: she was aware of this and we weren't a couple.

I knew after Lori died that we both needed to grieve, me for my twin and she, for her lost husband. At the onset of 'post-Lorien', I hadn't even thought about wanting her for eternity, but now - now that time had passed... I knew in my heart, even without Lori's blessing, I would still want her and figured it would be with a guilt-free heart. It was still a futile argument between my good and evil internal twins though Journal, as neither of them would get to gloat their victory.

I turned for home not long after I started as I hadn't brought my water bottle and, in this heat, it was abject stupidity to be out in it, let alone running through it. As a doctor, I was well aware of this. I all-but collapsed in the back yard, leaning over my knees to capture my breath as Ash went inside to get water for me.

I sat on the steps with Mercy when I was breathing regularly again, and asked her what she was up to. Making a potholder for Mum was her response and then told me her next project was to make a bead dress and matching headband. I laughed. If anything, she would certainly give it a good go. She was smart, our girl, like her mother... like her father.

When Ash came back out, I stripped off my gym shirt and took the bottle from her, drinking half of it straight down. With the remainder, I poured it over my head in an attempt to cool off my body. This didn't make Mercy happy; I splashed her. In true antagonistic form, I splashed her again, this time by shaking my wet hair at her. She wasn't happy, and moved farther away up the verandah from me. I couldn't help but smile and Ash laughed, asking if I was going to have a shower. I told her I was going to mow the lawn, and that I could take a hint.

Several minutes later, I was still not mowing. I called the mower a few choice words, which caught Ashlyn's ear, but I hoped not Mercy's. I didn't often swear and tried to avoid it altogether in front of Merce. Not being one to give up, I checked the petrol and there was plenty, so pulled the spark plug from it. I gave it a clean and tested its spark against the body of the mower. It was still working, so reinserted it.

I then heard a bang and looked up to see what had been its source. Ash was now sitting forward on the sun lounge, her book on the ground beside her. She was looking at me with a lopsided grin. The reason for this was my white thighs. Having no other option of course Journal, I grinned at her and gave her a partial flash, pulling my shorts halfway down my arse to show her more glimpses of white.

She blushed and pulled a face at me, reaching for the dropped book. I chuckled to myself and tried the mower again. It started this time, so assumed the spark plug had been the problem. Giving her a thumb up, she was still watching my little mower struggle, I commenced the fifteen-minute job of mowing the lawn. She was right; this was something that I could achieve every weekend. It wasn't a big job.

I was nearly finished when I went to grab a swill of water, remembering I'd dumped the last of it over my head. I turned to see Ash looking in my direction and mimed refilling the bottle for me. She disappeared inside and I kept working.

Her touch was feather light, brushing over my shoulder to alert me to her presence. Hell Journal, hadn't this girl ever heard of poking a finger, or a firm tap to get someone's attention? Did every move she make have to entice me so? Just to bring that point home ever further, her hand then slid down over my back as she retracted it. She had this weird look on her face, and I asked her if she was OK. She was, and went inside to make lunch.

I kicked off my shoes at the back door, looking forward to a cold shower. The droplets fell like icicle needles against my hot skin, melting instantly, immediately dropping my thermostat. She'd done the washing recently and there were no towels in here I realised, so called to her, as I was nearly done.

A few seconds later, the door opened and there she stood before me. I wasn't worried about her seeing me naked - it wasn't the first time. I asked if she was going to take my picture as I waited on her to pass me the towel. She backed out quickly and I had a silent laugh. This was a good thing, I believe.

I dried off quickly and didn't bother to dress; I had no clean clothes down here anyway. Tucking the towel around my hips, I joined the girls for lunch. I was starving.

She wanted to talk about our upcoming holiday to Forster and I played with her a little, making Mercy giggle. We always got into trouble together and we took it like a team. I eventually brought her back on track and then proceeded to discuss the packing routine. I assured her I would have it all done today, just to make her happy.

When I had finished my packing, I stood at Mercy's door. Ash looked like she was ready for a breakdown. I could see why. Mercy had a huge pile which I assumed was what she wanted to take with her, the smaller pile already worked through, discarded items. I took over and left

Ash to put all of our clothes together as I managed to talk Mercy into a much smaller pile of things she simply couldn't do without. These all fit into one bag and I shook her hand, telling her it was a job well done. She nodded and took the praise. I loved this girl; she could always make me laugh.

Ash was a little weird with me again over breakfast and I tried to do a quick manual calculation of when her period was due. She didn't normally act this way when she did have PMS, but could think of no other reason for her to be acting strange. She even jumped a little when I asked her if she'd checked on the still sleeping Mercy when she came down. Wherever her thoughts were today, they weren't in Sommersett. She went in search of her, and I went to get dressed.

There was a knock at my door a few minutes later and I told whomever it was to hold on, I wasn't decent yet. It was Ash, and I smiled, wishing she had burst through the door anyway. We did respect each other's privacy though, so I knew she wouldn't do that.

She was bored apparently, and one thousand thoughts danced through my head Journal, when she asked for me to 'un-bore' her. She wasn't impressed with my plans for the day, tending to the garden again, and wanted another fun-filled option. Mercy came into the room just then and dramatically collapsed on the bed, face down. A tickle-fest finally got her up and active and this alleviated Ash's boredom for the moment, following Mercy into her room to dress and then ready her breakfast. I solved my own problem of what to do today and decided to catch up on some emails, starting with Mum and Dad. I'd been very slack of late in returning their weekly newsletter.

The smell of baking brought me from my concentrated ramblings of life in Sommersett and I followed my nose downstairs to a 'good twin', 'evil twin', assortment of cupcakes. The green ones looked sickly with only the barest hint of green colouring poking out from under the treasure-trove of lollies on top. Instant insulin requirement for any adult! I took a pink one instead.

Journal Entry – Sunday 3 January: 10.00 am

It's been a whirlwind of a few days since I last wrote in you Journal. We made it to Forster by lunchtime and after a quick lunch, headed for the shore. It was a beautiful day and I spent most of it in the water with Mercy, tossing her about, looking for weird and wonderful things and watching her mother from the corner of my eye. We were there for hours.

Later, with Mercy in the tub, I went out onto the verandah to shake the sand from me, knowing I'd get the last shower. When Ash joined me, she sat down and grimaced and I laughed, stripping off under the towel and shaking most of the sand off. I teased her that men had it easier as I moved the towel over me to remove the last stubborn grains. Ash laughed and looked toward the glass sliding door where my arse was in full-mirrored view.

I sat on her knee with the towel retaining my modesty, calling her a perve. She told me to get my 'bare arse off her' and I went to get up. Unbelievably her arm stole around my waist and she lowered her cheek to my chest. She smiled up at me so warmly; it was she who had instigated this embrace. I wanted to blurt out my feelings for her right then, but Mercy coming out of the bathroom fortunately interrupted me. I went to help her change and backed away from Ash, making a deliberate point of shielding myself from her this time.

After dinner, Mercy started to argue with Ash as to the sleeping arrangements that night. I was lying on the single bed where I was supposed to be, listening with an attentive ear. This was one argument I wanted Mercy to win. She wanted the single bed, which would force me into bed with Ash. To end the fight, I got off the bed, telling Mercy it was OK and that I'd sleep with Mum tonight. Oh God, how I wanted to sleep with Mum....

I climbed in and rolled away from her, wanting her to feel at ease. I was tired from an active day with Mercy and was asleep almost instantly. Knowing she was beside me no doubt aided in my relaxed state.

I was the first to wake and I found myself spooned into Ashlyn from behind. I didn't know when this position had evolved through the night, and smiled. Could I be so bold as to pretend to be asleep? I had to make a decision about this, and quick, for when she woke, she'd feel my erection pressed into her. I would then have to explain, if I wasn't asleep, what was going on. I also had no intention of drawing away from her. I'd waited years for this...

What the hell, I thought; I had an excuse fully prepared. I gently ground myself against her, and Journal, it felt so fucking great! I gravitated my hand down over her arm to rest on her thigh, moving in closer again, allowing my lips to brush against her nape.

I whispered her name, taking the boundary even further. I was chancing it, even if the dice were loaded, but her reaction would let me know if anything was possible for the future. If she jumped out of bed, her face would betray exactly how she was feeling and that would be the end of it. But, she didn't jump out of bed; instead, she nestled in closer to me and I moved my determined hand to play under the edge of her shortie pyjama bottoms. A little subtle hand flirting could breach concrete walls for the moment. I myself had turned into concrete, aching to lie within the softness of her. I shuddered, then froze. Mercy jumped onto the bed, waking her mother with a flurry of good morning kisses and I rolled away from Ash, knowing Merce would want to lie between us for a morning snuggle. I adjusted the covers to hide my straining sectional upright currently holding up the tent, and then adjusted myself. Ash then looked down at me.

She wanted to know if Mercy had woken me and of course I said yes. I then had to stop Mercy a second later as she went to climb on top of me, wanting her morning cuddle from Daddy too. I told her I had to pee first, or she'd hurt me otherwise. Acceptant of this, she was content to lie between us. It took a few minutes before I could get out of bed.

When in the bathroom I let my mind tug-o-war over whether Ash had been awake or asleep. As much as I wanted to believe she was awake, and therefore wanted me to tease her in such an intimate way, I couldn't allow it to cement my acceptance when I knew it was not necessarily the case. I was then embarrassed as I'd whispered her name. What if she *had* heard? What was I *doing*?

I avoided her as much as possible over breakfast, which was a hard thing to do. There was only so many times I could get up and down from the table, only so many refills of plates I could manage to choke down. For once, my appetite wasn't great. I kept my eyes glued on the scenery outside the window for most of the meal and only as we were finishing up, I turned toward my family. I was surprised to see Ash looking at me, and it wasn't with daggers. I relaxed the tiniest smidge.

Another romp at the beach made me feel a lot better. The fact that Ash hadn't said anything, nor made me feel weird had also helped. By the time Mercy and I got out for lunch, I had returned to my normal self, realising I had made this into the drama I then suffered through all morning. Ash was the same as usual. I was also excited as to whether Mercy would kick up a fuss again tonight over which bed she would sleep in.

Sure enough, I was back in bed with Mum. That was fine by me, but I found myself lying as far as possible from her as we watched a movie. She didn't seem concerned about the distance between us, not moving any closer to me either. In fact, we were lying there like two planks. I knew why I was lying like this, but why was she? *Was* she aware of what happened this morning?

I realised how ridiculous this was and eventually moved into the centre of the bed, raising my arm to let her in against me. She either would, or wouldn't. Thankfully, she did. I was then able to concentrate on the movie, for what it was worth. I still wanted to know if she had been conscious or not, finally deciding to ask her a loaded question; her answer would tell me everything I needed to know. 'Was she OK about this morning?' She told me that these things happen, which meant she *had* been awake. *It was all a misunderstanding, Your Honour*!

She then surprised the shit out of me, mentioning Christmas night. This was a new one to me. Pressing her for information that she was reluctant to give, I asked if it was akin to what happened this morning. Big mistake, she then wanted to know what *had* happened this morning –

from my point of view. I didn't know what to say to this. I thought she'd been asleep, she thought I'd been asleep. What would it mean if we were *both* awake? I lied and told her I was asleep until Mercy landed on us, but was aware that I had her in my arms at the time and we didn't go to sleep like that.

It was similar to what happened in the waning hours of Christmas night except I was in her arms and I 'copped a good feel' before she managed to get out from under me. Oh, go you good thing Eli, and that was in my sleep! She then made a suggestion that was right on the money, wanting to sleep in my arms so it wouldn't matter if she woke in my embrace the next morning. I pulled her to me tighter, never wanting to let her go. If only I knew what was going on in her head... That conversation has played over in *my* head many times Journal.

The trip home took longer than the trip up, and it was mid-afternoon when we finally got to Michael's. Mercy of course got straight into the pool with Glen. Although we'd eaten lunch, I still helped myself to a steak sandwich, adding all the trimmings. My appetite was back to normal again, as was our relationship with each other, her currently teasing me about being a bottomless pit.

Ash helped me cart three single mattresses from the garage when I had eaten, knowing Mercy would be ecstatic again that she had another night in a single bed. She then joined Glen and Mercy when they got out of the pool and I decided to set the beds up now before she had a chance of any input. I arranged Mercy near the TV on a single mattress, and then set the other two up as a double bed. If asked about it, I would blame it on the lack of covers. I knew this wouldn't wash very well, especially if Michael was in earshot at the time. He had more bedding than a factory outlet. I would love to have been able to pinpoint the exact moment I'd become such a schemer... I also noted Michael's watchful eye on me from the kitchen. I knew he was no fool. Would he click as to my objective? He didn't say anything, which was always a good thing.

Michael and I walked back out together, and Ash got up with the intention of making the beds, I assumed. I stopped her, not wanting to see the layout of the bedding with enough time then up her sleeve to brook interference and move them around. Would she though? She sat back down, and I dragged her to her feet again, wanting her to come for a swim with me.

I was already in the pool when she came to join me, not mentioning the beds, thankfully. Perhaps she had already rearranged them. I would find out soon enough. Her careful entry into the pool was unacceptable however, and I pulled her in on top of me, straddling her around my waist. So many years ago, the wakening of our physical relationship had started after a day spent in the pool, much like this. Would she remember? She did, and we had a laugh about it, although I was more than serious. I hugged her and then let her go, not wanting any paranoia to surface. I didn't let her far from me during our swim. On more than one occasion, I brushed against her, teased her, and chased her around the pool.

When Bree and Simon got home, Mercy was given another Christmas present – Barbie's house. She was elated. Simon and Glen helped her set it up as I watched Ash disappear into the kitchen with Michael and Bree. I wondered if I'd get a mention.

I grabbed Mercy's new Barbie and started fiddling with it absentmindedly, not realising I had stripped the poor girl until I heard

Simon ask what I was doing. I told him I was just seeing if she was more anatomically correct - a lame excuse. Mercy put an end to this thankfully, taking Barbie back from me to re-dress her. Simon told me I was in desperate need of a woman, which I knew, and glanced toward the kitchen where the woman I loved had gone. I didn't realise they were watching us from around the corner and I didn't know where to look. Would she have understood my reaction to Simon's statement? Did I care if she did? Yes.

Michael and Mercy had a round of Twister after dinner; we couldn't all play for fear of crushing her under the adult weight. She was so flexible though and absolutely adored Michael. More games were in store for later, Michael informed Ash, something special we hadn't played for a while. Ash went out onto the patio with Bree, and I was hoping it was Truth or Dare, as much as we'd outgrown it.

Mercy wanted another swim, looking decidedly hot after her third round of Twister with Uncle Michael. I told her we'd have to ask Mum, but to put her swimmers on just in case. She grinned at me, knowing we were working as a team again. She came out with the bottoms on but the top still in her hands. She couldn't get the 'damn thing' on. Such a passionate little thing; such a foul temper... I told her not to swear as I wriggled the offending garment over her head and arms. It was such a cute little outfit - a red and white two-piece with frills around the bottom of the top and at the top of the bottoms. She looked gorgeous. I was so proud that she called me Daddy; I hoped she would always call me Daddy.

She reminded me that Mum and I swore, as she followed me into the laundry so I could change back into my boardies. I answered her through the closed toilet door, telling her that it didn't mean she could. I told her why people did swear, explaining they were being lazy and didn't know enough good words to describe what they meant. She said she didn't want to be lazy, but were Mum and I? I laughed; there was no answer I could give to that one, not without it becoming an hour-long explanation.

I led her to the lounge room and told her to stay there until I'd asked Mum. The sight of her already in her swimmers may have turned a yes into a no, and I knew how much she wanted one last swim. It was getting near her bedtime though so this could go either way. Ash reminded me I was also Mercy's parent and didn't need to ask her permission. I led Mercy outside, making Ash laugh when she realised she was already dressed in her swimmers.

It was nearing dark when I dragged her out, taking her straight up the back stairs to the bathroom. As our bath at home was the massive spa, she usually had a shower, so a bath at Uncle Michael's was always a treat and he kept a stock of bubble bath on hand for this very reason. She'd been in the pool most of the day so only had a quick tub before drying off and dressing in her pyjamas. Ash must have laid these out prior, thank God, as I'd forgotten to grab them before getting in the pool.

Mercy knew the drill and also knew she'd been allowed to stay up later than normal and proceeded to dole out the goodnight kisses and hugs to everyone before Ash and I took her into the lounge room to get her comfortable in the special bed. Another treat tonight was allowing her to fall asleep watching her choice of DVD. I didn't think it would take long.

It turned out we were playing Truth or Dare, and Michael finally picked on me first after sparring with Ash over who got first choice. I went the dare – the look in his eyes as I set up the beds was too much of a risk for him to mention. And, I knew he wouldn't pull any punches.

I was to give Ash the frigid test but had no idea what it was. Michael got Ash to her feet and put her through the paces, much to my amusement. Oh yeah Baby, let me at her.

I placed my flattened hand on her forehead and smiled at her, starting the slow glide downwards. Simon told me to space my fingers out and I wanted to kiss him fully on the mouth. Thanks Simon! You could always rely on him in times of need. The span of my spread hand was wide enough to brush over both of her nipples as I passed, and they sprung to attention at my gentle touch.

Finally, I was cupping her totally, so warm and inviting. I wanted to stay like this for the rest of the game. Would someone dare me to do that? When she asked if I was done, I gave her the lightest of caresses before letting go. She blushed. A great reaction…

Ash then took her go and of course, Michael was the target. She got a little shitty though when he picked truth, but made the most of it. She asked him whether he had the hots for Lori and me when we started at Sommersett High. Great, bring me into it… Michael still wouldn't kick me out of bed it seemed, and everyone thought it was hilarious except Glen. I was still 'fucking gorgeous' apparently, yeah thanks Michael, and this time Glen laughed with us. I shot him a playful wink and he blew me a kiss, but this was not the person I wanted to be flirting with tonight.

It was nearly midnight when Bree noticed the time, and I'd already worked out it would be me and Ash sharing the New Year's kiss. All the others were couples. We gathered out on the patio and I came up behind her, placing my hands gently on her waist. The others were already in each other's arms, waiting on the last second. She turned to face me when I informed her of our kiss requirement, and she smiled.

When the countdown was complete, I went for it, nothing sweet and syrupy, but a real kiss, barely restraining myself from slipping my tongue over her lips and into her mouth. She kissed me back. When I finally drew away, she said 'wow' and I wished her a Happy New Year and pulled her back against me. In addition, I wished her a year full of wonderment and surprises - for us both, and she said she'd drink to that. If only we were on the same wavelength Journal.

It was well after 1.00 am when we all went to bed. Ashlyn had made no mention of the bed setup prior to this, but certainly brought it up as we got in next to each other, noting the intimate arrangement. I cuddled into her, draping my arm over to capture her against me, then asked her to roll over so I could form myself into her from behind. We were a perfect fit. Her silken hair smelled of shampoo and it shone in the moonlight. My hand went to it without consulting my brain. I asked her if that was OK, not wanting to push too hard. She nodded and wriggled further against me and I took her hand in mine. I could get used to this...

It was certainly a wonderful holiday and New Year Journal, and my intention of reading her body language now has me confused. It appears to be a great vibe I'm getting, but am I reading more into it because that's what *I* want? Watch this space...

My entries may be a little lax over the next few months, I just don't get the time to write in you when I'm back at work, but I will no doubt have plenty to go over with you. I certainly hope so.

AUTUMN

Meeting the staff

THE ART STAFFROOM was a small one, housing two Music and three Art teachers in total. Our five desks were placed around the wall at sectioned intervals and a coffee table surrounded by a chair and two small sofas took pride of place in the centre. The small, battered fridge had seen better days and I was thinking of replacing it myself; no point in waiting until the school budget would make it a priority.

I took my lunch from it and sat in the chair to eat. Kari Donovan walked in, the new commercial printmaking teacher, and grabbed her lunch as well, sitting with me for a chat. It wasn't often I didn't eat at my desk, instead working through the lunch break. It meant there was less I would need to do when classes were dismissed, less I had to do in the morning or when I got home. I had other things to do, more important than catching up on my own homework. I liked Kari though, she was about my age and was full of exciting plans she and her boyfriend had been up to, or were about to unfold. They both shared a love of the outdoors and more often than not, were off hiking, camping or boating.

She was in the midst of telling me about last weekend's fishing trip when more of the staff came in. Andrew Dean, the other Music teacher who went to his desk briefly before darting out again, and Janet Kowalenko the ceramics teacher. As usual she had an apron on, liberally covered in smears of various thickness of clay. She pulled it off and draped it over her office chair before taking her lunch from the fridge and joining us at the coffee table. Janet was an older woman, about forty-five I guessed, and was confident and took no crap from anyone. Not that this made her a tyrant; the kids respected her, as did her peers. She was not averse to opening the staffroom door and dragging the kids screaming past into our quarters for a stiff dressing down. You'd think they would have learnt by now to haunt some other area of the school during breaks. "Where's Damon?" she asked. I looked around, assuming he'd walked in with the rest of them.

"Haven't seen him," I said.

Damon Weber had replaced Karen Smith at the start of this term as the new Art teacher, a handsome young man in his mid-twenties with a mass of blond hair and a proudly sculpted set of angled sideburns. The female student body were all in love with him of course, junior and senior. He was a nice enough man though, always polite and considerate, never encroaching onto my space from his desk situated next to mine. The last inhabitant of that desk, Mr Turner, never had such problems with personal space, and the number of times I had to move his stuff from my desk to the floor became quickly annoying. No amount of ordering, pleading or bribing ever changed it. "I think he fancies you," she said and dropped me a wink. I laughed,

"He's a little young," I answered.

"Pish tosh, it's all about chemistry Ashlyn. Once you're legal, age has nothing to do with it." I should have known this would be her reaction. Her long-standing girlfriend since I had worked here was now thirty-one years old, and they'd been together for five years. She was no ageist.

"He's not really my type," I said, a little baffled. I'd never thought about dating a colleague. I was sure it would be a lovely cool pond on the outside but wrought with many underlying snags ready to ripple and undulate the surface once you'd carelessly dived in.

"He's single, handsome and breathing, what more do you want?" Why was she driving this point so hard? Having our desks next to each other, I spoke to Damon a lot, and he was an early starter, as was I. He was very easy to get along with, to talk to, but nothing had ever ventured past a professional relationship, not even hinted at, and I was happy to keep it this way.

"I'm not really into dating; I have a five year old who started school this year."

"Have you dated anyone since Lorien died?" This question took me by complete surprise. They all knew him of course with exception of Damon and Kari; he shared this staffroom with them when he was relieving for Alan O'Dowd, my predecessor, whilst on leave.

"No Janet, I'm not really into dating," I reiterated. Damon walked in the door and I threw her a look, letting her know this conversation was over. She either chose to ignore my glance or didn't see it, as she continued.

"Time to get back out there girlie, and there's no time like the present. You must be aching for sex by now at the very least."

"Ahh, I'd rather not talk about it here Janet," I said and got up to throw my wrappers in the bin.

"What's the topic today, ladies?" Damon asked as he sat with Kari and Janet, taking the space I'd vacated.

"Ask her," I said, motioning to Janet, "she's leading it." I grabbed my folder and took off for the Music room.

The next morning, I arrived as always at 8.00 am. Damon was already there, making coffee. "Want one?"

"Thanks." He sat at the coffee table and I joined him, thinking it would be rude to position myself at my desk and ignore him whilst I worked.

"Interesting conversation I interrupted yesterday," he said, smiling at me over the rim of his mug.

"Oh?" I said, not picking up the thread.

"I didn't know you were a widow, uh, single, sorry."

"It's OK Damon, and yes, I am."

"But you don't date."

"Haven't been on one in over eleven years, as a single girl."

"That's sad," he said, and I wanted to smack him over the head with my briefcase. It was not sad! He caught my mood and jumped back in, trying to explain himself further. "I didn't mean that to be so rude Ashlyn, I just meant that if you aren't sharing yourself with another you aren't truly living."

"I thought you were single?" I asked.

"Guilty as charged, but I still share myself with others." I raised my eyebrows at him, unsure exactly what he meant by that. He didn't add anything more.

"Well so do I," I ended up saying. "I have a five year old and she takes up most of my spare time." I was starting to feel like a broken record.

"I'd like to meet her one day."

"Why?"

"I love kids."

"Do you have any?" He shook his head.

"No, never settled down. I have plenty of time for all that in another few years."

"Is that why you became a teacher? Because you love kids?"

"And that we also get all the school holidays off." I laughed with him.

I took my cup to the sink and rinsed it, ready to get some pre-class work done. He came up behind me and I took his cup from him, rinsing it also and putting them both on the drainer. "I guess there's no point in me asking you out for dinner this weekend?" And there it was, he had passed over the unspoken line drawn in the sand.

"That's very sweet of you Damon and it sounds lovely, but I don't think so. We have to work together."

"I didn't mean for us to get involved in a heated, erotic relationship. Just dinner."

"Maybe another time, OK?"

"OK," he said and grinned at me. "I *will* ask again, you can be sure of that."

"I can handle it," I said. He smiled a little sadly and said,

"He must have been very special."

"He was."

The weekend blew by again as they always do. Elijah and I took Mercy to Glassread for a picnic on Sunday and she rode her bike around for ages, leaving me alone with Elijah. He was, as always, ready to listen whenever I needed or wanted to talk. I thought that by bringing Damon into the conversation it would also let him know someone was interested in me, maybe shoving his feelings a little more to the surface. "Do you like this guy?" he asked.

"He's easy to get along with, handsome I guess, but too young."

"How old is he?"

"Twenty-four."

"It's hardly like you're from a different generation Ash."

"I told him I had my hands full with Mercy," looking around to see her bent over something she'd found on the grass, prodding at it with a stick. "Mercy, what are you doing?"

"Just watching the ants eat this worm." At least she hadn't been trying to anger a King Brown... I turned back to Elijah and he was studying me, a thoughtful look on his face.

"Do you feel like you've lied to him?"

"No, I love the time I get to spend with our girl, and with you," I answered a little too keenly. "We're a family," I added, to smooth out the obviousness of my statement.

"We are, but won't you want to settle down again one day?" I did, but the man I wanted to do this with hadn't shown any interest other than waking in each other's arms once or twice.

"I do, but I'm still not ready for that Elijah. I like my life the way it is."

"Maybe it's going to change sooner than you think."

"I don't think dating a colleague is a good idea."

"Maybe not," he said elusively.

"Why don't you date, Elijah?" He didn't answer right away, then looked at me and smiled.

"I have my hands full with Mercy and her mother." I laughed.

"No seriously Elijah, why?"

"The only women I meet these days are patients and it would be wrong for me to date them."

"Really?" I asked. I always feared this would be how he'd finally meet Mrs Right. Possibly coming in with a sprained ankle he'd have to wrap, her long coltish leg all he could see before him, the maddening touch of her skin under his fingers... I shook myself a little and fobbed off the image. I was glad to know this wasn't going to happen.

"I wouldn't feel right, and as you said, dating a colleague isn't a great idea and I think that includes doctor/patient relationships too. They're someone I would have to see again in the future if it didn't work out, and I'm there to help the community, not make them uncomfortable. A doctor can also find himself in the media or losing patient trust when things go wrong, regardless of whether they're at fault or not. People expect us to be Gods."

"I thought of you as an Adonis when we were going out, a God."

"Do you still think of me in that way?" he asked playfully, puffing out his chest and beating on it. I didn't get a chance to answer as he called Mercy over for lunch. Yes, would have been my whispered answer if I had the courage to admit it.

After we'd eaten, Mercy wanted to look for crustaceans and shells in the weed and at the tideline. We didn't get much of that kind of thing on the shores of Lake Macquarie, but she grabbed her bucket and I followed her, leaving Elijah to have a sleep in the sun. He didn't seem to be getting enough these days. Often when I woke through the night and checked on Mercy, light would be coming from under his door.

Our girl swam like a fish, but she was forbidden to go near the lake edge on her own. On one previous scrimmage through the tideline, we'd found a blue-ringed octopus which we presumed was dead, but I was against her foraging alone; they were still deadly, dead. At least she knew what one looked like, so knew never to go near it. "Look Mum!" she cried and ran ahead. "Oh, how sad." She'd found a small seahorse caught up in the weed. I was sure it was still alive as its tail flickered and moved independently from the light motion of the waves.

"Catch it in your bucket Bump and we'll put it out further where it can swim away." She scooped it up gently, not wanting to hurt it, and we walked a few metres down the baths until we were past the shallow weed. It swum quickly out of sight as she upended her bucket near the waterline.

"Do you think his family will be waiting for him?"

"I'm sure they will sweetheart."

"Mum?"

"Yes?"

"How do you tell a boy seahorse from a girl one?" She was the girl of a thousand questions and sometimes I didn't have the answers for her. Elijah may have been able to answer it but probably not. He wasn't a vet.

"The girls have eyelashes, and the boys don't." Although this is how Pixar would no doubt conceive them, I knew she wouldn't accept that.

"Mum!" she admonished. I laughed.

"I don't know Merce, but I'm sure they can tell each other apart."

"It's hot, can we go swimming?" Wham! New subject.

"We didn't bring our swimmers."

"So?" God, she was so much like her father. Nothing would get in her way if she wanted to do something. My lack of an instant reply made her grab on with her teeth. "Please Mum! Please!"

"OK, but just a quick one." I looked around before stripping off to my bra and briefs and Mercy stripped down to the buff, jumping straight in. I went in directly after her. Although she knew she wasn't to play near the water alone, when an adult was around, she was fearless and claimed the water as her own. I treaded water near her, watching her dogpaddle from one side to the other, occasionally using me as a buoy to catch her breath and take a break. She always slept well after being at the pool, lake or beach and I knew she would be out to it by 8.00 pm tonight.

We moved into shallower water so I could stand up and she hooked her feet into my clasped hands, gripping onto my shoulders.

"Ready?" I asked. She nodded and wiped the hair out of her face, her semi-toothless grin confirming this. "One... two... THREE!" I called and threw her into the air, landing in a splash. This was one of her favourite games in the water. She preferred to play it with Elijah at the beach though, as he could throw her farther. After several goes at this, I was beginning to think I would also be sleeping well that night.

"Hi Daddy!" she called, and I looked around to see Elijah perched on the boards, watching us with a smile on his face. "Did you have a good sleep?"

"Yes Honey, a very good sleep."

"Are you coming in for a swim?"

"It's getting pretty late ladies..."

"What time is it?"

"Nearly five."

"Come on Mercy, it's time to go."

"One more!"

Elijah counted with us and she attempted a backward somersault, something they'd been working on when last at the beach. She didn't quite pull it off but we both clapped loudly when she surfaced.

Elijah had the picnic blanket with him, and he wrapped it around Mercy first and dried her off. I helped her dress before draping it around my shoulders and grabbing my clothes off the deck. Little was said as we walked back to the spot where we'd sat, Mercy running ahead and executing several cartwheels on the way. "Where does she find the energy?" I sighed.

"Has she worn you out Mum?" I laughed and nodded.

"Shame, I had some plans for you this evening." *He had what for who now*? I thought to myself. What were these plans exactly?

"Oh, what plans are those Doctor Standish? Don't forget the doctor/patient rules of yours," I said flirtatiously. *Shut up Ashlyn!!!* I internally screamed, realising that comment pushed him away.

"I was thinking of a game of cut-throat 500, she'll be in bed very soon I imagine."

"Sounds like an awesome plan," I said enthused, yet feeling disappointed. I knew of a few other games I'd rather be playing with him. "Maybe strip 500," I offered with a laugh, hoping to reverse the negative comment from before.

"Considering your current attire, I already have you beaten," he said lecherously and hugged me to him, smiling.

"Not without cards in your hands!" I leant into his chest briefly, pulling away almost immediately and smiling up at him.

When we got home, I ordered Mercy straight into the shower then also went and showered, washing Lake Macquarie from my hair. When we were both out, we all had dinner together. Elijah had made hotdogs and baked beans, another one of Mercy's favourites. It was also a favourite of ours on a Sunday night as neither of us usually felt like cooking.

I wasn't really up for a game of cards once we'd put Mercy to bed, and decided on watching the movie of the week on Fox instead. I put my pyjamas on and made some tea, crawling onto the sofa with Elijah. He patted his thighs and I lay my head on his lap, stretching out. His hand worked soothingly into my hair, reaching out for his mug every now and then. Even though the movie was full-on action, I was asleep within half an hour. "Babe," he shook me lightly, bringing me from my slumber.

"Hmmm?" I said, not wanting to lose the wonderful dream I'd been having. We were re-enacting the scene out of 'From Here to Eternity', with the breakers crashing over Elijah's broad back as he kissed me passionately in the wave-wash. It had seemed so real.

"Honey, wake up, it's time for bed."

"It's never time for bed," I grumbled, which woke me further, assuming he hadn't caught my underlying inference to never being time for bed with *him*. I looked up and he was smiling down at me, his hand stroking my hair.

"What Babe?"

"Nothing," I said and got up, heading for the stairs. "Night Elijah."

"Night Honey." He went to lock the doors and turn off the lights as I made my way to my room, closing the door behind me and climbing into bed. As I drifted off, I wished he were lying here beside me so I could cuddle into him and sleep the sleep of the secure and loved.

Monday morning, 8.00 am, Damon was at my desk waiting for me to arrive. "How was your weekend Ash?"

"Fine. Yours?"

"Not bad," he said and pulled his arm from behind his back, presenting me with a bouquet of flowers.

"What are these for?" I asked.

"Does there have to be a reason?"

"Usually..." I said. He laughed.

"I told you I would ask you out again and I intend to greet you every Monday morning like this until you say yes."

"So, are you asking me out again Damon?"

"Yes."

"And will do so every Monday until I say yes."

"Yes."

"I'm going to have to start taking Mondays off then," I smiled. He laughed again.

"Well?"

"I'm afraid not Damon," I said, picking up my briefcase, "but thanks for the flowers."

"Where are you going Ash?" he asked as he saw me heading for the door.

"I don't want to cop a ribbing from the rest of the staff. No one else needs to know about this, I'm taking them home." He smiled, which I returned as I walked out of the staffroom.

When I got home, Elijah was just about to leave for school with Mercy. "Hi Mum, what are you doing home?" Elijah was eyeing the bouquet curiously.

"Just dropping these flowers off. There isn't enough room on my desk."

"Who gave you flowers?" Mercy asked, tugging her backpack on. The smaller the kid the larger the backpack it seemed these days.

"Just a friend."

"Are you coming to school with me and Daddy?"

"Since I'm here I think I will Sweetie." I smiled down at her and ran my hand over her hair. Daddy had put it in pigtails this morning. She took my hand and Elijah's, and led us out the door.

Sommersett Public School was just as close to us as Sommersett High. It was across the road on the Eastern side of the house; we were surrounded by schools. Mercy gave us each a kiss and ran off into the playground, spotting a group of her friends playing hopscotch. "Have a good day!" I called out, but she didn't hear me. I turned to Elijah and smiled.

"So, who's this friend then?" he asked, checking the road for drive-by-mothers before we crossed over to our house.

"Damon." He didn't say anything more for the moment.

When we got home, he put on the kettle. "Do you want a coffee Ash?"

"Sure." I didn't have a class until third period and my morning had already been interrupted, and so rarely this happened. I may as well make the most of it. "Don't you have to get to work?"

"No rush." We were both silent as he made the brew, coming to join me at the dining room table with the mugs. "So, he's asked you out again?"

"Yeah."

"When's the big date?"

"I said no, but he said he's going to ask me every Monday morning until I say yes, complete with floral arrangement."

"What did you say?" he asked, sipping at his coffee.

"That I was going to start taking Monday's off." Elijah laughed loudly, shaking his head.

"You're a classic Ash. Is he a bit of a try-hard?"

"No, I think he's genuine, but I still don't think dating a colleague is a good idea. But..." I cut myself off, leaving the point alone. I didn't want to explain to Elijah that I wanted sex, and with him would be especially nice... There were very few opportunities for me, and I would never dream of seeing someone from an online dating service. The thought made my stomach crawl. I'd rather stay single. I also knew that if I dated Damon, I would want to bed him, which was possibly another subliminal reason why I didn't want to go out with him. I knew what I wanted from that date...

"But?" he asked.

"Nothing."

"Come on Babe, out with it, there's nothing you can't tell me." I smiled shyly and dropped my eyes, peering into my mug. "Come on Ash, tell Unkie Lie..."

"I'm horny," I said quietly.

"I see..." he mused, but didn't comment any further. The silence was deafening.

"What do you do Elijah, when you're feeling like this?"

"I either take care of it myself or ask a woman out on a date or two. As a last resort, I pay for it." I looked at him in surprise. I suspected his hands were his best friends at times, as was a casual encounter, but I never dreamt of him actually going to a prostitute. And since when did he date?

"You're kidding me, aren't you?"

"No Ash, sometimes it makes more sense that way. It's perfunctory and uncomplicated and I get exactly what I want and need."

"It seems a shame that someone as handsome as you has to go to a hooker."

"I don't 'have' to, I choose to." I wasn't sure how I felt about this information, wasn't sure I wanted to know. "Are you OK with this?"

"It's not really any of my business I suppose."

"Do you want to help me out instead, in the future?" How I would love to...

"It would certainly be a wonderful arrangement for both of us, hey?"

"It would indeed," he said, smiling at me over his mug. I sighed, if only it was that easy.

"Have you ever double clicked your mouse?" he asked. I laughed.

"Once for the camera, but I don't want to just have a good time, I want the intimacy that goes with it. I miss my cuddles and snuggles, laying in the afterglow and all that good stuff." He smiled and nodded.

"I miss it too... Can *I* have a hug?" he asked.

"Anytime," I said and got to my feet as he rounded the corner of the table.

He drew me into his arms and held me against him firmly, but tenderly. It was a wonderful hug and I melted into it. He sighed deeply and ran his hands slowly over my back, then tightening them around my waist, pulling me closer to him. "This is nice..." I said against his chest.

"Hmmm," he agreed.

We stood like that until the commencement bell rang at the High School. "I should make a move I suppose," he offered.

"I would love to chuck a sickie."

"Why don't you?"

"I've already been in, Damon saw me remember."

"No reason you didn't get a headache once you were home." It was tempting, I had to admit. "I'll give you a doctor's note," he sing-songed to me. I laughed.

"No, I should go in." He smiled down at me and kissed my forehead before releasing me. We grabbed our respective bags and headed for the door.

Telling Michael

I WAS SURPRISED TO HEAR MUSIC roaring from inside the house when Mercy and I got home from school, more specifically, Nickelback. Full volume. "What's that Mum?" she asked.

"Daddy must be home early," I said and put a finger to my lips, wanting her to be quiet. "Let's peek!" I suggested. She nodded and crept in behind me as I slowly opened the door.

It was hard not to laugh aloud at the display before us. Elijah was rocking around the kitchen, having been cutting up vegetables at some stage. He was in the process of singing into a zucchini and throwing his head around with one hand in the air, finger pointing to some unknown icon. In a Tom Cruise action, he slid from one end of the kitchen tiles to the other. Spinning around, he opened his eyes. When they finally met mine, the look on his face caused me to laugh uproariously. He had been so busted.

Mercy laughed loudly too as Elijah ran to the stereo, silencing it. "Why did you stop Honey? We were enjoying ourselves, weren't we Merce?"

"You're funny Daddy!" she said and tinkled out her bell-like laughter again.

"Nice way to announce yourself ladies," he chastised. I could tell he was embarrassed, and it wasn't easy to embarrass a Standish.

"Don't stop singing Dad, I like to hear you sing."

"Maybe later Mercy," he grumbled and went to the fridge to get a drink and snack for her.

I flicked on the kettle, not overly trying to hide my smile. "Funny?" he asked.

"Very," I answered. He grabbed me and started to tickle; Mercy joined him. "OK, not funny!" I screamed and tried to wriggle away from the onslaught of my family's tormenting. Elijah pulled me to him in a bear hug, looking down into my face.

"I owe you one Ash," he promised.

"You won't ever bust me doing anything so hilarious," I promised.

"If that's a dare, I'll lie in wait until I catch *you* at something...," he threatened, one eyebrow raised with innuendo.

"You won't catch me doing that either," I scoffed and pulled away to make the coffee.

We sat at the table with Mercy, and I smiled at her and nudged Elijah. She rolled her eyes and grinned back at me. "Mum?"

"Yes Bump."

"Why aren't you and Daddy married?" Where had this come from?

"You know Daddy's not your birth father. We had this conversation before."

"I know."

"So, you know I was married to your real Daddy?"

"Lorien," she said.

"That's right and he was this Daddy's brother," I said, pointing to Elijah.

"Unkie Lie," she added.

"Correct Honey. And Unkie Lie - Daddy, and I are just good friends." She chewed her cracker thoughtfully for a few moments and I stole a glance at Elijah. He was grinning at me. *You can help*, I mouthed. *Why? You're doing fine,* was his answer. *Thanks!* Was my reply.

"So why do I call Daddy 'Daddy' and not Unkie Lie?"

"You started calling him that when you were young, after your father died. We thought it would be good for you to think of him as your Daddy as he nearly is. Being Lorien's brother, he was as close to a real father as you were going to get, and you know he loves you just as much as your father did."

"If you marry someone else will he become my *new* Daddy?"

"Elijah will always be your Daddy Honey, despite what happens." She seemed happy about this.

"We're a family," Elijah added, "and we always will be Mercy, no matter where you live or who Mum marries one day."

"I want her to marry you Dad, so we can always be together."

"Marriage doesn't work that way Bump. Mum and I need to be in love to get married. That doesn't matter though because we always will be together or living very close by at the least." His words comforted me...

"Why aren't you in love with Mum?" she asked. That was a question I wanted answered too. He thought for a few minutes before finally looking up and smiling at me.

"Because she won't have me," he said, and I laughed with him. *Yes, I would...*

"What's made you ask about this anyway Merce?" I questioned.

"Well, MaryAnn Butler told me that I shouldn't call Daddy, Daddy, as he *wasn't* my Daddy. My real Daddy was dead, and this Daddy was only my uncle and I should call him Uncle out of persrect for my dead

Daddy." I think she meant 'respect' instead of 'persrect', however these shotgun words didn't sound like they came from another kindy goer.

"What grade is MaryAnn in?" I asked.

"Year 6."

"Does she have a big sister called Lizzie who goes to high school?"

"Uh huh," she nodded and resumed eating.

"In-bred white trash," I mumbled to Elijah. "Lizzie is in one of my classes and if she could get onto her back during class, she would."

"Sounds like a girl I want to meet," he laughed.

"You *know* the mother Hon, think about it." He did and realised that these were two of the Butler kids, seven in all and to six different fathers. I remembered Elijah complaining how hard it was to find them in the surgery records, as their mother could never remember what name any of them were under. Real classy people, and it was no surprise that MaryAnn was giving Mercy a hard time. She would have to be jealous of the loving family Mercy came from, regardless of who was her father and who her uncle. "You just ignore her Bump, nothing she has to say means anything to you, or me and Dad. OK?"

"OK Mum!" she chirped. Nothing got her down for too long. She planted a kiss on both of our cheeks and took to the stairs.

"That sucks," I said to Elijah.

"It won't be the last time she goes through something like this Babe. We are a rather unique family."

"I know, but what business is it of theirs? Most of the venomous crap that comes out of kids mouths comes from the parents first."

"Jealousy Ash."

"I know that too, but I want to protect her. Losing her father is enough for her to have to deal with, at this age especially. She shouldn't have to ward off these arseholes at five years of age. *Or* feel that what she is, or has, is anything less than what she deserves."

"She's tough Babe, just like her mother." He came in behind me and hugged me. I wanted to turn in his arms and press my lips into his, savouring him. Instead, I ran my hands over the forearms wrapped around me and tilted my head back. He kissed my brow softly. It wasn't enough, but it would do. For now.

The next afternoon I rang Michael to see what he was up to. I needed to talk to someone and when he was serious, he was an excellent Agony Aunt. "Come over for dinner Ash. Leave twin a note and get him over here too."

"Are you sure Michael? We don't want to put you out."

"Just get over here woman." I laughed.

"OK, be there soon. I need to talk to you."

"Sounds fascinating..."

"Oh, believe me Michael, it's a beauty!"

I went in search of Mercy and told her to grab her swimmers; we were going to Uncle Michael's for dinner. "Yay!" she called and dropped the play doh she'd been working on. It was the first play doh I had allowed in the house since the 'making breakfast' episode when she was three. She changed in the dining room whilst I wrote out a note for Elijah. 'Elijah - we're at Michaels and staying for dinner. Come over when you get home. We'll be waiting for you. Ash xxx' "Put my name on it too Mum!" Mercy insisted, so I added 'and Mercy xxx'.

I clicked her into the seatbelt and as I went to slide into the front seat, she stopped me. "I forgot my album Mum. I *have* to take it with me!" Her album was a manila folder of her latest work. Each time we went to Michael's he got to pick his favourite and it replaced what he'd chosen the last time, taking pride of place in the centre of the fridge door. I went back inside to get it for her.

On the drive over, she told me she was going to marry Uncle Michael. "I think you should tell him that when we get there Bump, it will make his day." And, it probably would. It wasn't every day a gay man was asked to marry such a beautiful china doll as my daughter.

"Uncle Michael!" she called as she unbuckled herself from the belt. She had seen him coming down the driveway, his languid stride becoming a slow run.

"Hi Honey! Got a kiss for me?" She pressed her little mouth against his cheek with a loud 'Mwuah!' She got one back.

"Where's Uncle Glen?"

"He won't be home for a while; he had to go out. Are you ready for a swim?" She pulled her T-shirt and shorts off and threw them to me as she took Michael's hand and walked back up the driveway with him.

"Yeah, thanks Merce!" I said and followed behind them. Michael turned and looked at me over his shoulder, grinning.

They had a system to get into the pool and as they neared, Michael stripped off his own shirt and swung Mercy up and onto his shoulders. "Ready?" he asked.

"Yep!" He walked down the pool stairs and kept going until he was waist deep. He then dove forward, skimming the top of the water as Mercy splashed around on the back of his neck, staying upright.

Eventually he pulled her under, and they surfaced together with her in his arms. He got another kiss. She *adored* her Uncles Michael and Glen. "I'm going to marry you when I get older," she told him, and I returned his smile.

"That would be wonderful Mercy; can I wear the bridal dress?"

"No," she said in her 'you're silly' voice. "I wear the dress, you have to wear shorts."

"Shorts? What happened to a suit?"

"Not at my wedding. I want to get married in the pool." Michael and I both laughed loudly at this.

"Let's discuss it when it gets a little closer hey?"

"OK," she agreed, "but *I'm* wearing the dress!"

"That's something else we can discuss, mermaid!"

He grabbed the floating bed and plonked her on it, wading over to sit with me on the steps. "So, what's in dire need of discussion Ash?"

"You won't believe me."

"Give me your best shot." I grinned at him like a lunatic and barked out a laugh. “Come on girl,” he prompted, shaking his head.

"I've fallen in love with Elijah."

"This has an eerie sense of déja vu about it Ash," he laughed.

"Don't I know it!" He laughed again with me.

"What are you going to do about it?"

"Nothing."

"And why?"

"If he doesn't feel the same it will ruin everything we have."

"What if he *does* feel the same?"

"I'm not prepared to take that chance. And, I thought you'd be more surprised!"

"I've watched him interact with you over the years, even before Lorien died, and I think he's always had a little something for you."

"Even if that were true Michael, that doesn't mean the 'little something' is a big enough something to build a relationship on."

"So, you don't just want sex?"

"It would be a great place to start, but no, I want him completely." He smiled and shook his head at me again.

"At least you aren't in a blind panic like you were when you realised your love for Lorien."

"I was seventeen Michael; nothing is as big an emergency now as what it was then."

"I guess not."

"I'm the most fickle person on the face of this earth, aren't I?"

"No Ash, I wouldn't say that. You've had two wonderful men in your life other than your father... and me," I returned his smile. "Why wouldn't they be men that you would want forever? Lorien is gone, but that doesn't mean you have to become a Nun, or get none." We both laughed at his homophone. "And, what better person for you to be with than the twin you started with? He's a great guy Ash, you couldn't do better."

"I know."

"I don't think sitting in a cinema with my arm around you will work this time." I knew that too.

I then went on to tell him about Lorien's last words. This was something Elijah and I hadn't discussed with anyone else, ever. "Jesus," was his response when I'd finished. "It seems a little pre-determined to me. Why fight it?"

"Fight what? He's never done anything inappropriate. Not sober anyway," I added, thinking back to his eighteenth, *or awake*, I reminded myself, thinking back to Christmas night and our weekend in Forster. "We flirt a little and have a cuddle and a kiss every now and then, but that's just what we do. It's not outside the boundaries."

"Don't you find it strange that these flirtations are deemed to be normal to you both? Do you think other platonic couples carry on that way?"

"I'd never really thought about it. You and I kiss and cuddle."

"I'm gay."

"Well duh!" I said.

"There's nothing sexual there smart-arse." I grinned at him. "You two are already involved; you just don't know it yet."

"How I wish that were true," I sighed.

"You seem pretty calm about it all."

"No point in getting worked up, is there?"

"I think you should get him drunk and throw yourself at him." I pondered that for a while. It seemed to be a possible scenario.

"It could make it worse..." I said. He didn't answer; he just raised his eyebrows at me and smiled.

"You're just wasting time Ash, get stuck into him." At this point Glen returned home.

"Uncle Glen!" Mercy called as he stripped down to his jocks and dove straight into the pool, giving her a hug and kiss.

"How's my girl?"

"I'm Uncle Michael's girl, we're getting married." Glen laughed loudly, his head thrown back.

"I can't wait to see that," he said. "Am I invited?"

"Of course, you can be the flower girl."

"Yet I'm not allowed to wear the dress?" Michael called to her from the stairs. I loved my extended family.

When I finally had Mercy out of the pool and dressed again, she went to play on Michael's PlayStation, and I re-joined the men outside on the patio. Michael had been filling Glen in on my predicament. "Being the newcomer," Glen started, which was amusing as he had been around longer than Mercy, "I see things more impartially than maybe you do. I think Elijah has always had a soft spot for you, and more recently seems to be having a hard time controlling it. Just because you aren't aware, are too involved in the issue to cohesively *be* aware, things are building - mark my words."

"So, you think there's a chance then?"

"An extremely good chance Ash. I'm not a betting man, but I would put the house on it." This made me glow a little. It was always great to get positive feedback, especially when it was what you wanted to hear.

"You're not just telling me what I want to hear are you?" I asked, wanting them to confirm this was not the case.

"No Ash, I think you have a great future together. For God's sake, Mercy calls him Daddy already," Glen concluded. Maybe they were right. I was too close to the subject to be able to see objectively. I sincerely hoped so.

I knew Elijah had arrived when Mercy called to him and I could hear her feet running to let him in. "Hey Pumpkin," he said, and then, "Where's your beautiful mother?" Michael and Glen smirked at me.

"Out the back, Dad." His footsteps preceded his arrival, and I couldn't stop grinning at the guys.

"Hey hot stuff," he said, sidling up to me against the barbecue bench, his arm wending around my waist. "How was your day?"

"Fine Hon, how was yours?"

"The usual." He leant down and brushed his lips across my brow. "Why are you blushing?" he asked me quietly. Before I had a chance to reply, Michael interjected.

"We're here too twin!" he said and laughed.

"I know it, but surely I can say hello to my favourite girl first."

"I thought that was Mercy?" Glen asked.

"She is when in ear-shot," Elijah grinned back at him. Michael and Glen continued their knowing smiles and eventually Elijah caught on.

"What's with all the shit-eating grins around here tonight?"

"Nothing in particular, just having a glorious day... Right Ash?" Glen threw at me. Elijah looked at me curiously.

"Don't worry Honey, it's an inside joke."

"I should have arrived sooner then, hey Babe?"

"Yes, that's right, isn't it *Honey*?" Michael asked Glen.

"Oh indeed *Babe*, too very right," Glen responded in equally pointed sarcasm. I got their point. I hoped Elijah did *not*. Well... maybe I did...

Bree and Simon came home just as we were sitting down to eat. Mercy had the choice of menu and hamburgers were the fare for the day.

Did I mention that Uncle Michael liked to spoil her? During the course of the meal, Bree and Simon gave us some news that made me want to cry. "We went to the Urologist today to get some test results back," Simon said and took Bree under his arm. What was wrong? "We found out we can't have kids." Silence followed, no one knew what to say. We didn't even know they'd been trying.

"I'm so sorry to hear that," I said, nowhere *near* hitting the level of sorrow I wanted to convey to them. "How are you holding up?"

"We had our suspicions. We've been trying since Mercy was about four," Bree said, stroking her hand over Bump's head softly. "And today it was confirmed." I felt Elijah take my hand under the table. I looked at him and the sadness in his eyes said it all.

"Bree, this must be so hard on you. Have you thought about surrogacy or implantation? Surely there must be *something* you can do?" I wish I'd taken more notice of exactly what Simon had said, wanting to swallow my head whole, once Elijah corrected me.

"Honey, Urologists deal with male reproductive problems." I understood immediately and apologised to Simon profusely. Here I was thinking it was Bree...

"It's OK Ash, either way, we can't have kids. Not unless one of you bludgers wants to give up some of your swimmers for us." He laughed loudly at his own suggestion. I wasn't sure whether he was trying to placate us, or whether he was truly OK with the situation. One look at Bree and I realised he was kidding.

"You can be my pretend parents Aunty Bree and Uncle Simon," Mercy piped up. I wanted to drag her to me and smother her in kisses. She would have had no idea of the worth her precious statement carried.

"We already are your pretend parents Merce," Simon said and leant over to give her a kiss on the cheek. Both he and Bree looked a little misty around the eyes. I leant into Elijah and he put his arm around me, pulling me in close to him. It was such a sad time.

Michael and Glen had been quiet during this conversation, which was a rarity. When I glanced at Michael, he had a pensive look on his face. "Were you serious about sperm donation?" he asked Simon.

"Not really, and we certainly wouldn't expect any of you to be involved in something this close to home."

"But it would work?"

"Yes, Bree's able to conceive and carry. It's *my* equipment that's in need of a recall." His mood was light, but this must have been hurting him so very deeply, not to mention what it must do to a male's ego.

"Elijah?" Michael asked.

"Hmmm?" he responded, removing his cheek from my forehead.

"What are their chances if they could find a donor?"

"Excellent. It's a pretty common thing these days."

"I think you should consider it then," Michael offered to Bree and Simon. "Make a few enquiries at least."

"Maybe," Bree said. "It's not the same as having your own." I looked at Michael curiously, wondering if he had himself in mind. He didn't offer anything further and it wasn't something I could ask him in front of everyone else. Certainly not at the moment.

Elijah insisted we all go home in one car, so I handed my keys to Michael, letting him know we'd pick it up tomorrow. On the way home, I brought the subject back up again to Elijah. "Would you ever donate your sperm?" I looked over onto the back seat to check whether Mercy was still asleep.

"To a bank or friends?"

"Friends I suppose, maybe to a bank too, whatever..."

"I wouldn't donate to a bank, but if Simon and Bree asked me, I would certainly think about it. I'm not sure though if I could go through with it unless it was a last effort."

"Why not? It would be an amazing gift you'd be giving to them."

"I know, but I would assume there would be no third parent permanently involved and I would have to deal with a child in my environment that was mine, not a random child of my friend's. I'm not sure I could get past that." I saw his point. "When you mentioned surrogacy, would you have carried it for them if it was Bree who was unable to carry a child?"

"Probably. I'd have to think about it first of course."

"Fair enough, but what if they wanted an egg from you as well?" Now I really understood his point. It would technically make it my child, regardless that Bree and Simon would be raising it as their own.

"It would be hard to deal with, you're right Hon. I could live with being the carrier, but knowing I was about to give birth to one of my own at the same time... It would be impossible to part with at the end I would imagine."

"That's why surrogacy is not an accepted practice in NSW and is illegal in Tasmania. Most States *do* allow it as long as there is no financial beneficial gain to the surrogate mother. Not that it would be an issue for you and Bree."

"Ewww, having sex with Simon is not on my top ten list of things to do today either," I added, turning the conversation back to a lighter note. Elijah barked out a laugh and quietened it immediately, checking Mercy again in the rear-view mirror. She hadn't woken.

"Oh Ash, you are so naïve sometimes…" he continued to chuckle. "His sperm would be implanted; you wouldn't have to bed him." I blushed in the dark and realised I should have thought before I opened my mouth. I knew in the back of my mind that I wouldn't have to have sex with Simon. "Do you want to have more kids?" I wasn't expecting this question and it surprised me a little.

"Yes, I do. What about you Elijah? Do you want to have a family one day?"

"I already have a family," he corrected me with a smile, taking a quick glance at Mercy again, "but I would like to have a larger one."

"It's a hard thing to achieve when you're on your own."

"Impossible, I'd say," he said and grinned at me.

"I'd do it, for you Elijah," I said a little sheepishly.

"You *do* do it for me Babe," he said. *What*? I thought. What exactly did I do for him? I looked at him to get a better understanding of his comment, but his face was blank. It softened as he looked at me, adding quietly,

"And I'd do it for you too Ash."

"We're talking about donating here, aren't we?" I confirmed.

"But ev cos," he answered in a feeble attempt of a French accent. "'Ow evair," he continued in poor dialect, "I believe zat… ow you say… 'intair-cos', iz zee best meh-sord zair iz."

"Want to run that by me again Pierre?" He laughed.

"I think the old-fashioned way, intercourse, is still the best method."

"I see." I would dearly love to put into practice what he was alluding to, tonight in fact.

'"Seriously though Ash," damn, he was only playing with me... "If neither of us have a significant other by the time we're thirty-five, let's have one together."

"Created via the best method or the clinical insertion?"

"That, my lady," he said, waggling his eyebrows at me, "would be entirely up to you." *Can we get some rehearsal in?* I wanted to ask, but of course, I didn't. I wasn't sure if he *was* being serious...

As per his promise, another bouquet awaited me on Monday morning. Damon was becoming harder to resist, but he was nowhere to be seen. In fact, I didn't see him until lunchtime that day; we were on playground duty together. "Thank you, Damon," I started, knowing he'd be aware to what I was referring.

"You didn't take them home today?"

"I didn't have time." He smiled at me.

"Has anyone asked about them?"

"No, so I assume you've divulged that information yourself." I had noticed a smug smile on Janet's face at recess and Kari was more than her usual cheerful self. She made a big deal of coming over and smelling them, taking one of the buds and tucking it into my hair.

"I divulge nothing," he teased, bending down to pluck a clover flower from the quad. He leant toward me and threaded it into my lapel buttonhole.

"Damon!" I said, glancing around the quad to see if any of the students were watching.

"If there's nothing going on between us then we have nothing to hide or have to justify ourselves over, is there?" His explanation was ice thin... "Have you got your excuse ready?"

"For when we get dragged into Mrs Lawper's office to *justify* our playground flirtation?"

"Are you flirting with me Ashlyn?" he asked, stopping his slow stride and turning to face me.

"No... I..." I spluttered. "That's not what I meant..." I blushed, damn me to hell! A slow smile lit up his face.

"Well?"

"Well what?" I asked.

"Do you have your excuse ready, for when I ask you out in about three and a half seconds?" I shook my head and smiled, meaning he was a fool, not that I didn't have an excuse. He misunderstood my reasoning, asking, a little in surprise, "So you'll have dinner with me on Saturday night then?"

"No Damon, sorry, that's not what I meant."

"Then why can't you make it?"

"I already have a date with a five year old." We resumed our slow march around the quad, and he stayed quiet, possibly thinking this over.

"I'm going to keep asking..."

"I'm going to keep saying no," I said and smiled at him again, trying to remove the starch from my stony promise.

"What about something less intimate then?"

"Like?"

"Do you play tennis?"

"Not very well."

"What about swimming?"

"What about it?"

"Are you always this elusive Ms Standish?" *Yes, because if we go on a date, I'll want to have sex with you Damon!* I screamed internally.

"Yes Mr Weber," I answered calmly. He laughed.

"I thought maybe we could go to the indoor pool and then get some lunch afterwards."

"Doesn't sound like much of a date."

"You are so frustrating Ashlyn. I am *trying* to remove the date scenario, so you feel more comfortable with it. I want to spend more time with you, and I don't care what we're doing, as long as we're doing it together." He had spun toward me during this dialogue, taking my upper arms lightly in his hands. I shrugged away from him and took another guilty glance around the quad. "We can do whatever you want Ash..." I sighed heavily. He was starting to wear me down.

"OK."

"OK?"

"Yes, OK, we can do whatever you want." He opened his mouth to speak, and I interrupted him. "Just don't go crazy with the plans. I don't want to be boarding a Concord and find I'm in Vienna." He laughed.

"Dinner's back on the agenda then?" I hesitated only briefly before saying,

"That's fine. But I won't be able to make it for a few weekends. I'm already booked out until the end of May."

"As long as you aren't going to keep postponing this…," he added suspiciously.

"I wouldn't have accepted at all if that was my intent, Damon." He nodded and grinned at me, reaching out to take my hand. "Damon…"

"Oh sorry, just a natural reaction. I'm a pretty happy guy at the moment. How's the first Saturday in June?"

"That's fine."

"You could be a little more excited Ash, I won't mind." I smiled at him, saying,

"I am. It's just complicated Damon…"

"I promise I won't add to the complications." I hoped not. *Must not have sex… must* not *have sex…* I reminded myself.

You Gotta Have Faith

I WASN'T SURE WHAT TO TELL ELIJAH when I got home. Would he even care? I had to admit I was a little excited at the prospect of going out with someone again. As wonderful as Elijah was in the comforting department, it wasn't quite the same, wasn't to the level that I wanted from him.

The house was silent when I arrived home. Mercy was at Mum and Dad's, so I didn't have to pick her up from school. "Elijah?" I called out. There was no response. I wondered briefly where he could be, then realised it was too early for him to be home. I grabbed my bag and headed upstairs. I could hear noises coming from his room and thought he'd left his television on. It seemed strange. I went to the door and listened; it sure didn't sound like the TV. I was going to open the door and thought better of it, knocking instead, just in case he *was* in there.

"Ash?" I heard.

"Yes Honey, it's just me." What was he doing home at this time of the day and what was he up to? A smile crept onto my face, I had a fair idea, and that idea included a major self-gratification scenario. He'd been watching porn. *Need some help there?* I thought to myself and laughed quietly, waiting on him to open the door.

"Hang on one second Babe."

"Babe?" I heard softly, in a girl's voice. *Oh my God, he wasn't alone in there!* I headed for my room and shut the door, never having felt so embarrassed in my life. A few seconds later, there was a knock.

"Ash, can I come in?" I stood and opened the door, blushing furiously.

"I'm so sorry Elijah, I had no idea."

"I didn't realise the time, *I'm* sorry Ash." He came and sat beside me on the bed. It was impossible not to notice his boxers were on inside out. He'd obviously dragged them on in haste.

"It's OK Honey, we're all adults."

"I wouldn't have brought her here if I knew you'd be aware of it." Did this happen regularly? Was I so naive? He took my hand, asking, "Are you OK Babe?" And then I got angry. I had no right to be, I knew I was jealous, but I portrayed it as anger toward him. So unfair, so out of my control.

"Just go back to what you were doing, she'll be waiting for you."

"She can wait." Why would he do that? I worked it out pretty quickly though when I realised who he was with. I looked up to see Faith standing at my door wrapped only in a towel. The smart-arsed expression she always held in reserve for me was clearly written on her face.

"I thought we had an agreement about her," I said lowly to Elijah. Since the night she'd spent here with Elijah when I was pregnant and the trouble she'd caused, he promised he'd never bring her here again. Yet, here she was.

"Hiya Ashlyn," she drawled. "Coming back to bed Eli?" Elijah looked at me in concern and I waved him on.

"You may as well finish what you came here for, but then get her the hell out of here!" I stood and walked into the bathroom, shutting the door behind me. I sat on the edge of the spa for a few minutes, crying. Life sucked and it kept proving it to me repeatedly. Why did he want her?

Why didn't he want me? I ended up filling the tub, adding bubbles and climbing in. Not that anything could help, but a hot bubbling spa certainly didn't hurt.

Several minutes later, there was a knock at the door. "Come in," I called. When he had entered and shut the door behind him, I let him have it. "Is she gone?" He nodded. "You broke a promise to me Elijah!" I accused. By the look on his face, he was aware of this. "Why? Why her?"

"She came into the surgery Ash and it just... sort of ...happened." I wanted to be cruel, to scream at him, to punch him in the face. However, I stayed silent, not finding his response an ample explanation. But then again, what explanation did he need to give? None really. He was not aware of how much this had hurt me, and I did not intend to tell him exactly why I was so upset.

"Just leave me alone Elijah."

"You've been crying? A bad day?"

"No, but it sure as hell got a lot worse once I got home."

"I know you don't like Faith, and I'm sorry Ash. I had no right to bring her here."

"Fuck you and fuck her too. Oh, you already did that."

"Why are you so pissed off? I know she's not your favourite person..."

"And neither are you at the moment." I sank further into the spa, the bubbles now covering my chin. I didn't even want him looking at me. He went to run his hand over my hair, and I jerked away from him. "Don't touch me!" I could tell he was confused.

"Would you be this upset if it had been anyone else?" he asked quietly.

"Yes, no, I don't know..."

"You know I have sex Babe." I was acting like a child and I knew it, but my mood was betraying my reactions and I didn't know how to stop it. "Babe?"

"Get the fuck out of here!" I screamed at him and he stood, looking at me dejectedly. He had no idea what was going on. He threw me one last glance and left. When I knew he would've been clear of my room I started to cry again, feeling so helpless, so hopeless. The noise of the spa was driving me crazy, so I turned it off, now hearing only the quiet sounds of my controlled sobs.

I had no idea of how long I'd been lying there, but I was freezing when I woke. "Ash?" I heard. Elijah was standing over me, a worried look on his face. "Come on Honey, get out, you'll end up with pneumonia." He had a towel in his hands, and I stood to allow him to wrap me in it. I was shivering so violently he had to hold it around me as he led me into my bedroom. He'd set up a little fan heater on the floor and turned it on, directing its flow in under the towel. It melted me immediately and I slumped onto the ground in front of it, capturing all of its warmth. "Babe, take this," he said quietly and handed me a pill and a glass of water. My teeth were still chattering as I held the glass to my lips to swallow the blue button. "Are you dry?"

"N... n... n..."

"Come here Ash, you need to dry off and get into bed." He helped me and then dressed me into my pyjamas. Under more aware circumstances, I would have died from the embarrassment, but I didn't care now. I felt like concrete.

"Eh... Eh... Elijah..."

"Don't talk Babe, we can do that tomorrow."

"Buh... buh..." I wanted to thank him and to let him know I wasn't angry with him.

"Tomorrow..."

He pulled down the covers and waited for me to slide in before snugly tucking me in. "Get... get in..." was all I could get out. He understood my reference though and climbed in next to me. He was so warm, and I hugged him to me fiercely. I soon felt like I was floating in a cloud of cotton wool and my blood had started to warm my extremities. I hazily recalled the blue pill I'd taken and then fell into the sleep of the dead.

I woke the next morning feeling groggy, vague and disorientated. There was a note on my bedside table from Elijah. *Ash, stay in bed. I will have rung the school by the time you wake up to let them know you won't be in. I also rang your parents, and they will look after Mercy tonight as well, so get some rest. I'll see you this afternoon. Love Eli xxx.*

I felt a little shameful about my tirade yesterday afternoon and knew there would be questions asked when Elijah got home. What on earth was I to tell him? Should I make something up, blame it on something else or just outright lie to him? A small part of me was screaming to tell him the truth. I also had to let him know about my future date with Damon. This was something I didn't want to talk to him about in the first place and now I *really* didn't want to. When did life become so hard? The overcast day outside seemed to reflect my mood so perfectly.

I found myself in the kitchen but realised I wasn't hungry, so went back to my room. I glanced at the clock having no idea what time it was, stunned to see it was well after 2.30 pm. Sitting on the bed, I did something I hadn't done for a long time. I spoke to Lorien quite often in my head, but this time I spoke aloud, as I did when he first died. "Lorien? Baby, it's me... I need your help... I need...," I sighed deeply and finished with, "I don't know what the hell I need." The clouds broke their coverage at this moment and a beam of sunlight poured through the window, creeping its way across the bedroom floor until it enveloped me in a golden caress. The trees outside whispered to me,

"Shhhhhh," and I smiled and looked up before bursting into tears.

"Oh Lorien," I cried. "Why did you have to leave me? You could have taken care of me better here on Earth than where you are now. Look at the mess I've made of my life." The trees continued to soothe, and the sunlight dappled and danced over me until my sobs lessened. "I miss you so much Sweetheart..." I sighed, and the trees sighed with me.

Then the day became dark again and the breeze stopped. "No, don't go!" I screamed. I heard the front door shut and footsteps running up the stairs.

"Ash?!" Elijah called as he flung open my bedroom door. He saw me in my miserable state, crying, sitting on the bed. "Oh Honey," he said quietly and came to take me in his arms. "What's happening Babe, what's wrong?"

"I just had a Lorien moment..."

"You should embrace it Ash, not reject it, not feel upset by it. I get them too..." he confided. "It helps." I sat on the bed and he sat with me, his arms still around me.

"It's because of why I asked him to come."

"Can you tell me?" I shook my head. No, I couldn't. "Has it got anything to do with yesterday?" he probed gently.

"Sort of," I sniffed and then told him about Damon and how I felt about Faith being here, carefully masking the jealousy factor.

"There's not much I can do about Damon, Ash. That's something you have to be comfortable with, but I can promise that you will *never* see Faith again. I'll never see her again." I looked up into his eyes, his image a little bleary considering the tears I still had in my own.

"I can't ask you to do that Elijah. You have your own life to live."

"We talked about this remember, how we get through our wants and needs? Well, Faith was just a band-aid for an itch I had, nothing more. She'll never be a part of our lives." *Our lives?* I thought. "I knew I shouldn't have brought her here Ash, and I am so, *so* sorry you had to find out. I was being selfish."

"No, you were just being a man," I laughed. He smiled at me and drew me close, kissing me on the forehead.

"Do you want to go out for dinner tonight? We'll have the night off."

"What time is it?" I asked and rechecked the clock. For nearly two hours, Lorien had been with me; that I'd spent in a daze. I did feel a little better for it though. "I don't really feel like going out."

"OK, I'll cook."

"Let's just order pizza," I suggested.

"Sounds like a plan Babe," he said. Neither of us made a move for such a long time. His strong arms were more therapeutic than any little blue pill.

Over pizza, I asked Elijah exactly what he'd given me last night. "Other than the shits?" he asked, grinning. I pulled a face at him. "Valium," he said, reaching for another slice.

"How much? I didn't wake up until the afternoon."

"Ten milligrams," he answered through a mouthful of pizza.

"Well, that explains the way I felt when I woke up."

"A little groggy?"

"I felt like I had a hangover!" He laughed.

"You were hysterical and then you were freezing, I didn't have much of a choice."

"Did you stay with me?" I asked a little sheepishly, looking down and toying with a piece of pepperoni.

"Uh huh."

"Thanks Elijah."

"Anytime Babe. Do you want me to sleep with you again tonight?" he asked quietly. I did, but didn't know how to voice this without it coming across as needy. I wanted him to be there because he wanted to, not because I asked him to.

"I'll be fine." He grinned a lopsided grin as he reached for a serviette, wiping off his mouth and fingers.

"You know where to find me." If only I had the strength to sneak into his room in the middle of the night, unannounced.

The next day at school I went in a little later than usual, primarily to avoid being alone with Damon before the rest of the staff arrived. I walked in just before the first bell rang. I knew all of their schedules now and the only ones who didn't have a class first up were Janet and I. I should have come in even later… "So, finally taking the plunge girl. Good on you." I assumed from her comment that the entire staffroom was aware of our upcoming date. It didn't take much for something to be newsworthy in this staffroom.

"What do you mean exactly Janet?" I really liked Janet and didn't want this to become an issue for me. I wanted her to keep her space and allow me my privacy.

"Going out with Damon."

"He's told everyone?" I asked, taking the steaming mug from her and sitting at the coffee table.

"No, just me and Kari."

"Well, that's nearly everyone!"

"Why does that upset you Ashlyn?" she asked, reaching over to take my hand.

"Because it's no one else's business and I have a slight issue in becoming involved with another staff member. I don't think it's professional."

"You can't hide away forever at home."

"Why not? It's worked for me so far."

"You are so young and have such a full life in front of you. Sharing it with someone makes it a more intrinsic life, a complete life."

"That doesn't mean I'm meant to share it with Damon though."

"No… you're right." She contemplated this for a few moments before adding, "But you have to trial-run them before you buy." I had to laugh at this, and she laughed with me. "I don't want to seem to be interfering Ashlyn, but you are a special young lady with a lot to offer someone. Don't keep it on the shelf letting the expiry date rule your world. You've got to get back on the horse girl!"

"I'm not much of a rider," I sighed. She patted my knee warmly and let the matter rest.

At lunchtime, I knew I couldn't dodge Damon any further. I wasn't sure whether I was actually avoiding him, or just avoiding what possible conversation could occur between us. I didn't want him fussing over me, and knowing I was off yesterday, was concerned he would do just that.

"Hey Ash," he chirped as he entered the staffroom. He glided his hand over my shoulder lightly as he went to the fridge to get his lunch.

"Hi Damon." He came and sat next to me, and smiled as he opened his lunchbox.

"What have you got today?" he asked with a grin.

"Tuna."

"I've got egg and lettuce, want to trade half?" I laughed and felt like I was back in kindy. But I did want to trade half.

"OK," I said, "we can be stinky together and in two different ways." He didn't mention yesterday, or our future date, and I began to relax a little. I had myself so worked up over this, which turned out to be futile. Maybe this could work.

The rest of the staff came and went over the next forty-minute break, some joining us, some not. When the bell rang signalling the end of lunch, I went to wash up the mugs and plates in the sink before starting on some work at my desk. "I'll dry," Damon said, suddenly beside me.

"Don't you have a class?"

"They'll be fine without me for ten minutes. They've got work to continue with." I smiled at him and put the plug into the sink, squeezing out the dishwashing liquid. I felt it being taken from my hands and turned to Damon in uncertainty.

"What -" He cut me off, leaning in to kiss me. I didn't fight it. I let him kiss me, but drew away shortly after as his arms wended around my waist. "Damon," I admonished softly, "you promised."

"I thought you'd stop me." I should have. I looked down and blushed. "No one's here..."

"I'm here!" I corrected him.

"And you're the one I want to kiss. Again..."

This time when our lips met my arms worked their way around his neck, pulling him closer. He took me into his embrace, and we were pressed so tightly together. It was wonderful and I went with it, knowing though it was so wrong. When I finally drew back, he grinned down at me. "That wasn't so bad now was it?"

"No," I mumbled, drawing right away from him and running my hands over my clothes, smoothing them into place.

"I wanted to give you a sneak preview." I smiled at him, which turned into a grin and then a laugh.

He Said

Journal Entry – Sunday 25 April: 11.20 pm

THINGS ARE CHANGING JOURNAL, and they're not changes to make me shout with joy. Although I've just come to bed after having Ash asleep on my lap for hours, I found out today that there was another wolf sniffing around my den, and that wolf's name was Damon Weber. And it started off as such a great Sunday.

I had to work yesterday as Doctor Wood was taking the day off, so you can imagine how much I was looking forward to the picnic that Ash had planned for us today. Just me and my two girls at Glassread Baths, one of our favourite spots. She obviously had something on her mind, but I knew she'd speak when she was ready. Soon enough Mercy straddled up on her bike and rode in large circles around us, leaving us to talk privately.

I wasn't aware of how little interest I would have in this conversation; it was about the new Art teacher at school, namely Damon. He'd asked her out and Ash was now looking for what I assumed was my permission to do so guilt-free; possibly by getting my permission meant Lorien had also given his blessing. I wasn't about to give that to her.

I wanted to get as much information from her about this guy without it looking like I was prying for any particular reason and started with a simple question - did she like him. It appeared so, from her answer, citing he was handsome and easy to get on with. I worried at times that Ash was not aware of the male wiles and how manipulative we could be. This Damon could possibly be putting on show what he *thought* Ash would like - no guarantee that it wasn't a tool to get her into bed, or just a downright lie.

She was a little concerned he was too young for her, although a few years did not make it a problem in my eyes. The *only* problem was that she was talking about Damon as I wanted her to talk about me. I wanted her eyes to shine when she spoke my name, wanted to be involved in the lead-up to a relationship with her, not sitting on the sidelines watching it unfold around me.

I was capable of burning this guy, so well that Ash wouldn't even know I was doing it, but was that right? Of course it was, no one could give her more than I. I hid a smile when she told me the excuse she'd finally used - she was too busy with Mercy. I wished she had mentioned me in her response, letting him know there was someone else around. He may then be a little more in tune with the possibilities at home than Ash was. Would this revelation make him fight harder for her though?

Our conversation had been interrupted with what Mercy was currently up to, poking at something with a stick. As Ash questioned her on what she was doing, I took this opportunity to study her, wanting nothing more than to reach over and drag her against me. Not giving her the chance to protest as I kissed her in full passion, making her understand immediately how I felt, making her understand immediately that she had to make a decision.

When she turned back to me, I continued the conversation from where she'd left off. I didn't want to leave it up in the air, so she was undecided on what was going to happen. I wanted it black and white, for my selfish sake moreso. I asked her if she felt that what she'd said about Mercy was a lie. She smiled at me warmly and shook her head, no; she loved the time she spent with Merce *and* with me. And with me! I knew it. That turned out to be because we were a family. Perhaps I didn't know it after all... so, I threw it out on the table, what did she want from life and surely, she'd want to settle down some day.

The wistful smile she gave back to me shot right through my heart – I wasn't expecting to react like that Journal. And she did want to settle down one day, but not yet, she liked things the way they were. I couldn't argue with that, but I could think of things being better, a whole lot better between us. If I could only get my way... Would she even stop to think I was including myself in those plans? Probably not...

She didn't believe dating a workmate was a good idea and I couldn't agree with her more. I was always concerned this is how I would lose her one day, some handsome new teacher taking an interest in her, falling in love with her and she in love with him. Taking her and Mercy from me... I was getting morbid with my musings, pulling myself from them when she asked me why I didn't date anymore. I wanted to laugh aloud. How could I tell her that the only person I wanted to date was sitting here in front of me? *I love you Ashlyn*, I wanted to say to her. Pick me, pick me!

She was waiting on my answer, so I duplicated hers and used her and Mercy as my excuse - I just didn't have any other time to spend with anyone else. Her not wanting to date a colleague gave me some further ammunition and I added that I thought it inappropriate to date a patient. There *is* no law against it, but she didn't need to know that. People did however expect us to be faultless and Gods in our own right, and she smiled at me in what I read as a flirtatious manner, before telling me that's how she thought of me when we were boyfriend and girlfriend, all those years ago...

I stretched out on the blanket when we'd finished eating, having a quick cuddle with Mercy who then wanted to invade the shoreline, picking up bits and pieces of debris and oddments to ponder over with us later. I was happy to let Ash go off with her, opting to have a nap in the sun instead.

I knew sleep wouldn't come easy for me; knowing that my two girls could be viewed by me without their knowledge. God, I was starting to sound like a stalker. But it does concern me that Mercy calls me 'Daddy'. I was not her father, merely an uncle, and one day some other gent could possibly be caught up in the fray, wanting her to call *him* Daddy. The thought of this broke my heart; the thought of them both becoming someone else's broke my heart. It also made me laugh a little; the thought of anyone ever owning either of those two high spirits was impossible. They belonged to no one except themselves, Mercy since she left the womb and Ashlyn, well, as long as I'd known her.

I gave up trying to sleep and sat up to watch them on the shore. Something was going on, as they were both crouching over the wave-wash. Whatever it was, Mercy put it into her bucket and let it go in the deeper water. She had no doubt saved something's life. That's my girl...

My eyes nearly goggled out of my head when I saw Ash looking around before stripping off to her panties and bra, Mercy down to the raw. She dove in and her mother followed quickly behind her. The wooden planks of the baths hid a lot of their playful action from me, and even when I sat up fully, I couldn't see them clearly. We had no towels or change of clothes, so I'd have to take the blanket to them when they got out again, cold and wet, with nothing else to dry themselves on. I took everything back to the car and made my way down to the baths to watch them from the side.

Mercy was such a great little swimmer, currently dog-paddling her way around the baths, showing no signs of tiring. Ash eventually led her into the shallower water where she could stand, and Merce started her new favourite trick, being thrown into the water backwards. She loved it. We'd invented this game at the beach.

The crystal glints of the sun reflecting off the water caught my eye time and time again, bathing them also in a dazzling light that made them seem surreal, not really there. How I wanted to join them, how I wanted to sit here and just watch them. Mercy caught my eye eventually and showed me her latest attempt at a backward somersault. She was getting very close to nailing it. She wanted me to come in for a swim too, but it was getting late, and I decided to be the fun police today.

I wrapped the blanket around her as soon as she was out of the water, drying her off quickly before Ash helped her dress. I was in no hurry to aide her. All I could see before me was her silhouetted form, near naked beneath the wet, white fabric of her panties and bra. Her nipples were straining under the transparent material, and the dark outline of her pubis was impossible to ignore. I desperately wanted to peel those wet garments from her body and warm her, dry her with the heat from my body alone. I imagined it would sizzle and steam off her in a rapid transgression, leaving her dry and possibly thankful, in no time. Instead, I handed her the blanket.

Mercy, in her usual manner, cart-wheeled herself back to the picnic spot in front of us. Ash wondered over her boundless energy and I asked if Mercy had worn her out. I also added that it was a shame as I had plans for her that evening. Would she ever notice my sexual undertones and flirtatious manner?

We had a relaxed and easy relationship, and well before Lori died we were comfortable hugging and nestling into each other. Now it meant something to me though, I took ownership of every nuance, every touch, kind word and look. Could she be so oblivious? When strip 500 was offered, I felt myself starting to rise and tried to quell it instantly. Mercy wouldn't understand but Ash surely would.

I mentioned that in her current state of undress I already had her beaten. Two quick rounds and I would have had her naked, one more round and she would have to pay the price for having no further clothes to add to the strip pot. Oh, what a wonderful scenario was playing out in my head. She hugged me to her briefly and let me go; content to travel home in the car wrapped in just the blanket. Her grip was a little slow at times...

I busied myself making a scrap tea whilst the girls showered. Neither of us really wanted to make a big fuss in the kitchen come Sunday night and I gladly prepared another of Mercy's favourites - hot dogs in baked beans. It wasn't too bad but the thought of it was a little off-putting at times. Still, she loved it and it took all of five minutes to heat up and combine. We ate together, as we always did.

Ash wasn't up for cards once we had Mercy in bed, and we were both content to watch the Sunday movie. She was asleep on my lap within half an hour of it starting, not that my fingers running soothingly through her hair had anything to do with it, I'm sure. It gave me a further chance to study her again.

Her profile beguiled me; a pert nose, a small smile, her flickering eyes hooded by those long dark lashes. I ran my hand over her shoulder lightly, causing her to moan softly and reposition herself further into my lap. Could I reach down and play a soft kiss to her cheek, her brow maybe, her mouth...? Would it wake her? Did I care? Yes, I did, and my growing groin was a testament to this. I refocussed on the movie, not wanting her to end up with a crick in her neck.

When the movie finished, I shook her gently, not that I wouldn't have been happier to snuggle in behind her and sleep the night here, holding her in my arms. I was sure even subliminally, she would have also liked it. But, the coward I was once again prevented me from acting on this.

It took a few moments for me to rouse her, prompting it was time for bed. Her answer threw me – it was never time for bed. What does that mean Journal? Did she mean with me? If you have any insights, I would love to hear your theories.

That is basically the outline of our weekend. And here I write, once again, on my own. What do I do Journal? Do I risk what we have and tell her how I feel? Will I lose her anyway, having someone else steal her out from under me? Should I take the chance to find out whether she has any feelings for me? If the answer was yes, that would be the end of the competition. If the answer was no... well, I don't know what that would mean. And here I am, back at square one.

Journal Entry – Monday 26 April: 9.20 am

Just a quick entry Journal as the morning has not been a good one. Ash left for work at her usual time today, around 8.00 am. I was surprised to see her back again within half an hour, a bunch of flowers on her arm. I didn't ask, didn't have to – Mercy did. They were from a friend and I knew this friend would be Damon.

Since she was here, she came with me to take Mercy to school. On the way home, I asked who gave her the flowers. Her answer didn't surprise me, and I asked when the big date was. She had turned him down, but Damon told her he was going to bring a bouquet in every Monday until she said yes. I knew it would only be a matter of time before Ash relented.

She was in no rush to get back to school, so I made coffee. I was in no rush to get to work this morning either. There was something else on her mind though and I wished I hadn't pushed her for the information. It was information I didn't want to know, although I would have been happy to help her solve the problem. She was horny, wanted sex. So, as per my earlier point Journal, I knew it would only be a matter of time before she relented.

She asked me what I did when I felt this way and seemed a little shocked when I revealed that I paid for it on occasion. Let's face it; it was an easier option sometimes! It was a shame apparently, that 'someone as handsome as me' has to go to a prostitute. I had to laugh at that. I explained to her though I chose this option, I didn't *have* to, and was concerned I'd divulged too much. She looked a little uncomfortable about it. I also offered her the chance to help me out in the future and she laughed, agreeing it would be a wonderful arrangement. That it would!

I asked her if she masturbated and was assuming she didn't. Her answer delighted me though; she'd captured herself doing it on camera once, for Lori's benefit I assumed. I would love to find that evidence and watch it myself. But she didn't just want to get off, she was missing the intimacy that accompanied lovemaking and I admitted I missed it too. I hugged her then, and we stood there in each other's arms until the High School bell rang and dragged us back to reality.

She didn't feel like going to work and I told her I'd write her out a doctor's note. I would then also ring in sick so I could spend the day with her. Work on my moves ha ha ha. We both ended up going to work...

And here I sit at work, writing in you. I have to get a hold on this.

Journal Entry – Wednesday 28 April: 10.30 pm

I took the afternoon off today Journal, for some reason I was in an elated mood. I wanted to get some research done which I never seemed to get around to these days and decided to get a few chores out of the way too. I put Nickelback on the stereo before I started in on the housework, realising it had been too long since I'd listened to music at this volume. It was energising.

Now I wouldn't normally be telling you this Journal, it's not a life-changing issue, but the aftermath makes it a worthy tale. Whilst cutting up the vegetables I reverted to my teens and sung into the zucchini in my hand, sliding across the kitchen tiles. I was having a great time. When I spun around however, Ash and Mercy were peeking through the front door, massive grins on both of their faces. I'm sure my face went beetroot red. I don't think I had ever been so embarrassed in my life. I turned the music down whilst Ash razzed me. Dear, sweet Mercy wanted me to keep going. God love her. Ash made coffee and the shit-eating grin was still covering her face, so I attacked with tickles and Mercy joined me. Any excuse I could muster to touch her I took these days, ending the torment in a big hug.

Sitting at the table, Mercy came out with a question that took us both by surprise; she wanted to know why we weren't married. Ash went through the explanation again, of how Lori and I fit into their lives and that I was really her uncle, not her Daddy. Ash shot me a glance, obviously wanting my assistance with this, but I was happy to let her go, much to her chagrin. Mercy was worried if Ash married someone else one day that he'd become her new Daddy. She wanted me to marry Mum so I would always be her father. I explained that marriage didn't work that way and people had to be in love to get married. Of course, she then wanted to know why I wasn't in love with Ash. How could I tell her that I was? Obviously, I couldn't Journal. I promised her that we would always be a family, whatever happened in the future, and this made her happy.

Ash then asked her where this conversation had come from and some older kid at school had been giving Merce a hard time. I knew the family; they were professional breeders and just above the poverty line. Most of the seven kids were half brothers and sisters due to their fathers being different men. Mrs Butler was certainly not selective when it came to choosing a man.

Ash took it hard that Mercy had to deal with this on her own at school, and I knew how cruel kids could be. It was all a part of growing up and was difficult to avoid. Mercy was tough though and I knew she'd always be OK, if not a little upset occasionally as these things happened down the track, from time to time. Of course, I took this opportunity again to hug her. I know, I should be ashamed of myself, but I just can't help it...

Journal Entry – Thursday 29 April: 11.00 pm

All was quiet when I got home from work today and I didn't know what had happened to my little family. I called out but there was no answer. I finally found a note on the island bench letting me know they were at Michael's and I was to go there when I got home. We were staying for dinner. Our girl saw me pull into the driveway and came running to open the door for me. After a kiss and a cuddle, she told me Ash was out the back with the guys and Merce went back to the PlayStation.

It was a weird situation when I joined them on the patio, as if I had interrupted something. I gave Ash a kiss and leant up against the barbeque, next to her, with my arm around her waist. She was blushing. When I asked her why, Michael interjected to let me know they were there too. It felt like he was directing the conversation away from her again. They then gave Ash and I a teasing, using our pet names for each other, namely 'Honey' and 'Babe'. I got the feeling I'd been the topic of conversation for some reason.

Mercy chose hamburgers for dinner and just as we were about to eat, Bree and Simon came home. And Journal, what sad news they had for us. We didn't know they'd been trying to have a family, but they found out this afternoon that they weren't capable. Mercy told them she'd be their pretend daughter, and the pride and love I felt for her nearly fell from my eyes as tears.

I took Ash's hand; I knew how hard she'd be taking this. She'd always hoped for them to have a child so he or she could grow up with Mercy. But this wasn't going to happen now. A few options were thrown around like surrogacy, implantation or sperm donation. Sperm donation was certainly their best option and the success rate was high.

I insisted we all travel home in the one car and Ash revisited the Bree and Simon issue, asking if I'd ever donate. I checked Mercy was asleep as I considered it. I believed I would help Simon and Bree out, but it would be difficult knowing their child was technically part of me. Not that it would ever be considered that way, and difficult to live with possibly. I posed the question back to her and when she realised if one of her eggs was involved, the implications were a little more intense.

She made me laugh when she thought she would have to have sex with Simon, and I reminded her that it was clinically inserted into the uterus. Sex wasn't required. I also asked her if she wanted more kids, and she did. I wanted a bigger family too, our own family enlarged, not with anyone else. She told me that she'd carry for me if ever needed and I reciprocated her offer, also offering my sperm donation services. I also let her know that the old-fashioned method was the best choice for pregnancy. I didn't mean this as doctor's advice either, I just wanted to find that intimacy with her.

We made a deal; if neither of us were with anyone else by the age of thirty-five, we'd have a baby together. That was only a little over five years away and if I had to, I would wait that long. She wanted to know by what method she'd be impregnated, and I told her it was entirely up to her.

Journal Entry – Tuesday 4 May: 11.30 am

Funny to think back to this same time yesterday, Journal. You won't believe the past twenty-four hours; in fact, I don't believe them either. Faith, of all people, came into the surgery yesterday. I should have recognised the name when I saw the new folder but didn't stop to think she'd come all the way to Sommersett to see me on a pretence. She had though.

After a few minutes into the consultation, she made it very clear to me why she'd come – she wanted sex. It had certainly been a while and unfortunately, I let my cock make the decision for me. I told her to meet me at home at 2.30 pm, giving me plenty of time to get her in and then out of our house. There was no way I wanted Ash to know about this. I felt like a bit of a prick just accepting the offer when I had no intention of going anywhere else down the road with this woman, but she had offered. Who was I to say no?

It was wonderful too Journal. God, I felt so alive again. I knew that I was using her when I closed my eyes and believed myself to be making love to Ash instead. Faith's problem though is that she never knows when to shut up, so the Ashlyn fantasy was difficult to hold on to for more than a few minutes. And then the fucking started.

We didn't make love, we fucked; rutted like two animals, over and over again. There didn't seem to be anything that could get my dick soft. Until Ash came home… and early. It disappeared in a flash. She knew I had someone in here with me too.

I dragged my boxers on and followed Ash into her room, a fact that did not sit well with Faith. Too bad, I loved this woman. She was embarrassed that she'd unknowingly caught me at it, but I told her it didn't matter and apologised for having her here. Ash hadn't worked out who was actually in my room with me, thank God. But, in true Faith form, she ruined it all, turning up at Ash's door. I should have known this was something she wouldn't be able to resist. Ash told me to finish up and then get her out, however only one of those points was now relevant to me.

I took Faith back to my room, handing her clothes to her. She wasn't happy. Then, in a blinding flash of understanding, she told me I was a stupid fool for falling in love with a woman who I could never have, who would never want me other than as a replacement for my dead brother. I escorted her down the stairs; no one talks about Lorien like that in front of me. Her words hurt though.

I could hear the spa running when I went in search of Ash and knocked before entering the ensuite. She was covered in bubbles, her modesty retained. And then she let me have it, reminding me of my broken promise never to have Faith in the house again. I knew I'd broken that promise when I brought her here, but never thought Ashlyn would ever find out. I garbled out some lame excuses, none that I knew would wash. I then realised she'd been crying. Why would she be crying? She screamed at me to get out, so I did.

Back in my room, I sat contemplating what just happened. If I didn't know better, I would have considered this a jealous outburst, but wishful thinking did not make it so. I knew how much she despised Faith and knew that was the problem, and not that I was having sex with someone else. If only this would be an issue with her, a jealousy issue. That would be something that could be resolved in an instant, making me the happiest man in the world.

I went looking for her after dinner. She hadn't come out of her room all evening. She wasn't in her bedroom and I couldn't hear the spa running so sat on her bed for a few minutes in case she was using the toilet. I still couldn't hear any noise, so quietly opened the ensuite door. I found her in the spa, which was now off and would have been freezing. I ran into my room and grabbed a heater, putting it on her bedroom floor, then going to grab a Valium and a glass of water. I went in and woke her; she *was* freezing.

She let me help her out and I wrapped a towel around her, trying to warm her. My God, she was like a block of ice. I sat her on the bed in front of the heater and aimed its flow directly at her. She wilted on the ground in front of it, and I passed her the Valium, instructing her to take it.

I dried and dressed her, all done with the eye of a professional doctor, not one who wanted her in other ways, and then tucked her into bed. She was trying to talk to me, but I shushed her, telling her tomorrow would be time enough for that. She wanted me to climb in with her, so I did. I didn't know whether I was warm or that she was so terribly cold. I was a little frightened that she'd overdone it and was glad she wanted me to stay with her, so I could keep an eye on her. She slept right through and didn't even stir when I eased out from under her in the morning.

Ash wouldn't be going to work today, so I rang the school and arranged for Anna and Dom to have Mercy again that night. With nothing else I could do, I left her a note.

When I got home, she was screaming, and I flew up the stairs to find her weeping uncontrollably. Lorien had been here, and my throat swelled shut as I choked back my own tears. She was in such turmoil and I didn't know what I could do for her. As a doctor, I had never felt so helpless.

I asked her about Lorien, and she told me the reasons she wanted to talk to him. It *was* about me, me and Faith and of course, bloody Damon. I told her there was nothing I could do about Damon, but assured her I would never see Faith again. Ash didn't want to infringe on my life though, but didn't understand that *she* was all I needed. My promise was one that I intended on keeping this time. It had hurt her, for whatever reason it had been.

She cheered up a little and we got pizza for dinner. She asked what I'd given her in tablet form last night and I told her. She felt it when she woke up this afternoon, which I knew she would. I offered to sleep with her again, for my own selfish reasons this time, but she declined. She didn't believe herself to be a very strong woman, but she was so wrong.

Journal Entry – Wednesday 5 May: 7.30 am

Great, one week after the first bunch of flowers show up and they're going on a date! It's my own stupid fault for leaving this so long. The knowledge that she was also going to have sex with this guy was enough to drive me insane. He had no idea of what he was being offered to him on a plate and I doubted he'd cherish it, look after it. Appreciate it! He would get to fuck her, and I hated him for it. I knew it was blatant jealousy on my behalf, but I felt like a witness to a plane crash, helpless to do anything but to stare in shock. There was nothing I could do in this situation either; not without embarrassing myself at the same time. Damn this all to hell!

WINTER

Bad Date

THANKFULLY, ONCE I HAD ACCEPTED DAMON'S OFFER the flowers stopped coming on Monday mornings. May flew by and date night was rapidly approaching. Damon was at my desk first thing Friday morning, ready to finalise the plans. "I've been pretty good, I haven't harassed you since you said yes." My smile was his response. He looked a little confused, and said, "We *are* still on for tomorrow night, aren't we?"

"Yes Damon." He exhaled in what appeared to be relief.

"Where and when shall I pick you up?"

"My place will be fine if that's OK with you, or I can drive and meet you somewhere..."

"No, no. Your place will be great. No point in both of us needing to drive. How does around 6.30 pm sound?"

"Fine. Where are we going?"

"I thought we'd try the Mexican place on the Central Coast since it's your favourite food."

"How did you find out about that?"

"I asked around." He threw me a sardonic grin and leant against my desk, his arms folded across his chest. I scoffed and shook my head. I wasn't going to give him points for asking the right people the right questions. "Second thoughts?" he asked in relation to my slightly rude reaction.

"No Damon, I'm really looking forward to it too."

"Excellent. There's a band on at Sommersett Golf Club. I thought we might catch them after dinner?"

"Sounds good." I smiled, giving him a little warmth. It wasn't his fault that I was trying to retain a semblance of a barrier between us, it was mine. My desire to avoid sex was making me cold toward him and that wasn't fair. I'd accepted his offer and I had to be the master of my own destiny; I couldn't treat him like a student and hold him at arm's length. This was something I needed to deal with.

When I heard a knock at the door at 6.25 pm, I muttered under my breath. I had taken *way* too long to work out what I was going to wear that evening, and Mercy wanting to play dress-ups in my wardrobe at the same time didn't help. I had decided on jeans and an A-line swing shirt with bell sleeves. It was dressy without being overly so, and it was one of my favourite smart-casual tops. Broad swirls of strong colours were emblazoned across it and it was a flattering length, especially when teamed with jeans. I was looking for my shoes now, which was holding me up even further. I didn't want to leave Damon downstairs for too long alone with Elijah. I wasn't sure why, but it was a gut instinct I was following. "Mercy?" I called out. She clomped into my room, wearing the heels I had been searching for. "Can I have those now Sweetie, Mummy needs to get going."

"Can I meet him?"

"Of course Bump." She kicked off the shoes and handed me my bag and coat off the bed.

"You look really pretty Mum. I like it when you put on makeup." I smiled at her and she led me downstairs.

Both men were sitting on the sofa, watching the Saturday footy game. My team - the Dragons, were currently giving the Roosters - Elijah's team, an absolute flogging. Both men stood as I reached the bottom step. "Wow, you look great," Damon said, sizing me up.

"Thanks Damon. This is my daughter Mercy."

"I'm five and a half," she offered and peeked around my legs a little shyly. Damon bent down to her level.

"What a pretty name. Do you know what it means?"

"It's unusual and dramatic, just like my father." Elijah and I burst into laughter.

"I'll explain later Damon. Now you be good for Daddy tonight."

"I will Mum," she said, and I leant down so she could kiss my cheek.

"I won't be too late," I told Elijah and he got up to see us to the door.

"She might be though," Damon added and winked at him. Elijah's face turned to thunder. I couldn't wait to ask him what they'd been chatting about before my arrival downstairs. "Don't wait up!"

"Call if you need anything," Elijah said quietly and hugged me to him in goodbye. A quick brush of his lips over my brow now changed Damon's expression into thunder. It must have been an interesting conversation I'd missed. Surely these two hadn't been jousting over me? It was too ridiculous to give even a moment's thought. It would also mean that Elijah wanted me. I *hoped* they had been jousting over me, but this didn't make it so. I sighed and followed Damon out the door.

"Bye," I called again as I got into the car. Mercy had joined Elijah at the front door to wave us goodbye. He hoisted her up on his hip and my little family waved until we were out of sight.

Damon was unusually silent for a few minutes; I expected him to be chirping like a bird. I glanced at him and he looked back at me. I smiled, which seemed to ease him a little. "Your daughter is really sweet."

"She can be deceptive," I laughed.

"What was the inside joke about her name?"

"Lorien always liked Mercy as a name if she was a girl, which of course she was. I liked it too as it was unusual and dramatic, just like her father. This point has been mentioned quite a few times over the years, but it's the first time I've heard Merce come out with it."

"And Elijah's story?"

"Meaning?"

"How does he fit into all this? I didn't know you lived with anyone else."

"He's Mercy's uncle, was Lorien's twin brother. We've been together since I moved in with the Standish's when I was nineteen. He got me through my mourning period when Lorien died, and I in return was there for him. We're a tight unit."

"It's pretty obvious. Did you two ever go out?"

"I was his first girlfriend when they moved to Sommersett and when we broke up, I went out with Lorien. You know how that turned out, married, kid..." I smiled at him again.

"I don't think he's ever gotten over it somehow," he muttered.

"Why? What did he say to you?"

"Nothing in particular, but it felt like you were his daughter, not his sister-in-law and I was picking you up with the intentions of ripping your virginity from you."

"You're about a decade too late for that," I laughed. He looked at me again and smiled. Whatever had been the problem, he now let it slide.

We chatted comfortably in the car. Damon was easy to get along with and I found myself relaxing, enjoying the ride, enjoying my meal and laughing and joking in the car on the trip back to Sommersett. It surprised me when I took note, not thinking someone outside my little realm could give me so much pleasure. I wasn't sure where we were when we pulled into a driveway, not far from the club. "What are we doing here?" I asked.

"This is where I live. I thought I'd drop the car off and we could walk to the club. I also need to use the bathroom and would rather use mine than a public one." He took me by the hand, leading me inside.

I looked around his lounge room and finally took a seat on the sofa, waiting for him. "There's wine and beer in the fridge if you'd like some," he called out. I would like some, but I also wanted to stay semi-sober; my plan to resist any advances still in the forefront of my brain.

"Are you going to have one?"

"Sure," I heard from behind me. "Come with me," he said and took my hand again, this time to lead me into the kitchen.

"White, red or beer?" he asked, pulling two half bottles of wine from the fridge and a VB.

"I thought you drank red wine at room temperature."

"What is room temperature in Europe during winter?"

"About the same as the fridge I guess," I said laughing, understanding his point. I wasn't sure if it was an accurate response, however. "I'll have a beer, thanks." He twisted the cap off and reached for a glass from the cupboard, pouring the beer into it perfectly. It had a nice inch frothy head and fit the glass exactly. He repeated the process with his own.

"Want to take your coat off? The fire's still going in the lounge." He stood behind me and took the coat as I shrugged it off my shoulders, taking it into his room to put on the bed. "Want the grand tour?"

"Why not," I agreed. His home was clean and cosy. I asked him about flatmates - he lived alone; girlfriends - hadn't had one in a few years. I was surprised at this. It would seem he would be a perfect match for an equally suited girl, not that I was lining myself up for the challenge. He was a little evasive on the subject, so I didn't push it.

I went to use the bathroom on our way past and he stopped me, telling me the ensuite off his room had just been cleaned this afternoon. Was he expecting me to be using it later tonight? In the morning? Was I simply *so* vain that I assumed these were his intentions? I really needed to get over myself. I slid the door shut and tried to pee as quietly as possible, knowing he was only on the other side of the thin internal door. *Go into the lounge room*, I willed him.

He was sitting on the bed when I came out and I looked around his room. "You're a very tidy man Damon."

"I hear it impresses the ladies," he laughed and passed me my beer.

"Like using black and red satin?" I asked cheekily, spotting the sensual linen on the bed, including pillow covers, and several candles on each of the bedside tables. My assumptions may have been correct after all. He winked but didn't answer.

"Come on, let's go dancing Ash." We finished our drinks and headed for the club, just a few streets away.

We walked to Sommersett Golf Club, hand in hand. Damon stopped me at the bottom of the ramp leading us into the venue, taking both of my hands in his. He had this goofy smile on his face and then leant in and kissed me lightly. It was nice. Nice is a word that allows you to make a judgement without thinking too hard about the answer. It wasn't an expected kiss, or a clothes-ripping, lustful kiss, it was simply a nice kiss. I thought it would also be nice if he kissed me again at some stage.

It took only a few seconds for our eyes to adjust, considering it was already dark outside. Damon generously paid our two entry fees and led me toward the bar. "I'll get the drinks, you paid for dinner and the band," I called over the noise. The music had already started.

"No need, I asked you out." I smiled then ordered and paid when the barmaid neared. "OK, you can get the drinks," he said and laughed.

I was glad that the barmaid from ten years ago no longer worked at the club. I would have found it difficult to come here if that was the case. I looked around the venue as we waited, thinking back to the nights that 'Listening at Keyholes' last played here. It seemed an eternity ago. "What are you smiling at?" Damon asked. I thanked the barmaid as she handed me my change and we found a vacant table near the back of the room. I then proceeded to fill Damon in on a little more of my background. He was impressed. "Wow, you were in a band?" I nodded.

"You met the bass guitarist tonight, and my husband was the lead singer, guitarist and writer of the songs."

"You are certainly some kind of family. I didn't know you were that musically inclined. Would never have guessed it in fact," he added.

"What do I do at Sommersett High Damon?" I challenged. He smiled in embarrassment, realising I *was* a music teacher.

"Being in a band is just so... cool!" he explained, then corrected himself. "Not that you aren't cool or anything..." He let it go, knowing he was sinking himself into deeper water with his comments.

"It's OK Damon, it was ten years ago, a lifetime ago."

"You'll have to play for me one day. I've never heard you perform."

"I'm not much of a public performer; it's just my students that hear me these days, and more often than not, on the piano. Sometimes I'll record myself playing and accompany it on the violin for class."

"I'll have to sneak into one of your classes then." I laughed.

All of a sudden, Kari's face was in front of mine. She was leaning down from my side. "What are you guys doing here?" she asked, dragging up a seat. I glanced quickly at Damon to gauge his reaction before answering.

"Just taking in the music."

"Are you here together?"

"Yes," Damon answered before I had the chance. Not that I was going to deny it. I wasn't ashamed or embarrassed to be here with him, but it would make life a little more difficult once it became common knowledge in the staffroom. Perhaps they were already aware of our date... I laughed a little to myself, remembering that Kari was.

"This is Tony," Kari said, introducing us to her boyfriend who had just pulled a chair up to the table. "Ashlyn and Damon," she said to him and he shook each of our hands. He wasn't what I expected of him.

Being an outdoorsy guy, I assumed he'd be tall and lean. He was about my height and a little podgy. A few years older than Kari too it seemed.

"Kari has told me a lot about you two." She elbowed him and he added, "In separate conversations of course." I raised one eyebrow at Kari and she suitably blushed. What had she been saying to Tony about us, I wondered.

"We were just going to dance," Damon said, holding his hand out to me.

"We'll join you!" Kari enthused. Damon didn't seem very happy with this arrangement.

On the floor, I saw Damon take Kari aside, and she nodded at whatever he'd said. This was getting curiouser and curiouser, not unlike Alice in the damn rabbit hole. The band was great though, and we were all wrapped up in the music before too long.

When we got back to the table, Kari leant in and stopped Tony from sitting back down. "We were just about to make a move, we'll catch you at school," she said. Tony gave her a weird look, but rose all the same.

"Nice to have met you," he said, and they disappeared into the crowd.

"Did you shoo them off?" I asked and laughed.

"Yes, I did," he said and grinned back at me. "We have all the time in the world to catch up with Kari at school. She doesn't need to become part of our date. Who knows when I'll get another one," he challenged me. I let the challenge go unanswered.

I could see myself getting involved with Damon, but did I want to? That was the question I needed to answer before it went any further. I didn't want to lead him on, and I didn't want my work environment to become an issue either. It was a hard question to answer, as I didn't really know him all that well.

He pointed to my empty glass, I nodded, and he took the glasses back to the bar, and to get us another. I was a little surprised to see him come back without drinks. "Bar closed?"

"No, I thought you might like to come back to my place for a while, listen to some music of my choice... Get to know my tastes a little better, Music teacher."

"What tastes exactly are you referring to Damon?" I asked.

"Are you flirting with me again Ms Standish?" I laughed. "So, do you want to?" My head was starting to pound a little, so I *did* want to, and I accepted his outstretched hand.

We could still faintly hear the band when we arrived back at his place and he danced to it a little as he stuck the key in the door, opening it before me. "Madam," he said and waved me through in front of him. "Take a seat, I'll be right back."

He went into the kitchen and returned with a bottle of wine and an ice bucket. Bending down he opened the small china cabinet and removed two crystal glasses. "I save these for special occasions," he said and passed them to me.

"And you keep the champagne in the fridge for special occasions too?" He grinned and popped the cork, allowing it to settle before placing it on the coffee table.

"Would you mind pouring? I'm just going to get changed."

He came back out in a pair of grey trackie pants and a T-shirt, barefoot. He took his glass from the coffee table and clinked it against mine. "Cheers beautiful." He watched me over the rim as he drank. "Any requests?" he asked, sitting down cross-legged in front of the stereo.

"I thought you were going to make the selection."

"That I was…" he agreed, and started to flick through the pile of CDs in the cabinet under the stereo. "Hmmm… Something not too brassy, but with plenty of rhythm… ahhh, the perfect thing." I couldn't believe it when Michael Bublé started to croon.

He stoked the fire and switched off the lights before stretching out on the floor in front of it. Its light was the only illumination in the room, and it captured his hair, highlighting embers of gold and auburn. It was a little hypnotic. He grinned up at me and took another swig from his glass, asking, "Romantic?"

"You've done this before," I said.

"Not for a long time."

"So why is it exactly that you're single Damon? I would have thought you'd be a big hit with the girls."

"Had my heart broken a while ago, it takes time to heal."

"What am I doing here then?"

"The time has passed. Has it passed for you too Ash?" he asked a little sadly. I sighed, wondering that very thing for such a long time. It had, I supposed, otherwise I wouldn't be here with Damon, wouldn't have allowed my feelings for Elijah to have bubbled to the surface. I looked at my champagne, alive with effervescence, and noted the irony. I glanced at Damon and he was waiting on my response. If I admitted my time of mourning was now an inbred emotion, regardless of my always loving Lorien, would he assume too much? I met him halfway, answering,

"Mostly," and left it at that.

"Toss me a pillow," he said, and I threw him one off the sofa. "Now come and lay here with me." The look on my face must have said it all as he added. "It's much nicer down here in front of the fire. Your honour isn't at stake." I knew the outcome of the mathematical equation of alcohol plus fireplace divided by two lying on the floor in front of it. I was aware of what the answer could be, would be... I hadn't had sex since Lorien died, naturally. I hadn't been on a date or met anyone who could even compare. I had managed to lock those urges away, and successfully so. But here they were, gushing from me like a broken water main, and I wanted him *so* desperately. *No, no, no* I reminded myself and then rose from the sofa to join him on the floor.

I lay next to him, and he rolled onto his side, propped up on one elbow. He smiled at me warmly and emptied his glass, reaching for the bottle to refill both. "You can get that look off your face Damon," I warned playfully.

"What look is that Ash?" he asked, eyebrows raised in innocence.

"The cat that ate the canary." He laughed loudly at my idiom, but didn't deny it. Instead, his face slowly lowered to mine, giving me time to stop him I assumed. I didn't though; I wanted him to kiss me again.

He drew back a few minutes later and smiled down at me. "That was magnificent 'Tweety'," he said, and I laughed. He put his glass on the table and took mine from my hand, placing it next to his. The crystal was radiant in the firelight. It sparkled and danced along with the fire in his eyes. Did they match my own?

His free hand travelled slowly over my waist and up my side as he wended his propped arm in under my head, shifting down to lay with me. This kiss was deeper and longer, holding more of promises to come. I resigned myself to its intention and moved with him on the floor. His soft moans were driving me crazy and when his leg moved between my own, I welcomed it in. I was so horny, and it had been so long... *You work together. Stop it!* my conscience screamed at me. My libido took the situation under control however, dragging the thought out the back door and beating it within an inch of its life. I kicked off my shoes.

When I felt his hands at my jeans button, I didn't stop him. When he eased his fingers inside, I didn't stop him. When he repositioned them inside my briefs, I didn't stop him. Hell, I did not intend to stop him, period. I knew I was aroused, knew it was obvious and his gentle caresses would make him aware of this too. I gave the pleasure back and reached for him. He was straining through his trackies and a small spot of moisture had formed. I knew he was just as aroused.

I was surprised at the length and thickness I found when I slid my hand into his pants. I assumed I had been lucky having had a well-endowed man in the past, but it was more common than I ever realised; Damon was also capably gifted. He groaned into my mouth and worked his lips down my throat before he sat up, startling me. "Sorry Ash, give me a minute." And with that, he disappeared back into his bedroom. What was he doing?

When he returned, he waggled a condom at me, taking the previous burning yearning into a somewhat less than romantic atmosphere. "Want to put it on for me?" Before I could answer, he stripped off his pants as he tore it open with his teeth, handing it to me. Lorien and I had often included the application of the condom into our foreplay when we still used them, his favourite being me rolling it onto him via my mouth. I had no such intention of doing that this evening however, pinching the tip with my fingers and manually adjusting it. He knelt down in front of me and pulled my legs into the air, dropping me onto my back. He yanked off my jeans and briefs and was on top of me in an instant. In one more instant, he was driving into me, riding me with quick, jabbing thrusts. His mouth was back on mine as he worked himself faster and faster. What happened to the foreplay? Was that it? Is this how the rest of the world made love?

"Damon…" I mumbled through the kiss.

"Fuck Ash, this is so hot, you're so fucking hot! Oh yeah, fucking take it, take it…"

"Damon," I tried again, but he was in his own world. He'd turned into a machine and I was the depot. Seconds later, he was yelling,

"Oh fuck Ash, fucking hell! My balls are going to explode… Jesus FUCKING CHRIST!" And then it was all over, and he came to lie beside me again, his head on my chest. "That was fucking great!" he said. I couldn't agree with him, I had never felt more wretched in my life. To make matters worse he removed the condom and threw it into the fire, which crackled and spat briefly, issuing a fine black smoke. It was enough to turn my stomach. I wasn't ready for this. "Stay with me Ash, stay the night," he mumbled sleepily.

"OK Damon," I lied, wanting to get out of there as soon as he was asleep. Thankfully, that was about five minutes later.

I eased out from under his arm and crept to the bathroom, grabbing my jeans and bag on the way. I cleaned myself up and redressed, closing his front door behind me quietly. I rang a cab from outside.

I let the tears flow freely on the way home. The cab driver wasn't one of the chatty varieties and he left me to it. It was less than a five-minute drive and if it hadn't been winter, I would have walked. I checked my watch when he turned on the cabin light so I could pay him, and it was after 1.00 am. The house was dimly lit and quiet, and I hoped Elijah had gone to bed.

He was sitting up on the sofa, asleep, the TV on. He stirred when I closed the door, even though I had done so as softly as I could. "How was your night Babe?" he asked, dragging his hands over his eyes, taking them from sleep into awake. My face crumpled, the slow leaking tears now expanding in the comfort of my own home. "Come to me Babe, tell me what happened," he soothed, his arms opening for me to envelope in. I did so gladly.

"It was horrible!" I said and sniffed. I felt so much better already; his strength had a comforting presence like morphine.

"What did he do to you?" he asked darkly.

"We had a nice evening," there was that word again, "and then we... we... he..." I started to blubber again.

"Oh Honey, please tell me, you're breaking my heart." I couldn't stop. "Ash, please Babe, tell me what happened."

"Is that how the rest of the world does it Elijah? Is that how *you* consider love making to be?" He stiffened a little. I was going to have to reveal what happened for him to know what was now wrong with me.

"You'll have to be a little more specific than that Ash, but I think I understand where you're going with this."

"Wham, bam, not even a thank you Ma'am."

"No Babe, that's not how the rest of the world makes love. Was he rough with you?"

"No, nothing like that, it was just... over. I *knew* I shouldn't have gone out with him."

"Sounds like a selfish prick. I didn't like him when I first laid eyes on him."

"That doesn't help Elijah," I said, and he commenced his soothing again, drawing his hand lightly over my back. "So much Lorien and I gave to each other when we made love. I'll never have that again!" Like an idiot, I started to howl. I buried my face into his shoulder, and he pulled me closer, holding me until the torrent started to slow.

"It's OK Babe, it's OK..." he soothed, his fingers feathering through my hair.

"Oh Elijah... I just... just wanted to feel... wanted again," I sniffed.

"I want you...," he said, his voice slightly hoarse. I smiled up at him, appreciating his attempt to pacify me.

"No one's *ever* going to want me again in the way I want to be wanted," I wailed, and started crying all over again. His sweetness had taken an opposite effect on me. He tilted my face toward him and smiled at me, running his fingers over my cheeks, removing the tears. And then, he was kissing me.

My eyes were wide as I stared at his closed lids, then fell into its rhythm and embraced the kiss. His lips were soft and searching and mine eagerly parted when I felt the first nuance of his tongue. My face was still in his hands and I crawled onto his lap to face him fully, deepening the kiss. His hands eased down my back, coming to rest on my rear, and he pulled me tighter against him. *Oh my God, this is incredible*, I thought, wanting to rip his shirt open. I could hear my own breath quickening. His fingers trickled lightly up over my back, ending once again on my face. Unbelievably he was then drawing me away from him, looking into my eyes. "Better now?" he whispered. *No!* I thought, *Don't stop Elijah!* "Ash?" he asked.

"Huh?"

"Do you feel better now Babe?" He drew me down to his shoulder and caressed his hands over my back again.

"Not really," I answered in all honesty, I'd wanted it to go a *lot* further.

"I tried," he said, and I sat up. He smiled at me.

"It was a wonderful kiss, thanks Elijah."

"It was the least I could do." He was right; it *was* the least he could do. I wanted more, but there was obviously not going to be any more. I needed to get away and clear my head, needed to be away from him. I wiggled back off his lap and sat beside him, his arm still around my waist.

"I think I'll check on Mercy and go to bed. How was she tonight?" His expression was one I couldn't read.

"We watched the Shrek trilogy and she fell asleep on the sofa. It was a pretty quiet night."

"Thanks for watching her Elijah, I appreciate it. Not that it was the evening of a lifetime." He now looked at me strangely and I wished I could read his mind.

"It's not like babysitting." He grinned at me and then helped me lock up before following me up the stairs. "Now you come and wake me if you need any more cheering up tonight." I didn't know what to say to this so muttered,

"Ahh, OK. Good night."

"Night Babe," he said and disappeared into his room. I was so confused as to what just happened.

After Effects

TOMORROW WAS INDEED, another day. I woke the next morning feeling a lot better than when I had gone to bed. I'd come to terms with the events of last night and shrugged them off, not giving them any power. I would deal with Damon as necessary when I went back to school on Monday.

Elijah was in the middle of making pancakes as I made my way into the kitchen. "I thought you were going to sleep the whole morning away," he teased.

"It was a pretty late night. How come you're up and chipper?"

"I got a few hours of sleep on the sofa waiting for you to come home. Do you want coffee?" he asked, flipping over the golden-brown pancakes and reaching for the pot. I did. He handed me a steaming cup of good morning and as I passed by my phone, it rang.

"Good morning caller!" I chirped.

"Hey gorgeous." It was Damon. I put my mug on the table and sat heavily onto one of the chairs. I wasn't expecting this phone call and I certainly wasn't expecting his mood to be so casual, considering what had happened last night.

"Ahhh, hi..." I answered eventually. *Who is it*? Elijah mouthed to me. I shook my head and turned a little in my seat.

"What time did you creep away this morning? I was depressed when I woke up alone."

"After you fell asleep."

"Oh. I thought you may have wanted to hang around for a repeat performance this morning." Was he *kidding*?

"What performance was that?" I glanced up at Elijah and he stood there staring at me, the muscles in his jaw working to harden his look. The batter was dripping onto the counter from the wooden spoon he still held in his hand. I gestured to it and he shook off his apparent seething, grabbing a cloth to clean up the mess.

"I'm not referring to the band, lover," he said and chuckled. "Are you going to come over today? I was planning on making you breakfast but you'd gone."

"So, your intention was always that I'd be sleeping over?"

"Aren't you glad you at least spent *some* time at my place last night?" No, I wasn't.

"It was fine."

"Fine? That's hardly a word I would have used," he laughed again. It appeared he had *no* idea of how I felt about last night. Maybe this was the way he made love every time...

"I can't really talk now. Can I catch up with you at school?"

"What's wrong Ash, you sound a little... down. Is everything OK?"

"Sure, everything is *fine*." I re-stressed the word.

"You don't sound fine... did I miss something last night?" He had missed several things, my G-spot for one, my desire to slow him down, and my arrival at orgasm. All of these things had been overlooked. I know we are each responsible for our own orgasms, but this was ridiculous.

"No, I just have to go," I said, and ended the call.

"What did *he* want?" Elijah asked.

"You know, I'm not really sure. It sounded like he was oblivious to the mess that last night became. He rang to talk I suppose, all happy and excited."

"I said it last night and I'll say it again - he's a selfish prick."

"No, I don't think that's it, I really believe he had no idea. Maybe he hasn't had much experience."

"Why are you sticking up for him? The state you came home to me in last night was inexcusable. You were so upset, don't ever forget that..."

"I feel a little sorry for him."

"Sorry?" he scoffed. "He needs a good kick up the arse. If he doesn't know how to treat women properly at his age, then there's no hope for him, is there?"

We sat and ate the pancakes in silence. "Where's Mercy?" I asked, noting he hadn't called her to breakfast.

"Your folks came and picked her up this morning. She'll be back around five." I nodded.

"Don't be angry with me Elijah," I said, trying to keep the plea out of my voice.

"I'm not angry Ash, I'm confused."

"Why are *you* confused?" I asked with a smile.

"I can't work out what you see in this guy and that you're prepared to give him another chance."

"I never said that."

"You're leaning toward it though, aren't you?" I thought about this. Was I? I didn't think I wanted to see him again outside of our work environment, but still, I found myself wavering. I truly did believe he was unaware of my feelings, the way the circumstances were last night. I didn't want to talk about it anymore and a few minutes later Elijah nodded, seeming to think that my silence confirmed his last question.

There were so few dishes I decided to wash up instead of stacking them into the dishwasher. Elijah came to help me. His disposition seemed to have ebbed considerably and he ended up nudging into me with his hip. I smiled at him and nudged him back, scooping some bubbles from the sink and wiping them onto his cheeks. "Don't start what you aren't going to finish Babe," he threatened. My response was to scoop up more bubbles and wipe them over his goatee. "Right," he said and put both hands into the sink, taking water into his hands with the bubbles, and dumped it down the front of my shirt. I couldn't help but laugh and I splashed him back, straight from the sink. He took one of the mugs and dunked it into the dishwater, turning to me as I ran from him, putting the dining room table between us.

"No Honey, please don't!" We were laughing and scamming each other into running around the table, making a break for freedom. Our hilarity was cut short by a knock at the door. "Saved by the knock!" I called, and ran for the door, Elijah directly behind me. As I opened the door, he wrapped himself around me from behind and yanked me in a half circle. "Elijah, stop it!" I laughed and turned to see who was at the door. "Damon," I said breathily as I wiped the back of my hand across my forehead, removing the frothy aftermath. Elijah let me go immediately, returning to the kitchen in a huff. I was sure I heard him muttering *selfish prick* under his breath.

"Have I caught you at a bad time?" he asked, looking past me into the kitchen at Elijah.

"No, of course not, we were just cleaning up after breakfast. Come in."

"Sorry to drop in unannounced, but you didn't give me much choice." He looked around the room and then out onto the verandah. "Is there somewhere private we can talk?" I led him outside.

He leant forward and took my hand over the table, smiling weakly at me. "To what do I owe this pleasure?" I asked, prompting him to start talking.

"I wanted to know if I did something to hurt you last night. You seemed really strange on the phone earlier."

"No, I just had a realisation was all. I upset myself."

"Want to tell me about it?"

"Not really, *you'll* get upset in the process."

"I'm a big boy." Yes, he was that. I lowered my face a little when I realised I was smiling, and blushing. "I think I understand your reaction," he said and sidled his chair over closer to mine.

"Want coffee?" Elijah yelled out through the kitchen window. He had seen the shift in Damon's seating also it would appear. Damon smiled at me and shook his head.

"No thanks Elijah," I called back.

"Did you enjoy yourself at all?" he asked, his face now a look of concern.

"Of course, the band -" He cut me off.

"I'm not talking about anything that happened before you joined me on the floor."

"Oh."

"Well?"

"I don't want to hurt your feelings Damon."

"That bad hey?"

"It wasn't good."

"Care to enlighten me a little?"

"Well, it was just all over so fast and then you were asleep."

"Fair enough, I can appreciate how that would have made you feel. I certainly can't put the blame on anything else but me, but the grog didn't help."

"I was pretty sure when you rang this morning you weren't aware of how I felt about it all."

"No, I wasn't. That's why I came over. I knew you were upset, and I wanted to speak to you about it before we had to go to work tomorrow. Clear things up."

"You need to understand Damon, what Lorien and I had was so special. I know I'm naive to think all sex is like what I was used to having, but I know better now."

"Normally I'm a very considerate lover Ashlyn. I can't change what happened last night..." he leant in closer to me, "but I'd certainly like to try again." His lips brushed lightly over mine and then he kissed me with more force. I felt myself falling under his spell and I kissed him back. A wave of heat flushed through me, reigniting the unsatisfied urges from last night. He stood, drawing me up with him and he moved in closer.

When the kiss ended, he held me to him, saying quietly, "I really want to get to know you better Ash, and I'm so sorry about last night. Can we go out again sometime?"

"I'd like that Damon."

I walked him to the door; Elijah was nowhere to be seen. "I'll see you tomorrow then," he said and kissed me again. "See you Elijah," he added and headed for the car. I turned and saw him standing near the piano. His face was dark, and his hands were bunched into fists at his sides.

"Elijah, what's wrong?" I asked. He choked on his words for a few seconds, struggling with what he wanted to say.

"Nothing," he finally said and headed for the stairs.

"Honey?" I reached out and grabbed his arm as he passed.

"Ash just let it drop."

"Let *what* drop?"

"I'm not in the mood Ash, let's talk about it later."

"Talk about *what* later? Surely I'm free to go out with who I want?"

"Yes, you are, but I can't be here propping you up each time you fall over, especially when you keep taking the same leap."

"I don't expect you to."

"Good, because I can't do it anymore Ash. Watching you get hurt hurts me, and if you aren't prepared to accept things as they are, then I can't help you."

"I understand." I didn't want to upset Elijah, or hurt him. If he only knew that one word from him would whisk Damon out of my life forever. If only Elijah wanted me in the way I wanted him, it would be an end to the situation. Damon would cease to exist.

We went out again the following Saturday evening. Elijah wasn't free to watch Mercy, so I took her to Mum and Dad's on Friday night. Mum was excited that I had a date. I had neglected to inform her that we had already gone out before. "Tell me about him," she asked. I gave her a general run-down, which prompted more questions. She already had me living with him it seemed. I still wasn't overly joyed with dating a colleague and explained this to her, wanting to get her spin on it. A fresh view. "What's the problem?" she asked.

"If things don't work out, we have to share a small staffroom at work. It could make it uncomfortable for not only the two of us, but the rest of the faculty as well."

"That's a very good point Ashlyn," she said, but I could tell from the look on her face that she was excited for me. It wasn't every day that someone like Damon came along, her dancing eyes revealed.

He picked me up at 5.00 pm and we drove straight back to his place. "Dropping the car off?" I asked.

"No, I'm cooking for you tonight."

"A man who cooks, how special." I actually had one at home that also cooked.

The sun had just set, and the night air was enveloping us already. It was cosy and warm inside though; he had the fire going. He took my coat and tossed it onto his bed, taking my hand again and leading me into the kitchen. It had a sense of déja vu about it. He motioned to a stool at the kitchen bench, and I took a seat, accepting the glass of wine he poured and handed to me. "I know you like tuna," he said. "I've made tuna mornay."

"I'm a fan," I said and smiled at him warmly before sipping on my wine.

"*I'm* a fan," he said and joined me on my side of the bench, instigating the next kiss. We at least made it to the bedroom this time.

He was like a completely different person, taking care of my needs over and over again. When coming down from the last orgasm, he smiled up at me and I released the grasp I had on his hair. "Better this time?"

"Yes Damon, that was sensational." He slid up my body and poised above me, ready to penetrate. He eased in and started to grind slowly.

Two conflicting emotions started to do battle in my head. The speed of the delivery from last week left me unprepared and confused. This week I was also unprepared and confused - primarily because I didn't expect to have such feelings for him so quickly. It was one thing being pleasured by oral sex, but when met with face-to-face intimacy, it made it real, made him a real person. I wasn't primed for my own reaction to this epiphany. I knew I couldn't do this again and I suspected the *main* conflicting reason was due to fear. Fear that I could love him, fear of my life changing, fear of the unknown.

We lay quietly for some time in the afterglow before finally returning to the excellent meal that awaited us. I didn't speak of my concerns to him, didn't want to ruin the evening. When we sat down to eat, it was an enjoyable meal filled with lots of stories and laughter. "You're a really good friend Damon; I want you to know that."

"More than a friend I hope."

"I still have an issue with dating a colleague."

"What does it matter Ash?"

"If things go wrong, it could make it a very uncomfortable situation."

"Do you see things going wrong?"

"How can I answer that?" I laughed.

"We don't have to label this you know. We don't have to become 'boyfriend and girlfriend'."

"I know, but I also don't want this to become anything too heavy. I really like spending time with you Damon, and we get on great. But I don't want a relationship at the moment." There, I said it.

"Can we see each other every now and then at least? I know I won't be able to change your mind, but perhaps with a little more insight into me you'll come around eventually."

"Come around? See each other every now and then? You mean we can be fuck buddies?"

"Ashlyn!" he said in surprise and I laughed. "I would never have thought something like that could come out of your mouth!" He laughed with me.

"In answer to your question though, yes, I would like to see you every now and then, casually. We can see where that takes us, I suppose."

"Great. I intend on using all of my concealed weapons to win this war." I just smiled at him.

Elijah was at the dining room table when Damon dropped me off. I know he would have heard the car in the driveway, realising it had been idling there for some time. Why would he care if Damon and I were in the car kissing? I still felt a little guilty when I opened the door. As per his request, I didn't mention anything about the evening. I wished him good night and headed for the stairs. I still felt a little weird about it all though...

Ash's Birthday

DAMON AND I SAW EACH OTHER three times over the next several weeks. We had also established some rules. All talk and touching were strictly off limits at school, the choice to stay over at his place was not compulsory and no arguments were to be entered into if a suggestion was rebuked. It seemed to be working well for us, although I felt a little guilty that all the rules were mine. He didn't have such concerns.

My relationship with Elijah during this time seemed to fray and crack. The previous easy and caring connection we'd always shared was evaporating and I didn't know how to deal with it. I still loved Elijah, wanted Elijah, but nothing had progressed in this department; was in fact, slowly eroding away. I felt helpless. I hated feeling helpless. I was starting to sense I was about to lose him, that he'd finally had enough of my erratic ways.

There was a little contention as my birthday approached. Damon wanted to take me out and so did Elijah. Fortunately, my birthday was on a Thursday this year, so I agreed to see Damon the weekend before, spend Thursday night doing a family occasion and the following weekend Elijah and I were going out for dinner – Griffoner's at Castlebrook no less. It had been a while since I had a 'top of the range' seafood dinner and I was looking forward to it immensely. I still didn't eat a lot of seafood, but had become partial to lobster, technically crayfish in Australia. Elijah said I had good taste. I was also excited at the prospect of spending some quality time alone with him again, time that he had suggested we share together.

I got to Damon's around 6.00 pm that Saturday and he met me at the door. "Happy birthday Ash," he said, taking me in his arms to kiss me.

"It's not until Thursday," I reminded him.

"That doesn't matter; you still get your present tonight."

"So, it's a present now is it? When did you decide to call it that?" I asked cheekily, and he laughed, leading me inside.

"I was referring to this," he said and pointed to the large, flat, wrapped package leaning against the coffee table.

"You didn't have to get me anything," I told him.

"I didn't," he said, and I sat on the sofa as he passed me the gift. "Open it."

"Don't tell me I finally get to see your works of art?" I asked playfully.

"You've never asked," he said and pointed around the room to the four paintings on the wall, "but these are all my work." I goggled around the room, having noted the framed works before but never attesting them to being his. I felt a little foolish, thinking back to our first date and how I had chided him for not realising I was a musician, and therefore no surprise I had been in a band. I had now done the same thing to him.

"You're a wonderful artist Damon, I had no idea these were yours." I went to stand, and he stopped me.

"Open yours first." I smiled up at him and tore at the paper.

It was an oil painting, an oil painting of me. The upper part of my body was in frame, ending just below my navel. I was lying back on his red and black satin sheets, my eyes closed and my back arching upwards. My head was angled back, and my glossy lips were parted slightly. The expression on my face was shear rapture. I imagined that the scene *not* captured in the painting included him making love to me. It was a sensual, yet tasteful painting and I found myself blushing, knowing that this was the image I projected to him when we made love. “Do you like it?” he asked quietly.

“Oh Damon, I love it. I look so… beautiful,” I offered a little shyly.

“You are the most beautiful and erotic woman I’ve ever met Ashlyn.” He smiled down at me before leaning in to kiss me again.

“You did this from memory?”

“I’ve seen the image a few times,” he chuckled, “and hopefully will again tonight.” My already blushing face went a deeper red.

Damon cooked for me again that night. As per a previous date night at his place, he made mention of his intention to spend as much time with me as was possible and therefore preferred staying at home. He was still working on getting me to 'come around' apparently.

Tonight's menu was spaghetti, salad and garlic bread. His style was usually a simple dish, but it was always tasty and perfectly cooked. Whilst eating, I pressed him for more information on where he had gained his skills in the kitchen. "I have a mother," was his straightforward reply.

Little was I to know that when we made love that night, it was to be for the last time. On the rug in front of the fire was attempted again, with a much better outcome that the previous try. Lying there in his arms after, he tilted my face toward him; a warm smile caused me to return it with my own. "I need to talk to you Ash."

"About what?"

"My feelings for you."

"We have an agreement Damon."

"I know, but I can't help the way I feel."

"I don't want a relationship. That's not going to change anytime soon."

"I know, but I can still feel the way I feel, can't I?"

"Not if it's going to end up hurting you, no, you can't."

"Don't you want to know how I feel?" I looked up at him, not wanting to see anything burning too deeply in his eyes. "Ashlyn, I love -"

"No Damon," I said, putting a finger to his lips to silence him.

"But Ash," he tried again.

"Damon, I do care for you, do enjoy the time we spend together, but you have to understand this is all it can be. I can't give you any more than I have." He was silent, but drew me to him tighter.

"It's OK Ash, I can live with it." I sat up and turned to face him. I placed my hand on his face gently and smiled, knowing that I had to stop this, now.

"That's not fair on either of us Damon."

"I don't know why you're intent on fighting this Ash."

"I told you at the onset the only way this could be, and you're moving the goal posts."

"They don't have to be moved; surely it was worth a try?"

"It's never going to happen."

"How can you say *never*?"

"Because that's where I am right now, and I don't want it to change."

"I care so much for you; I want it to be different for us."

"I'm sorry Damon," I said and leant down to kiss him briefly, tenderly. "We can't do this anymore." I felt terrible, but it had to be done. He had taken his feelings further than he was supposed to. I know that it's impossible to govern at times, but I couldn't give him what he wanted, and I wasn't about to take him further down the wrong path. I did care for Damon, very much, but he wasn't where my current or immediate future paths wended. I couldn't hurt him.

"Please Ash, don't do this. I can work around it."

"Damon, it will only keep getting stronger and I can't do that to you, regardless of what you think you'll be able to cope with. I'm not that much of a selfish bitch."

"Be a selfish bitch." I smiled at him wanly. If only I could. "Will you at least stay the night?"

"It's not a great idea."

"Please?" I nodded and lay back with him, soaking up the warmth and bliss of the fire, and each other.

I snuck out around 3.00 am when I knew he was fast asleep. I thought that waking up without me would cement this decision for him, make him realise that it was indeed over. I still felt like I had done him wrong, and I was sneaking out of the house like a thief. But, I had to put him first. There was no point in debating this issue any further, and I knew if I stayed, we would be reliving it in the morning. His attempt to coerce would still go unheeded and it would only make it worse again for him. I truly wished that life could be simple.

Regardless of my obvious stealth, I got a phone call the next morning. Elijah's mood managed to fall into aggressive silence once he realised who was on the other end. I took the call outside, not wanting to put Damon through a public negation. We spoke for only a few minutes. During this time, he managed to amend the situation moreso to his liking. We would be friends - no longer friends with benefits, solely friends. This also included no intimacy of any kind, at any stage. He was still confident that by being around me I would 'come around' eventually. Maybe he was right, but I couldn't keep sleeping with him and having his feelings grow more intense if this didn't end up being the case.

Work went smoothly on Monday and he seemed acceptant of the new boundaries we were to work with. I was glad in a small way that we had been able to resolve this a little better than my suggestion of complete cut-off. At least I still had him as a friend, although the temptation to want him physically would no doubt rear its ugly head at some stage in the future. However, I would deal with that when, or if, it happened.

On Thursday morning, I was awoken by Mercy and Elijah bringing in a tray so I could have breakfast in bed. “Happy birthday,” they chorused, and I smiled, sitting up in bed as Elijah tucked the tray over my lap. He leant in and kissed me softly on the lips, the first proper kiss we'd shared since my first date with Damon. No cheeks or foreheads today, and it elated me.

“Thanks Honey,” I said softly and smiled at him as he sat on the bed. Mercy made her way across and sat up next to me, wriggling in under the covers.

“Is that you Mum?” she asked, drawing my eyes from Elijah's. She had noticed Damon's painting.

“Yes Merce.”

“You've got no clothes on.”

“It's considered a ‘nude’ and it's a very artistic form of painting. You'll see more of these when you get to high school and do Art.”

“You look really pretty Mum. Are you taking a nap?”

“Yes Bump,” I said and turned to Elijah with a grin.

His face was dark, his brow drawn. When he finally turned to look at me, he didn't return my grin. Instead, he scowled. "I won't be able to make it on Saturday," he said. "Looks like I'll have to work."

"Oh no Elijah!" I complained, "I was so looking forward to it."

"Were you Ash? I imagine it would be getting in the way of your other more important social engagements."

"No Honey, nothing is more important than spending time with you. You and Mercy." She beamed at me - he continued to scowl.

"You could have fooled me," he scoffed and tossed me a small package. "Happy birthday." He got up and left the room.

I hadn't told Elijah about my not seeing Damon anymore. He'd said he didn't want to know about our relationship, and I supposed that included when we were no longer having one. I wasn't sure it would make a difference anyway. I was not vain enough to assume that what Elijah had been putting me through was jealousy; I wasn't one hundred percent sure what had been his problem since I'd started seeing Damon. Was it even related? I knew I was going to have to tackle him over it eventually, but didn't look forward to doing so. I might not like what he had to say to me.

I sighed and opened the small package. Inside was a gold Pandora bracelet, and he'd started to fill it for me. It contained four charms already: a little girl, an angel, a jigsaw of hearts and a heart set with a ruby – my birthstone. The heart charms I considered very apt. He'd also bought the security chain to avoid me losing it and I felt the tears welling as I slipped it onto my wrist with Mercy's assistance. "We have more for you Mum," she chirped.

"Thank you Bump. If they're anything like this I've been very spoilt today."

"Did you get the painting for your birthday?"

"Yes Honey, Damon painted it for me."

"When am I going to see him again? I liked him."

"He liked you too Mercy, but I won't be seeing him again."

"Why not?"

"It's a complicated adult thing, but basically I couldn't give him what he wanted so there was little point in continuing to see each other. Do you understand?"

"Wouldn't you share with him?"

"Like biscuits and ice cream?"

"Yeah." It was hard not to laugh.

"Adults share things in different ways to children Merce, but you are a little bit right."

"Oh well, that's the way the cookie crumbles," she sighed, and I couldn't help but laugh.

"Where did you hear that?" I asked.

"Daddy," she said and grinned.

My other presents were stacked on the dining room table. A puzzle book and some hair products from Mercy, the pair of heeled black boots I'd been eyeing off the last time we shopped in Castlebrook, from both of them, and a final present with a gift tag simply saying, 'Love Elijah – don't open in front of Mercy'. "How about you run upstairs and put your uniform on for school?" I suggested, fingering the edging of the wrapping.

"Do I *have* to go to school on your birthday?" she whined.

"If I have to go so do you, now scoot." She trundled off up the stairs.

Inside was a sexy matched set of a bra and panties complete with a garter belt, all in a peacock blue colour, and sheer stockings, in black. Why had he bought these for me? Surely he wouldn't be sending me off to Damon with these as a weapon? Surely he didn't want me to wear them for him? It was perplexing and I wanted him to walk through the room so I could ask him about it. But I didn't see him again that morning.

When I arrived at work, Damon was already there. "Happy birthday Ash," he said and came over to hug me.

"Damon…" I said.

"What? Can't I even give you a birthday hug?"

"I don't want to hurt you."

"Can't I worry about that?" His voice matched his face; it had a slight pleading quality to it.

"No Damon." I didn't want to reiterate our conversation from early Sunday morning. He nodded and gave me a slight smile.

When the bell rang for recess, I went home sick. I could have stayed, didn't feel all that bad, but my stomach was queasy, and I wanted to go back to bed and sleep it off. I could also try to make use of the time I'd be able to spend alone, working out what was going on in my life. Nothing seemed to be a good fit at the moment, and I wasn't sure how to get things back on track.

I stripped off and climbed into bed naked. The cool linen felt good against my heated body and I slipped into a dreamless sleep. "Honey," I heard. I cracked open one eye and glanced at the clock. It was just past noon.

"What are you doing home?" I asked.

"Kari rang me from work when you left, to let me know. How are you feeling?"

"Not too bad. A bit nauseous, but nothing too serious." He placed his hand on my forehead and then took my pulse.

"Here, drink this." He handed me a cold glass of ginger ale. "It will make you feel better." I sat up, ensuring the covers were in position, and sipped from the frosty glass. It was good.

"Ash..."

"Hmmm?" I asked, still drinking deeply.

"I'm sorry about this morning, about the way I've been acting lately."

"Care to tell me why?"

"No," he laughed. "Not really, but I know I owe you an apology."

"You had me worried Elijah, I thought I was going to lose you." His look became confusion.

"Why would you think that?"

"We seem to be drifting apart. I thought you may have finally come to your senses and realised what a pain I am," I laughed.

"That would never happen Ash, I love you Babe. You and Mercy are my world."

"As you are mine."

"What happened with Damon?" he asked.

"How did you find out about that?"

"Mercy mentioned it to me this morning when I took her to school."

"Oh."

"Do you want to tell me?"

"Do you really want to know?" He nodded and took my hand, fingering the Pandora charms. "He wanted more than I could give him, and I wasn't ready for it. I'd told him months ago that I didn't want a full-on relationship and I knew he wanted a lot more. I think he's in love with me, but I wouldn't let him speak the words. That was Sunday morning and I ended it right then. It was never my intention to hurt him."

"You can hardly blame him Babe. You're a very special woman."

"Thanks Honey." I smiled at him and pulled a face.

"I mean it." My smile was more genuine this time.

He lay on the bed next to me and worked his arm in under my head, cradling me to him. "Are you going to leave that up?" he asked, referring to Damon's painting.

"I think so, it's a beautiful painting. And, we're going to attempt being friends."

"Pretty obvious what's happening," he said quietly.

"Not to Mercy, thank God." He chuckled and drew his arm across my stomach. I realised all that was between us was the covers and I was lying next to him completely naked. My body flushed and I knew it wasn't from the stomach virus that had sent me home.

"You're still hot," he murmured and brought his lips down to my forehead. A mother's thermometer… "If things were different, a lot different I suppose, could you see yourself and Damon making a go of it?"

"That's a futile point now Elijah. It no longer matters."

"You didn't answer my question…" I sighed.

"I guess if my life had evolved in a parallel universe and I had never met the Standish family it could be a possibility."

"So, you do like this guy?"

"We got on really well and I liked what he gave me."

"Sex?" I nodded. "I'll have sex with you Babe," he offered, and I smiled at him.

"I thought that was a five or so years down the track plan?"

"Practice makes perfect." He grinned his dazzling smile at me. I grinned back. If only he wasn't kidding...

"Don't you have to get back to work?" I asked.

"Doctor Wood will ring if he needs me. Now, how about a little something to eat. Are you hungry at all?" I wasn't sure. "I'll bring you something and you eat what you can."

I flicked on the TV when he left the room and got out of bed to use the bathroom. I also put a nightgown on, assuming my beloved doctor would be by my side for the rest of the afternoon. The midday free-to-air TV was crap, and I flicked through a few subscription movie titles to make a selection. The opening credits to 'Notting Hill' were playing when Elijah came back into the room.

A bowl of chicken noodle soup and dry toast with black tea were my lunch, but I found I couldn't eat much of it. He'd put honey in the tea though and it was very soothing. "Do you want me to close the blinds?" he asked, and I nodded weakly, slumping further back into the bed. He did and then came to lay beside me, checking his mobile and putting it on the nightstand before tucking into his own three-sandwich lunch. "Do you want anything else Babe?" he asked.

"Not right now, thanks Doctor Standish." He smiled at me.

When the movie ended, I sighed deeply. "I thought 'Notting Hill' was your favourite?" he asked and pulled me to him for a cuddle.

"It is, but I don't know why people can't just come out and say how they feel about each other. Why does it have to become some form of complicated dance?" He was silent for a few minutes before answering.

"I don't think people want rejection Babe, and if that's what they're expecting they hardly want to put themselves out there for fear of it," he smiled down at me, adding, "and the movie would have been over in ten minutes." I laughed. "It had a happy ending though." It certainly did and how I wished I would have a happy ending one day, a day that encompassed me, Elijah and Mercy as a real family. I was going to have to learn to live with my feelings for Elijah, as I knew that there could never be any more than what we already had. Regardless of what Michael said.

"Would you put yourself out there, put your cards on the table?" I asked.

"Not if it meant I was going to be rejected."

"What if you weren't?"

"We never know that until we're honest though, do we?"

"I guess not."

"Would you?"

"No," I admitted and laughed. I wasn't being honest with him now and hadn't been since January. Michael truly believed that neither of us wanted to talk about the elephant in the room. I still thought that the conversation was one sided and I would not, could not, ever take that risk. I was a wuss.

"Want to watch something else?"

"You pick this one," I offered, expecting an action flick. I was surprised when 'An Officer and a Gentleman' started.

I woke with Elijah sliding out from under me. "Go back to sleep Babe, I'm just going to pick Mercy up from school."

"What time is it?"

"Ten past three."

"Do you want me to come with you?"

"No, I want you to go back to sleep. See you soon." He crept out of the room and closed the door quietly behind him, but not before kissing my forehead softly. It made me feel much better. It wasn't a huge family birthday for me in the end; I slept through most of it.

When Saturday rolled around, I felt a little humble, not sure in the heat of his cancellation on Thursday whether we were going out tonight. I certainly wasn't going to bring it up though. Since he'd found out about my and Damon's break up, his mood had been so much more relaxed, reverting back to our prior state of mellow with each other. It was a wonderful place to be again.

At 6.00 pm he was at my door. "Aren't you getting dressed?" he asked.

"For what?" I played the innocent.

"For our date tonight." This was an actual date? It was hard to contain my smile, let alone the smug elusiveness I was trying to maintain.

"What date?"

"We're going out for your birthday, remember? Griffoner's?"

"I thought you had to work?"

"No, it didn't pan out," he said, looking a little embarrassed. I wasn't going to make him squirm through this any longer and got off the bed, marking the page in my book.

"Give me twenty minutes," I said and beamed at him.

"Give me fifteen," he said and laughed.

I started with a quick shower, and then put on my sexy birthday present from him. What I wouldn't give for him to see me in these later tonight. Maybe he'd ask? I knew I could drop a hint that I was wearing them without it being too suspicious. I went all-out, wearing heels, a somewhat low-cut dress, and makeup. Being winter, I would have to wear a coat, but not once we were inside the restaurant. I was looking forward to this immensely. Just to be spending time with him...

When I came down the stairs, Mercy ran up to me. "Mummy, you look beautiful!" She wrapped her little arms around me, and I picked her up for a cuddle. She breathed in my perfume and smiled at me.

"Hmmm, Mummy, you *do* look beautiful." Elijah came and enveloped us both in a family hug, and the arm around me sunk lower down my back so it was sitting just above my bum. There would be no need to tell him that I was wearing the lingerie; his fingers traced the waistline of the garter belt, then down over the suspenders. He had found them himself. He leant in to my ear and growled, "Hmmm Mummy!" again. I blushed and he chuckled. "Come on then, let's go."

"Aren't you forgetting something Elijah?" I asked. He drew in his eyebrows, not understanding me.

"Bree and Simon aren't here yet. Do you plan on leaving Mercy here alone?"

"Oh right," he said and laughed. Fortunately, they arrived five minutes later.

It was a wonderfully romantic evening. A few times our eyes locked over the candles and I thought there was something he wanted to say to me, but stayed silent. There were several things I wanted to say to him, but kept my mouth shut too. We ate, we danced a few times and then relaxed over dessert, a shared cheesecake, which made me laugh as he insisted on spooning it into my mouth.

"It's your birthday Babe. I should chew it for you too."

"Like a baby bird?" He nodded and smiled.

"Do you want to get going?" I didn't, I wanted this night to go on eternally. My thoughts were on my sleeve it appeared, or his thoughts were in line with my own, suggesting, "Shall we take the rest of this date home? Have a few drinks?" I was out of my seat immediately.

The drive home was as romantic as our dinner, he even took my hand and we drove in silence for a while. "What are you smiling about?" he asked eventually, not realising I had been.

"I feel like I'm seventeen again Elijah."

"Too young to be fooling around hey?" What did he mean by that?

"I was fooling around with you when I *was* seventeen," I corrected him.

"Too young to be taking it any further then?" he winked. "Ash..." he started tentatively. *Yes Elijah? Yes, what do you propose? Anything you ask of me will be yes. I want to scream out Yes! Yes! Yes! under you in full body connection...* "Are you listening to me?" he asked and laughed. I wasn't sure what else he'd said, if anything at all. Had he been waiting on my attention to speak? Had I lost the moment as I carried myself away in a little daydream again?

"Yes Honey, what did you want to say?" I asked, surprised at the calm tone in my voice. He didn't respond immediately and when I glanced at him, he seemed to be struggling with the sentences.

We pulled into the driveway, leaving room for Simon to get their car out. "What were you going to say Elijah?" I prompted again before getting out of the car.

"Nothing Babe, nothing important." Was it possible that he was going to broach the subject I had tried to suffocate within myself all these months? *Was* it possible? I supposed I wasn't about to find out. I sighed and climbed from the car.

Simon and Bree seemed intent on hanging around and spending a little time with us. Elijah eventually explained that he still had plans for me to finalise my birthday. Simon raised his eyebrows at him in surprise at that information, and Elijah told him to get his mind out of the gutter. After a quick run-down on their evening including how Mercy had behaved, they finally left.

I dropped my coat over a dining room chair and sat on the sofa. "What do you want to drink Babe?" he called from the kitchen.

"Whatever you're having is fine." He came into the lounge room with two glasses of champagne; he knew how I loved it. We had a toast and he put the stereo on, playing some soft instrumental music.

"Will you dance with me again?" he asked, and I smiled as I rose off the sofa. I leant into him, making his embrace tighten around me. His hands slowly wended down over my back, coming to rest on the ridging of the garter belt, tracing its lines through the fabric of my dress. I said nothing, not wanting to interrupt whatever notions were currently going through his head. They did appear to be about me however, and that's what I wanted him thinking of.

He chuckled eventually and drew slightly back from me. "You've got your birthday present on, haven't you?"

"I know you've already worked that out." I rasped, wanting my head back on his chest.

"Do I get to see them?"

"It's not *your* birthday," I teased, resting my head back on his shoulder. *Damn! What a stupid response!* I chastised myself. I'd missed my chance! It was only a few hours ago I was hoping he'd ask to see me in them, and I'd blown the opportunity! Damn!

"Ash?" he asked, drawing my face up with his finger.

"Yes Elijah?" I said and gulped. Was it finally going to be the sealing kiss that would take us to the next step? Again, he was silent for a few moments, then said somewhat dejectedly,

"Happy Birthday Babe." He did kiss me though, a sweet kiss like New Year. In fact, it could have been New Year as I could hear whistles and bells.

I was disappointed when we went to bed about an hour later, separately, once again. Was I going to have to do something about this myself? Was I game? I still wasn't sure that we were on the same wavelength. How could I admit that without him admitting it first? We were certainly dancing around the maypole. *Or are you dancing there alone Ashlyn?* my conscious asked me. And that was what I feared...

He Said

Journal Entry – Sunday 6 June: 1.45 am

IT WAS FINALLY DATE NIGHT last night, Journal, and he was an eager bastard, I'll give him that much. Arriving early, and with me the only one downstairs at the time, I had no other choice but to answer the door. Ash was running late or possibly on time, since he was early. He looked a little surprised to see me, and I assumed Ash hadn't mentioned our living arrangement. He went to shake my hand when he'd regained his composure, which I ignored and went back to the sofa, watching the footy game so I didn't have to speak to him. He sat next to me and fidgeted around a little, obviously wanting to kill time with conversation. I found that I *did* want to speak to him, get some information on his plans for the evening, his expectations, what he planned to do with, or to, the girl I loved. I ended up asking him a few questions, which he was happy to answer. Yes, they worked together, they were going out for dinner, he then wanted to go to the Golf Club and see a band. I was firing them out as quickly as he could answer, and I sensed he was starting to get a little riled at my inquisitiveness. Too bad mate.

I finally asked what his intentions were for Ash, reminding him she was a mother of a little girl and that her time was precious to Mercy. He loved kids apparently. Well, not my kid! I wanted to drag him out the back and beat the shit out of him, but knew this would not curry any favour in Ash's book. I'd also hate to think what Mercy would feel about her Daddy's choice of actions.

When Ash and Mercy came down the stairs, we both stood to great them. Ash looked stunning and I felt my ire rising again. Damn it, this guy was going to fuck the most gorgeous thing in my life tonight, and there was nothing I could do about it. And, in doing so, he may very well fuck my chances for the future. Mercy was a little shy, but he went to work schmoozing her regardless. I just wanted them out of here...

This had turned into a competition and my fist nearly found his chin on its own when he told me not to wait up. Reasserting my authority in this house, I took Ash into my arms, telling her to call if she needed anything. She let me do this, didn't pull away, so I kissed her lightly on the forehead, sealing my intention for Damon's sake. This made his face drop, and I knew he wasn't happy. At the very least, he would now be considering his competition. Ash had no idea how I felt, but I was sure he did, and I was not going to let her get away without a fight - with or without her knowledge of this.

We waved goodbye at the door, Mercy on my hip, and I felt my heart sag. I hadn't felt this low since Lorien died and I never wanted to feel this bad ever again. What do I do Journal? Fight for her? Let her go? I didn't think I could just walk away and leave it up to fate. On the other hand, I didn't believe I could tell her how I felt. On the third hand, and I was rapidly running out of limbs, if I was going to lose her, what was the harm in opening up to her? I feared that my ego was the problem. If she knocked me back it would hurt, and so terribly. I didn't want any more pain if I could help it. It was going to be a long night.

With Mercy fed, we snuggled on the sofa to watch the Shrek movies. She was asleep by 9.30, not quite making it through the third instalment. I carried her upstairs and tucked her into bed, leaving the night-light on, as I knew Ash would want to check on her when she got home. Was she coming home? I didn't even want to consider that as I could feel myself getting worked up again. I was going to wait up for her though, so went back downstairs and got comfortable again on the sofa. She found me there asleep on her return.

The sound of the front door closing roused me. She was crying. This realisation snapped me into instant awake. What had the bastard done to her? I opened my arms to her, and she came to me, curling onto my lap. I asked her what happened, and she said the night was wonderful, but the end result was what had thrown her. My poor sweet girl, wanting sex but not knowing how different it was going to be for her; Damon was no Lorien. When she asked if that was how the rest of the world made love, I knew right then that he'd had his way with her, my statement holding more worth than I realised. He had literally had his way, and Ash felt broken and used. I assured her not everyone was like that. I would love to prove this to her, but not now, not with another man's passion still on her mind. I just prayed they'd used a condom.

She was unimpressed with my verbal slaying of him, telling her I didn't like him from the start. I wasn't helping apparently, so I shut up and just held her, running my hand over her back. Maybe I should get her to sleep in my bed tonight.

She calmed down shortly after and I moved my hands into her hair, stroking softly, soothingly. I loved her so much and I didn't want to see her in this pain. She felt terrible, feeling that no one was ever going to want her again. I took a gamble, telling her that I wanted her. Never before had I spoken such a truth. She thought I was just trying to appease her, so I decided to bite the bullet and prove it to her. I wouldn't say she was reluctant at first, but I had taken her by surprise. Then she was kissing me back and we moved with each other, feasting, lips, tongues, teeth... When she climbed on top of me to better seal ourselves together, my hands glided down her back and came to rest on her rear, pulling her against me. I didn't ever want this to end.

But damn my principles, wanting me to remember where she'd been and with whom. The last thing Ash needed tonight was another round of sex, and to be honest I didn't want to go there, following in someone else's wake. I wanted our first time to be magical and special, not the result of a half-arsed apology on someone else's behalf. It was difficult, but I ended up taking her face in my hands and moving her away from me. I smiled and asked if she felt better. She didn't, and I was crushed. At the least, I was hoping to stir something within her that would result in an 'Elijah' moment, if not now then for the future. I think she realised how that sounded and she confirmed the kiss was wonderful before moving off my lap.

The subject changed quickly, and she asked how Mercy had been tonight, thanking me for watching her. I didn't know how to feel about that. Mercy was as much of my responsibility as she was Ash's, and I didn't feel the need for thanks was in order. If anything, it hurt a little. I just added that to the ever-increasing pile of resentment that started growing the moment she left the house those few hours ago.

Ash helped me lock up before going to bed; she seemed averse to leave my side. Maybe I *should* have asked her to spend the night in my room with me, for comfort's sake of course, Journal. Instead, I told her to come and wake me if she needed any further cheering up. I was pathetic!

Journal Entry – Sunday 6 June: 10.20 pm

I was up early this morning, having caught a few hours on the sofa before Ash got home. I didn't expect to see her for a few more hours and I was right; it was nearly 10.30 am when she finally surfaced. I was cooking pancakes at the time. Perhaps their aroma worked into her dreams, bringing her from sleep, awake and hungry. She seemed in much better spirits this morning and I hoped that was the end of the Damon situation. The ensuing phone call proved me wrong.

I didn't want to hear but it was impossible not to, with her standing right in front of me. I was unaware at first who it was, but after her comment about leaving after he was asleep, I knew it was Damon. She gestured at me and I realised I was leering at her, the batter on my spoon oozing onto the counter. She went outside to finish the call. How I wish I could hear what path the conversation was following...

She seemed willing to forgive him after she got off the phone, and I couldn't understand why. I reminded her how she felt when she got home last night, adding my reiteration of him being a selfish prick. She truly believed that he was unaware of the situation last night and it had been a mistake. She actually felt sorry for him. We ate the pancakes in silence.

She eventually asked where Mercy was, and I told her Anna and Dom had picked her up early this morning. She then broached the Damon subject again and I didn't want to talk about it. There was only one resolution I wanted to hear, and it didn't seem my wish was about to be granted. She sat thoughtful for a while and didn't revisit the conversation again.

Doing the dishes, we fell back into alignment with each other. Regardless of any fights or distractions, Ash and I would also be 'Ash and Eli'. Nothing could ever destroy that, unless it became my choice to do so. We ended up in a frothy bubble fight, starting with her wiping it over my cheeks. I was not as gallant, throwing bubbles and water at her as I chased her around the dining room. There was a knock at the door, which she thought would save her, but I had other ideas. As she opened the door, I swung her around by the waist; we were both wet and laughing.

Our frivolity instantly abated; Damon was standing at the door trying to work out what he was seeing. I let her go and removed myself from the situation, returning to the kitchen, but not wanting to be too far out of earshot. She led him onto the verandah where he commenced asking her about last night, wanting to know why she was distant on the phone. What kind of a wanker was this guy? I didn't believe he had no idea; he just wanted her to fall into his trap again. Why wouldn't he want that? To break the conversation I offered coffee, which neither of them wanted.

When I saw him kiss her, no, when I saw her *let* him kiss her, I knew I'd seen enough and went into the laundry to finish folding the washing I'd done last night. I couldn't look at her. When I heard them back in the dining room, I assumed he was about to leave, and unable to stop, found myself standing in the hallway watching his departure. Did I really want to see the kiss goodbye? Was I so much of a masochist that I needed to witness it again? Obviously, as there I stood. When Damon caught my eye after breaking from the kiss, he said goodbye to me and I was involuntarily moving toward him, unrealised intentions of punching him. I made it as far as the piano before Ash noticed me.

I wanted to bite my own tongue off when she asked what was wrong. She had no idea, and I knew I was just wasting my time waiting for her. She was never going to want me in return. This was the living proof. However, I was not going to be the good buddy every time she wanted to talk about Damon, or fall over again in his inability to care for her. And this was what I told her. I wanted no part of it anymore.

Journal Entry – Sunday 13 June: 1.40 am

She's out with him again tonight Journal. I feel a little guilty as I told her I wasn't available to watch Mercy as I had plans for the evening. I wasn't even sure if I was trying to make her jealous, or whether I didn't want to give her the freedom she needed for this date to occur. No babysitter, no date. It was ridiculous though, of course Dom and Anna would never say no. I made sure I wasn't home when he picked her up, but I sure as hell was when he dropped her off. The car idled in the driveway for a good fifteen minutes, so I knew either: a. this date had gone as badly as the previous one and he was pleading with her, or b. it had gone exceptionally well, and they were saying their goodbyes. It was a horrible thought, but I was hoping she'd come into the house in tears again...

She didn't though. She looked as bright as a button, alive and vibrant. Like a woman who had just been well fucked. As per her promise, she said nothing to me. She smiled slightly and then went straight to bed. Serves me right. I should have realised that getting the information was better than not knowing what was going on...

Journal Entry – Wednesday 21 July: 11.30 pm

I've decided that these musings can only be a tribute to my lost moments with Ashlyn, because let's face it Journal, that's all I write about in you. The fact that I have regressed from a late twenties professional into a blubbering teenager again has amused me though, and also surprised me with the honesty in which I have scribed within you. I suppose you are the person in whom I feel I can confide. There is no way I could speak these words to anyone else. Life seems so unfair sometimes. I spend my life helping others yet there is no one who can help me. I am really missing Mum and Dad too. Dad was possibly someone I could speak to about this. Maybe...

Anyway, they've been out on a few more dates, but not as many as I was expecting. I haven't asked though, and she hasn't offered. In fact, I found myself avoiding her when I could, especially when Mercy wasn't around. Maybe it was time I thought about moving out. There was nothing I could do to stop this roundabout, nothing I was prepared to do anyway, and I figured it was too late now.

One minor piece of solace I had gained though - I was taking her out for her birthday. Well, the Saturday after; it fell on a Thursday this year. I also knew what I was going to get her. She'd fallen in love with a pair of boots one weekend we took Mercy shopping in Castlebrook, and I'd already bought those for her. I'd also ordered her a gold Pandora Charm bracelet from the local jeweller, the few charms being very symbolic I thought. I knew she'd love it. As a last-ditch effort, I also bought her some lingerie, more specifically a garter belt and stockings, with a matching bra and panties set. They would look so hot on her, and in my favourite colour. The thought that Damon may get to see them didn't excite me, but I found myself buying them anyway. I wasn't giving them to her until her birthday next Thursday and not just because they were going out this weekend as an early birthday celebration. I was hopeless... I was in love...

Journal Entry – Thursday 29 July: 9.00 pm

I woke Mercy early this morning and she helped me make Mum's breakfast. I was a sucker when it came to Christmas and birthdays. I loved to spoil her especially, and my mood this morning was light and bright. Mercy wanted to make a cake for breakfast, but I finally managed to talk her into some toast and cereal. I knew who wanted the cake...

When I put the tray over Ash's lap, I leant in and kissed her. Not on the forehead or cheek this time, but on her magnetic lips. Feeling so elated at the time, I wasn't aware that within seconds my happy mood would come crumbling down around me. Bloody Damon. Mercy asked Ash about a painting on her wall and when I looked to see what she was talking about I could feel my face harden into a sneer. It was a painting of Ash and she was lying there naked on a strange bed. I didn't need to be Einstein to work out whose bed it was either. Her back was arched, her full breasts pointing upward. Her eyes were closed. It was obvious what was going on in that painting, and although it was well painted, I didn't want to accept this was an image *he* had been privy to. He was making love to her, not that you could see him, but the look on her face said it all. I did the only thing I could. I cancelled our date for Saturday and all-but threw her birthday present at her, stalking out of the room.

I sequestered myself away in my room until she left for work, then went in search of Mercy. On our walk to school, she enlightened me with some rather wonderful information. Mummy wasn't seeing Damon anymore. Mercy was a little sad about this as she did like him, but I on the other hand wanted to jump up and click my heels together. At work, all I could do was think about it. I basically got nothing done that morning and Doctor Wood ended up seeing more than his share of our patients. It wasn't often that I had an off day, but I certainly made up for that today. I realised I'd been given a second chance. Was I going to waste it as I had done so far this year? I had to work out what I was going to do and had two options. One was to bite the bullet and go for it, regardless of the outcome. The second was to simply get over it and walk away. I didn't want that though.

When the phone rang, I jumped a little, I had been so deep in thought. It was Kari and it took me a second to place who she was. Ash had gone home sick around 11.00 am and Kari wanted to let me know. My bag and jacket were in my hand before I'd even hung up the phone.

I opened her bedroom door and peered in. She was sleeping. I roused her gently so I could get her to drink some fluids and then sat with her on the bed. I apologised for my behaviour over the past several weeks and I felt a little sheepish when she asked me why I'd been in such a foul mood. I didn't enlighten her of course, although it would have been a perfect window of opportunity. I had to contain a laugh when she told me she was scared of losing me, as my behaviour had led her to believe. Like I would ever be going anywhere. I hadn't planned to bring up Damon, but the question of what happened was out of my mouth before I'd even granted permission for myself to ask it. She couldn't give him what he wanted. I felt like I'd already won. I knew she would and could give me what I wanted, if we ever managed to work this out; knew that her life with me would be barely a change to how it was now, with exception to a most vital part of course, Journal.

I sidled in next to her on the bed and realised she was naked beneath the sheets. What I would give to get in there with her, or to pull them down her body. Possibly offer a hands-on check-up? Not very professional, I know. Returning to the Damon conversation, I wasn't happy about her decision to leave the painting up, but she liked it. I asked her if she liked Damon, would have made a go of it if the timing was different. Her dialogue of being in another parallel universe where there was no Standish family, it may have been a possibility. Did she mean all Standish's, or just Lori? Was it possible that by being here I was blocking her view? I could only hope. She was going to miss having sex and I told her that I'd look after her. She thought I was joking. What would make her think I would put something like that on the table in a joking manner? It would hardly be considered a very funny situation. She was still burning up and I pressed my lips into her forehead, testing her temperature before going to get her some lunch.

'Notting Hill' had just started when I returned to her room. I was happy to sit there and watch it with her whilst eating my lunch. It was her favourite movie. When it was over, she sighed, musing how much time had been wasted by the characters not coming out with how they felt. I reminded her that no one wants to be rejected, especially if they expect it, and that the movie would have been over in ten minutes. This made her laugh. She asked if I would 'put my cards out on the table' and this made me laugh. I told her that I wouldn't if I knew I would be rejected, and posed the question back at her. Her answer was also no.

We put on another movie, my choice this time and I wanted to keep the romantic 'chick flick' vibe going, choosing 'An Officer and a Gentleman'. She fell asleep in my arms watching it. She woke as I tried to climb out of the bed, going to pick Mercy up from school. I told her to go back to sleep and kissed her before leaving. Her gentle smile warmed my heart.

Journal Entry – Sunday 1 August: 2.20 am

I was surprised to see Ash wasn't getting ready for our date come 6.00 pm last night and I wondered briefly as to what was the problem. I then remembered how I'd cancelled on her when I saw Damon's painting. I felt a little foolish. I panicked slightly, thinking she may no longer want to go, regardless of the offer being valid again. I thought I'd play the innocent and simply asked her why she wasn't getting ready. She thought I was working, as I'd told her on Thursday, and I said it wasn't happening now. A lie, but it got me out of the otherwise embarrassing explanation.

When I came downstairs, my two favourite girls were in the lounge room, Mercy hugging her gorgeous mother, telling her how beautiful she looked. I took them both into my embrace and agreed with her. My arm dropped lower down Ash's back to better hold her to me and I could feel the line of the garter belt around her waist. My fingers then went exploring, trickling down over the line of the suspenders and back to the waist. I purred at her, which made her blush. I loved getting that reaction from her.

On so many occasions over dinner I went to tell Ashlyn how I felt about her, what I wanted us to have together; to become a true family. But each time, I chickened out. I led her onto the dancefloor a few times and my body was intoxicated with the feel of her soft curves pressed into mine. We were a perfect fit, mind, body and soul. This felt like a real date, the kind where you may end up in bed or at the very least, a long goodnight kiss at the door. Maybe when we got home, I should escort her to the door and go through the motions of a formal end of date ritual. Would she let me kiss her, kiss her properly?

On the drive home, I took her hand in mine. She was smiling and I asked her why. She felt like she was seventeen again. I knew what she meant; I was feeling the same. I teased her about being too young to play around and she reminded me that we'd had our share of fun together when she was seventeen. When I spoke her name, I knew what was about to come out. I was about to tell her everything, 'put my cards out on the table', as she had previously put it. My courage had finally won out over my yellow streak and it was with bold bravery I started to speak. I knew it would all be OK, one way or another. She was smiling and looking out the window and I faltered. She wasn't paying attention to me and when she finally did, the moment had passed. I wasn't going to tell her anything now, even though she prompted me a few times.

There was to be no kiss at the door either, I'd forgotten Simon and Bree were there, looking after Mercy. They'd hear the car pull up and would come looking for us eventually, wondering what was the holdup. After a brief highlight of the evening, I was all-but ejecting them from the house, wanting to get back into the swing of things.

When they left, I poured us some drinks, champagne of course, and I put the stereo on softly in the background. I asked her to dance with me again, and I pressed into her as close as I could, revelling in the warmth and feel of her smooth body under my hands. I let them wander again over the garter belt lines and she didn't say a word, didn't stop me, and I eventually laughed quietly and drew back from her. I asked her if she had her birthday present on, and she knew that I was already aware of this. I asked to see them, and I was told it wasn't my birthday. If I still hadn't made my move, I certainly intended on asking her again come Valentine's Day, my birthday. She nestled back into me and I lifted her face up to mine. I looked into her eyes and she seemed to be waiting on me to make a move. But I still wasn't sure. I had managed to talk myself into this not occurring and once again lost my nerve, but not so much that I didn't kiss her, and kiss her properly. She let me, and our mouths moved together in a sweet symphony, tasting and teasing. I let my tongue run lightly over hers and she opened for me, letting me in. How I wanted to sweep her into my arms and carry her up the stairs to my room, but I ended up in there alone, again.

Journal, I am now reminding myself of the promise I made to you at the end of last year. That this year was to be *the* year and it was halfway through already. I know you are nothing more than an inanimate object, unable to advise or sympathise with me, but after reading this shamble of a tale, it's hard not to laugh at my months of angst written on your pages. I make you a promise Journal; come Christmas there will be a resolution. I hope it will be one to make the rest of my life complete.

SPRING

She Said

IT WAS THE LAST DAY OF TERM and I was looking forward to two weeks off. When we both got home from school, I dropped Mercy at Mum and Dad's and I was glad they were taking her for the first few days; I wanted a lazy weekend. Last term had been rough, knowing that the last-minute preparations before final exams next term were to start; ensuring the entire curriculum had been covered. Don't even start me on the HSC! We were expecting Simon and Bree over tonight, and possibly Michael. Glen had to work so we knew Michael might be a no-show.

Elijah was already home by the time I got back, having spent a little time with Mum and Dad before leaving. Two bottles of tequila were on the island bench, which he had no doubt picked up on the way home from work. I'd forgotten we were doing tequila shots tonight – not my idea, but nonetheless it was going to happen. A saltshaker and a dozen limes were also on the counter and I knew we were all going to be in for the long haul.

He came from around the corner balancing half a dozen shot glasses in his hands. "Hey Babe!" he called, leaning down and giving me a kiss on the cheek. My reaction to draw into him was quelled, difficultly so, but repressed all the same. He always took the school holidays off so he could spend them with Mercy and I. We were all officially now on two weeks leave.

I thought back to past school holidays and found myself daydreaming about the morning I woke up with him. Elijah's mobile ringing brought me from my reminiscence. "Can you get it Ash?" He was in the middle of slicing the limes and had citrus juice running down his fingers. It was Bree.

"Hi Ash," she said, and after I'd returned her greeting, she informed me that none of them could make it tonight. Could we possibly reschedule for tomorrow? I put my hand over Elijah's, stopping him from cutting any more limes, shaking my head when he threw me a quizzical look.

"Just hold it for a second, looks like they aren't coming." He grimaced and motioned to the already sliced limes, then gave me a cheesy grin, meaning we would have to use them on our own. I pulled a face at him and returned to the conversation with Bree. She apologised again and then reconfirmed we were on for tomorrow night. I told her it was fine and hung up.

"What's going on?" Elijah asked.

"They have to go to dinner with Simon's parents and Michael wasn't coming anyway. They'll all be here tomorrow night instead."

"OK, looks like there'll be a lot for us to get through tonight though. I'm not wasting these limes." I rolled my eyes at him but took the shot glass from his outstretched hand.

"Can I get changed first?"

"Knock yourself out Ash."

"No, I think the tequila will do that for me." He laughed as I took to the stairs.

It was hot for October and I dressed in a short, loose shift, adding a pair of cut-off tights so my reputation wouldn't be in question if the alcohol made me forget to sit like a lady. Elijah had moved the party onto the verandah and had hooked his phone to the music system. It was a lovely spot to spend the afternoon and I was glad he'd thought to position us out there.

He handed me the full shot glass again and waited with the salt in his hand for me to lick mine. He was eager and I laughed, licking my hand, holding it out to him. He licked his own and then sprinkled us both with salt. "Ready?" I was. We licked, we sipped - actually, we downed the shots, and then we sucked. I squidged my face up at the bitterness of the combination, making Elijah laugh. "Come on, round two..." I went to protest, and he goaded me into another quick lightning round. "One more and then a rest, OK?" It seemed a reasonable request, so I complied.

I had never drunk tequila before and was feeling no pain after the second, surprised at how well they were going down. "Wait," he said as I went to lick for the third and final time. He went inside and brought out a schooner glass of water each, letting me know it would help us avoid feeling like crap tomorrow if we kept hydrated whilst drinking. If you couldn't trust a doctor, whom could you trust? We took our final shot then drank the water.

Not long after, I really needed to pee. "You'll have to beat me in there," he threw at me, and took off for the bathroom, leaving me outside the door, banging on it for him to hurry up. He laughed as he came back out, stripping off his shirt. "It's making me hot!" It was making me hot too...

I realised he wasn't kidding, and I patted some water onto my face, cooling myself considerably. He was waiting outside the door for me, taking my hand to lead me back to the verandah. "Ready for the next round?"

"Not yet."

"Sook!" He refilled his glass, and mine. He surprised me by grabbing my hand, licking it for me. "One more at least for now?" I shook my head and laughed, feeling decidedly whacked already. He winked at me and licked the salt off my hand before downing his shot, sucking the lime into his mouth. "Shit, that's good!"

"I can't believe I'm sitting here with a doctor getting smashed on tequila shots," I laughed.

"We're on holidays Ash. Get into the swing of it Babe." He stood and took my hand again, dragging me to my feet. "Come on, dance with me."

He swung me into his strong arms and twirled me a few times around the verandah. Feeling his hard, hot body under my hands took me back to the carnal feelings I'd been having earlier, and I lowered my head, not wanting him to read the lustful thoughts in my eyes. "Do you need to watch your feet? I won't let you fall, I promise." I smiled up at him, thankfully oblivious to what my reaction had actually meant.

He pulled me closer and started to sing softly. It reminded me of when Mercy and I had caught him in the kitchen singing and dancing around, thinking he was alone. It also reminded me of the awkward conversation we then had to have with her. I couldn't help but smile. When he questioned me on it, I told him. There was no point in hiding things like that from him; he *was* aware of what went on in this house. It made him laugh which drew me into his up-beat mood too. "Don't you like my singing?"

"You have a beautiful voice Elijah."

"You're beautiful...," he said, and all expression abandoned his face. We were staring at each other, no longer dancing, just standing there holding on and I truly thought he was going to kiss me. As he cleared his throat and led me back to the chairs, I was glad I hadn't assumed that kiss, closing my eyes and leaning toward him. "Hungry?"

"I suppose."

"Want to make some burritos?"

"That sounds great, and I will *definitely* need to eat something." I followed him into the kitchen, but not before grabbing the tequila. The water had helped a lot and I was ready for a couple of fun shots whilst preparing dinner, and a couple we both had.

I felt a little less inebriated once I'd eaten and a nervous tingling sat heavily in my stomach. I didn't know how to seduce a man, especially this man and I was unsure what to do to keep this going. Eating seemed to have signalled a change to the early flirtations and I didn't know how to get it back on track. I was having a hard time keeping my eyes off his torso, but it was so prominently before me and all I wanted to do was to stand behind him and run my hands slowly over his broad chest, trailing through the hair as I pressed my cheek against his hard back. I kept my eyes from his, not wanting to have a neon sign posted to my forehead. 'Take me, I'm all yours', it would flash in gaudy pink lightning. I smiled at him shyly and went back onto the verandah, hoping he'd follow. He did. "Ready for another?" I asked in an attempt to take us back to where we were before we'd eaten.

"Let's do body shots!" was his response. He sidled closer and played a big lick up my face.

"It's not icing!" I said, laughing. He waggled his eyebrows at me and tilted my head to the side to apply the salt. He licked if off and completed the routine.

"Have you got anything on under there?" he asked, eyeing off my dress curiously.

"Of course!"

"Lift it." I raised my eyebrows at him, and his eyes crinkled in a smile. "I'm not going in for the boobs; I want to lick it off your stomach." I couldn't see anything wrong with that, naturally.

His tongue slid slowly over my abdomen, taking longer than necessary, not that I was currently in any position to judge time. The salt he applied was a generous amount and it took him a long time to get it all. "Tequila is everyone's friend," he said once he'd finished, grinning lecherously at me.

"You're a tequila slut," I offered, and he laughed, placing his next lick across my knee. "How many shots do you plan to take off me?" I asked and laughed, noting he was now up to his third. "Isn't it my turn?"

"Can't wait to lick me, hey?" he said with a sly smile. "And I think four should do it. Where do you want the last one taken from?" I wasn't sure what to say. Did I make it a good one and go for broke or should I play it safe and offer the back of my hand again?

"Ahhh, wherever you want, anywhere is fine..." He surveyed my body and went in for the crook of my neck. He didn't lick, he worked his lips against me instead, and I wanted to grab the back of his head and force my tongue into his mouth, with or without the salt, alcohol and lime accompanying it. He *had* to be flirting with me; he wouldn't be doing this to Bree surely? He obviously forgot where he was, or who I was, as his lips worked across my throat, feathering up to my ear. I didn't know what to say but couldn't let a drunken encounter possibly ruin the rest of our lives. "How much salt are you going to put on there?" I asked feebly, trying to return the situation to fun and playful. He chuckled and nuzzled into me for a few lingering seconds before drawing back, smiling.

"And now the salt..." He took his time licking it off, covering areas I was sure he hadn't reached during his first explorations. With his final four finished, he handed me the saltshaker with a triumphant smile. "I get to choose from where."

"Not fair," I answered.

"Why not, I *gave* you the option; you just didn't take me up on it."

"Play nicely Elijah," I warned.

"Oh, I will, and you can start here." He offered me the inside of his elbow. I gave it a quick swipe with my tongue, and he told me I could do better than that, so worked my way up further. I wanted to keep going, securing a nipple between my lips but stopped myself. "Hmmm, nice," he murmured, and then hooked his hands behind his head as I sunk the shot. The next one was taken from around his navel, all the way around his navel, and then the next from between his pecs. "Where shall I have you take it from last?" he questioned playfully. I knew there was no way he would want salt sprinkled on his genitals, so felt that it would be a harmless final turn. I was right, but only just. "The nipples I think..." Could he read my mind?

I leant in nervously and flicked my tongue over his left one briefly. "No, no, no Ash, you need to have enough moisture on them to make sure the salt sticks. Try again," he instructed, and I thought what the hell. I worked my lips against him, first the left and then the right and when removing the salt from them I bit lightly. I felt his hand move to the back of my head, holding me to him, running his fingers softly through my hair. "Ohh… Babe…" he groaned, slowly moving his hands to the sides of my face, tilting my head back to look up at him. His eyes flashed darkly as he drew one finger across my bottom lip. I opened my mouth to allow him to play that finger tentatively over the tip of my tongue, before lightly sucking it into my mouth. No hint of playful whimsy was evident in his eyes as he claimed my face with his hands again. With his head slightly angled, he lowered his full lips towards my own and I moved in to meet him halfway. As the space between us continued to diminish, the electricity shooting between us was a nearly visible arc. Time stopped, we continued to draw together, and as our lips were about to meet, he snaked his tongue over his bottom lip and softly groaned.

That soft groan was now echoed as a loud moan, in direct response to a knock at the door. "Who could that be?" I whispered, realising my breath was coming in short gasps and he looked at me, so intensely. What would have happened if we weren't interrupted? I couldn't have imagined what was unfolding before that damn knock! Surely?

Neither of us had made a move for the door and the rapping came again, more insistent. "Come on, we know you're in there!" It was Simon. They'd made it after all. I looked at my watch, it was just after 9.00 pm and the sun had set; a fact of which I had been unaware of until now. I stood to let them in, and Elijah smiled lazily at me, making my stomach roll. He followed and grabbed me from behind, holding me in his arms as I opened the door. I could feel him hard against me, of which he did not try to disguise, and I knew I had not fantasied our responses from a mere 10 seconds ago.

"Christ, you guys are plastered!" Bree laughed as she came in, Simon right behind her. "I hope there's some left!" There certainly was but we'd managed to get through nearly a whole bottle on our own, and over a four-hour drinking bout.

We sat and drank more, laughing with our friends. Sometime later when Simon suggested body shots Elijah caught my eye, his burning into mine. I blushed and lowered my face, making Elijah laugh. "Did I miss the joke?" Bree asked, refilling the glasses. They were taking two at once in an attempt to catch up. *Very responsible drinking by adults*, I mused.

"Only by about an hour," Elijah answered elusively and grinned at me again. I was on fire, my entire body, not only my raw throat.

"I think I'm going to have to go to bed," I said and yawned dramatically. I needed to get to bed to think over what it all meant. Would the situation be the same again tomorrow? Was this just a night of drunken fun? I sincerely hoped not, but if it was, I would be glad it hadn't gone any further. I could live with the consequences thus far, but what if Bree and Simon hadn't shown up? What then?

All three of them complained loudly at my suggestion. "I'm going to have to take a shower at the very least; I need to sober up a little." This met no objections and I headed for the upstairs bathroom.

I stripped off, slowly. My balance was currently a little off, and the last thing I wanted to do was crack my head open on the vanity. I ran a brush through my hair quickly, tying it back into an elastic as the door slid open.

Elijah just stood there, his eyes graduating over my naked body and I made no attempt to cover myself, instead turning to face him. His lips parted slightly, and he ran his tongue over the bottom one, making it shine. Were the goods good enough? Would the non-verbal offering be accepted? His nostrils flared and his breathing quickened as he crossed the short space between us fearlessly. His mouth was hot and hungry as he fused himself to me, running his hands down my back and rear, raising me onto the counter.

I drew him to me, wrapping my legs around his thighs, sealing him against me. My hands left the curls at his nape briefly enough to undo his shorts and I dragged them down his hips with my feet. He kicked them off as they hit the ground. "Lock Mercy's side," I mumbled, and he lifted me, moving me to the other end of the counter so he could reach the catch.

"Hang on, she's not here," he said, drawing back, then the urgency reclaimed him when he saw me smile, realising.

He dropped his hand down between my thighs, which parted even further for his touch. And oh, how sweet that release was as I writhed against his palm, his fingers provoking me into a higher and higher state.

His mouth moved to my neck as I hit my peak and I heard him chuckle lowly. "Oh Babe," he crooned. His croons became breathy moans as he thrust into me, keeping me finely balanced on my still burning high. "Fuck Ash, oh shit…" he whispered, building his force. I lowered back slightly so my head was against the mirror and he leant down to work my straining nipples with his tongue. "Oh God, Babe, I'm going to come…"

He lifted me from the vanity and suspended me in mid-air. Only his hands gripping under me and the connection of our bodies held me upright as he finished off in a roaring burst, biting his bottom lip between his teeth. As he shuddered within me, he drew my lips back to his, urgently at first and then slowing to a more controlled pace.

My feet eventually found the ground as our arms wrapped around each other, holding ourselves as close as was physically possible. He reached out and turned on the shower, leading me into the recess. Once in there we simply stood under the tepid water, still locked together at the mouth.

When we finally drew back, he looked at me so tenderly, his eyes so full of love. His hands ran down my hair, tucking it behind my ears, drawing in to kiss me again. His lips worked to my ear and he whispered, so very quietly, "I love you Ash."

"I… I…," I stammered.

"It's OK Babe, you don't have to say it, you don't have to feel it."

"I do though Elijah, it just feels so…" he drew back again.

"Wrong?" he asked, a slight frown on his face. I pulled him to me tightly.

"No Honey, not wrong. Weird maybe, unexpected, but definitely not wrong."

"We have a lot to talk about…" His mouth trailed around my throat and I angled my head back, letting him forage.

"We don't have time now though. Where did you say you were going when you disappeared up here?"

"To have a shower too." He drew back and kissed me once more before turning off the tap.

"What do we do when we get downstairs?"

"What do you want to do?"

"I want us to talk about it first, see what our expectations are before we go 'pashing' around in front of Bree and Simon. What if what I want isn't what you want?"

"I doubt that's an issue Babe, but you're right, I think we should cool it publicly tonight." I smiled at him and stepped out, throwing him a towel. As I bent to pull up my tights, he whipped the towel over my bum.

"Ow! I'll get you!" He opened his arms to me,

"Well come and get me," he replied cheekily.

"Do you want them coming to find us?" A smile was his response.

I sat as far from him as was possible, knowing the temptation to run my feet up his calves or to reach out and touch him would be too great. It was hard enough dealing with the smouldering looks. My heart was beating so rapidly, fully loving the anticipation of the days, weeks and years we possibly had in front of us. "So, you suggested body shots before Simon?" Elijah threw into the conversation.

"Hell yeah!"

"Random ones or matched duos?" He knew damn well that Simon was *not* going to let him lick salt off his girlfriend, but I admired his adeptness at making it look like Simon's idea.

"You team up with Ash, Bree and I will go against you."

"Teams?"

"Yeah, you have to take them off each other from the same place we do or it's double shots."

"You're the boss Simon," Elijah said and moved over to sit next to me. I was trembling…

"I can't believe you're nearly thirty Simon," I added for good measure.

"Are you OK with this Ash?" Bree asked in a flash of recognition, realising how my and Elijah's relationship was to each other. She had no idea...

"I think I can live with it... just!" I smiled at Elijah and he rose one eyebrow, smirking.

"Are you sure Babe?" he drawled, putting it back into my hands. I poked my tongue out at him and Simon said,

"We're not at the salty head-jobs stage yet Ash, put it away." I looked at him shocked. How would this have all been if Elijah and I hadn't already made the moves on each other? Completely embarrassing I would have guessed, for me anyway. I knew I wouldn't have gone through with it, so should I now if it went too far? I would call it as I saw fit, I supposed. "Come here Bree," Simon said and drew her close. He licked the tip of her nose, salted it, licked it again and gulped down the shot. He didn't even bother with the lime. "Your turn Elijah." He licked his lips and drew me to him, tortuously slowly. I wasn't sure whether they noticed but his tongue started from the top of my lip before grazing up and over my nose. Instead of licking off the salt, he sucked, making them laugh hysterically. Just a hint of a kiss stirred in that movement.

"Hmmm?" pondered Bree, surveying Simon, ready for her turn. She slowly worked her tongue around his outer ear, taking her time, likewise as she removed the salt. I was so impatient for my turn...

When she'd finished, she looked at me with a smart-arsed grin, thinking she had me in a compromising position. I pulled Elijah in front of me so they couldn't see my mouth behind his profile, and he slipped his arm down my back, pulling me close. I teased at him with my lips, tongue and breath, forgetting to grab the salt. "You're enjoying that a little too much, man," Simon laughed. "Your eyes are closed."

"Don't forget the salt!" Bree said and handed it to Elijah, who then drew back, smiling as he passed it to me.

"Don't forget the salt Ash," he whispered and moved the side of his face back to my mouth. I didn't even bother, they couldn't tell and probably didn't care, and I went back to my aural ministrations, loving every second.

Whilst Simon was working out his next launch-pad, I looked down and noticed Elijah in a fully tented-out state. He grimaced and took my hand, running it slowly against him. My eyes widened and I snatched it back, *way too obvious mister*! I mouthed at him. He laughed and sat back, waiting for his next turn, with a little too much glee I noted.

Right down the centre of Bree's cleavage was the next chosen spot and Elijah smiled at me wickedly as he waited on them to finish. "Go for it Standish!" Simon said, laughing.

"That was *just* the cleavage wasn't it?" Elijah confirmed before moving in closer. I smacked him lightly on the arm.

"This time…" Simon said, forewarning what was possibly to come.

"Do it Elijah," I said, making them laugh and easing the pressure a little.

"You're sure?" he teased.

"Just get on with it!" I said and they laughed again. He nuzzled into me and ran his tongue slowly between my breasts, edging it underneath.

"Oh Babe," he moaned quietly, his hands wanting to grasp them. For a second they flittered toward me, but he managed to remain composed. He pretended to add the salt, as I had, and bent to form his tongue once again to my curves, savouring it for as long as he was game. He looked up at me as he drew back, and I wanted to throw Bree and Simon out so he could take me right there on the table. Some friend I was!

"I've got one they won't do," Bree said, and I groaned inwardly. I was prepared to stop it at the next round if Simon went in for the nipple, but it looked like Bree was going to top him first. She leant in and kissed him deeply.

"What's that got to do with salt?" I asked, attempting diversion. When she pulled back, she smiled at me and said,

"I'm going to lick it off his tongue." Elijah laughed and Simon said,

"Not too much Bub." She barely upended the shaker before going back in for the kill. I looked at Elijah and rolled my eyes upward, resting my hand under my chin, covering my lips with my fingers. He licked his lips sensuously and my body flashed in anticipation.

"So, going in for a double shot?" Bree asked, assuming we weren't going to reciprocate.

"It's not like we haven't pashed before," Elijah said, not as elusively as he could have.

"When?" she demanded. We had her full attention.

"About twelve years ago," Elijah answered. "Ash?" he prompted. He patted his thighs, saying, "Climb onto my lap Babe, it will be less awkward."

"It's a good thing I'm drunk!" I said with enforced exasperation, straddling over his lap. I leant in and kissed him. His hand feathered to my jaw, wanting to pull me to him so much deeper, but I drew away from him after a few seconds, knowing there was more to come. "You taste like tequila," I said, lightening the mood again. They laughed. "Salt," I said and held my hand out to Bree. "Tongue out!" I instructed. Elijah poked it out and I shook the tiniest amount I could. "Ready?" He smiled and nodded. The kiss lasted a little longer than the first. He brought one hand up to tease between my splayed thighs, knowing there was little I could do about it. At least Bree and Simon couldn't see. I wanted to rock against his hand and ride him to a crescendo, but I eased away when he started to get more intense. He sighed and ran his hand over my back, drawing me to him. He planted a kiss to my forehead, alluding to our usual comfortable relationship with each other. I had forgotten to drink the shot.

"Happy now?" he asked Bree and Simon.

"Not as happy as you must be," Simon chuckled.

"I bet you're glad Michael's not here," Bree said. She was right on the money with that call. It would have been impossible with him casting out boisterous comments and possibly making the gameplay even more insidious.

"Are we still going through all this again tomorrow night?"

"Yes!" Bree and Simon answered together, laughing.

"Well then I'm going to bed," I told them.

"Me too," Elijah added. "I want to be able to stomach a drink tomorrow."

Bree and Simon relented and decided it was the best idea; it was well after midnight. I went in to pull the sofa out for them as Elijah headed for the kitchen, returning with four schooners of water. "Drink these before you go to bed guys, you'll thank me in the morning."

"Thanks Doctor Standish," Bree said and laughed. I went into the back bathroom and pulled out the Panadol, taking a couple for myself and handing two to Elijah.

"Help yourselves if you want them." I gulped mine down and finished off the water, saying my goodnights as they both crawled into bed. Elijah switched off the lamp and followed me. I was waiting in the hall for him.

"Well, goodnight," I said and reached up to kiss him briefly.

"Goodnight? Aren't you coming with me?"

"Do you think that's a good idea? What if they barge in on us in the morning?"

"Have you ever known either of them to come into any of our rooms whilst they've been staying here?"

"I guess not." He drew me to him and hugged me tightly.

"Please Babe, don't make me spend another night on my own…," he whispered, and that was the end of that.

"Your room or mine?" I asked cheekily.

"Mine," he said and dragged me through his door.

Fear gripped me like a knot in my stomach when I woke, alone, in Elijah's bed. I didn't notice the background noise of the shower until it stopped. I glanced at the bedside clock; it was 9.00 am. I was aware that he was quite possibly the first one up and when I heard the door slide open quietly, I rolled onto my stomach and closed my eyes, pretending I was still asleep.

I tried to remember if we'd made love again when we got into bed last night. I recalled talking to him in the hallway about the sleeping arrangements and I was currently naked, but could not put the pieces together from the hallway to now, or when my clothing disappeared. I was not only naked, I was also lying bare-arsed on the bed, no sheet or covers were even lowly draped over my legs or feet. Not that it mattered, but I was still hesitant as to how he would feel in the bright light of morning. I didn't know what he was doing, couldn't hear him moving around the room, but I wasn't game to crack an eye open to seek him out, for fear of being caught feigning sleep.

After what seemed like half an hour, I felt the mattress dip as he climbed back into bed. He lay over me, slightly lowered, with his stomach over my rear. The skin between my shoulder blades was ignited by his warm slow kisses and I tried to remain still, retain my sleeping façade. I didn't know why I felt compelled to continue this charade, he was obviously OK with what happened last night, but I wanted the whole thing, not just a sexual relationship to keep us both satisfied. Not that I intended to stop him now.

He was also naked I realised, the hair on his thighs tickling against me as he drew his knees out, easing my legs apart. He moved down slightly and positioned himself at my entrance, hardening against me. He slid in and started to grind slowly. Oh my God!

He slipped a hand up the side of my torso, up and across the underside of my arm as he rocked and drove. Each time his hand trekked from my waist through to my elbow I shuddered as he passed over my armpit. I wasn't sure if he noticed, but his lips were now nuzzling at my ear, exhaling in an erotic sensation, causing any anxious resolve I had to liquefy. My hands betrayed me as they started to clutch at the sheet, and when completing the next body-sweep he ran his hands in under mine, replacing the sheets. I ran my fingers slowly over his before entwining into them, holding him now in my grasp. "Are you awake, Babe?" he whispered.

"Uh huh," I moaned, arching my back, now meeting his thrusts. He pushed one knee further out and rolled me onto my side, still under him, still connected, and he lowered his face to nuzzle his cheek to my forehead before finally working his lips to mine, to kiss me. He tasted sweet and minty from the toothpaste and I had a horrific thought as to what I must have tasted like. Stale tequila was my first suggestion, but it didn't seem to dampen his intensity any.

Still sealed in the kiss I rolled onto my back; his movements became more aggressive, and he snaked a hand down between my thighs, readying me for the inevitable build up. Within seconds, he had me flying, then removed his dextrous fingers, using the grind of his pelvis against mine to keep me going. He fit within me so well, and as he ended his torture, he came to lay with me, running his hands over my nipples and purring into my ear. He manoeuvred me back onto my stomach and half-lay atop me, forming his curves into mine. His hands crept beneath me to cup my breasts, his lips back at my nape. "Good morning!" I said and he laughed quietly.

"Good morning."

"I like the way you chose to start the day."

"It's a brand new day Babe."

"Can I ask you something embarrassing?" He rolled off me and onto his back, sliding me over to lie across his broad, hairy chest.

"Anything." He smiled at me in encouragement.

"Did we do it again when we came to bed?"

"No," he laughed, "we were both ready for sleep."

"Why don't I have any clothes on?"

"You don't usually keep a change of pyjamas in my room Honey." I hadn't thought about that.

"Have you been downstairs yet?"

"They're both still out to it, we have plenty of time. We need time to talk." It sounded ominous.

"Go ahead."

"Are you going to meet me halfway Ash?" he asked, sitting up slightly to better see my face.

"If I knew what you were going to say I would."

"What do you think I'm going to say?"

"God, I keep forgetting how much you two are alike; this is such a Lorien conversation."

"I'm not Lori Ash, I can't be, and you need to accept that now before this builds into something neither of us can contain anymore."

"I know you're not Lorien, Elijah. He's been gone for over two years now, and although I will always love him, as will you, there's room in my heart to love you too. Just as intensely, just as intimately."

"I can't be his replacement."

"You're not. In fact, you're the only other person I could ever be with. No one else can compare to a Standish." This made him laugh.

"What about Peter?"

"He may be your cousin, but he's not a Standish." He laughed again and then became serious.

"I can't promise you miracles in the bedroom department."

"Huh?" I had no idea of what he was referring to here.

"I can't have sex all day every day like you were used to getting from Lori. For one, I won't have the time and secondly, I don't think my body would allow it. I'm not twenty anymore." He laughed quietly at his own admission. "More like a few times a week than a few times a day."

"You've done pretty well so far," I told him.

"Well, it's a bit like Christmas day isn't it? When the drudgery of life kicks back in things will possibly change."

"Do you love me Elijah, I mean really love me?"

"Yes Ash and I have for a long time."

"No, I mean are you *in* love with me?"

"Yes Ash and I have been for a long time."

"I'm scared."

"Of what?"

"That you don't really mean that, and I'll end up with my heart broken. I couldn't take it Elijah. I had resolved to stay single after the disaster with Damon; it seemed easier that way. But then there you were and when my eyes were opened to you, I couldn't shut them again."

"And when did this happen?"

"You first." He laughed and stretched, and I rolled off him, thinking he was getting out of bed. His body cracked as he twisted it in various directions and then came to lie with his head on my chest, a finger rolling over one exposed nipple, watching it stiffen to his teasing.

"So tiny, so erect... so responsive to my touch," he whispered and leant forward to kiss it tenderly. It made my body tingle. Then he explained the way he felt so marvellously. "For me, I knew there was something stirring when Keren and I started to have problems. As you know she was always jealous of you, and when someone is constantly pointing out the wonderful things in a person that they are envious of, it's hard to ignore. The real turning point was after I had Faith here when you were pregnant. I realised how much I'd hurt you through her and on the way back from taking her home, wondered why the hell I was so worried about it... then the realisation hit, and I had to admit it."

"Not at the Club when I asked you to kiss me?"

"No."

"So why did you *want* to kiss me but wouldn't as *I* would regret it?"

"We always had chemistry Babe, why wouldn't I want to have kissed you? And, you'll also remember this was around the time Keren and I were having problems." I smiled up at him warmly, feeling loved. "Your turn," he prompted. I rolled onto my stomach, hiding my face into the crook of his armpit. This was so embarrassing. "Come on Honey, I gave it up for you..." I didn't move my position but began to speak.

"It was Summer, and you'd been out running. When you got home, you decided to mow the lawn whilst you were still sweaty. Mercy was playing out on the back verandah and I was sitting on one of the sun lounges pretending to read. I was actually watching you cussing out the lawnmower that you couldn't get started. Watching your muscles stirred me and it was just like BAM! I realised I was in love with you. There was no going back from that point."

"What about when you were dating Damon?"

"I never thought you would feel the same way for me, and I had no intention of putting myself out there. If you had refused me, where would it have left us Elijah? All three of us? I couldn't risk tearing our lives apart..."

"So, we've wasted over nine months? We have a *lot* of time to catch up on..." He leant down and kissed me. I wanted it to build again, to have my way with him again and so totally, but he reminded me we had other things to discuss before leaving this room.

"I need to ask you one thing first," I said.

"Shoot." I lowered my face again, feeling a little shy as I glided my hand over him slowly.

"When you said you were... unable to recover as quickly as... you might want to... did that mean you can't go twice?" He grabbed my hand and kissed my palm, laughing quietly.

"No Honey, I can go a second time..."

"There's one other thing..." He smiled at me, raising his eyebrows when I hesitated a little.

"You aren't really into... oral, are you?" I still had reservations with open discussion like this. It had taken all of my time and effort to be able to discuss it with Lorien successfully over the years, and here I was starting again from scratch.

"Whatever makes you think that?" he asked incredulously.

"Well..."

"Because I haven't?"

"Yes." His smile broke into a wide grin before saying,

"That's your fault!" I was confused, how could it be my fault? "It's *most* what I want to do to you Ash, but every time so far when I've thought about it, I was ready to... ahhh... relieve myself a little too early in the game."

"So, it turns you on then, just thinking about it?"

"It drives me wild Babe, and just the thought of it." He chuckled lowly and pulled me tighter, dropping a kiss to my forehead. "We can talk about this later; we need to work out what we're doing outside the bedroom."

"OK."

"You first this time."

"Why me?"

"Because you have a child, so the decisions need to be made initially from your point of view. We can work on them from there." I didn't want to, really didn't want to open up to him so completely. Even though we were lying here obviously in step with each other and what we both assumed our futures were going to hold, but... "Do you want me to start?" I nodded and looked up at him, hopeful. "I want to spend the rest of my life with you Ash; I'm in love with you. Does that make it easier for you now Honey?" It did.

"I feel the same and I also want you to be Mercy's proper Daddy, maybe look at officially adopting her?" He nodded and smiled at me to continue. "I'm not sure what you want to do about the sleeping arrangements. Do you want to move into my room?" He didn't and I felt a little perplexed; surely we'd be sharing a space now?

"It was yours and Lori's Babe, I would rather you move in here... for now at least. Now what about Mercy? When do you want to tell her, how do you want to tell her?"

"When we pick her up on Monday afternoon."

"And your parents?"

"I want Mercy to know first."

"So... all beating around the bush aside," I smiled at him slyly and he placed his hand on my stomach, laughing and running his fingers over me lightly, "we're a couple?"

"Yes," I said and leant up to kiss him.

"And when we get downstairs, we'll be open and tell Simon and Bree?"

"I guess so."

"If you're not ready yet Babe, if you want some time to adjust...."

"Elijah, Michael and Glen already know..." He drew in his brow and looked at me for an explanation. "I spoke to them when I started having feelings for you. Can you imagine how they'll react when they find out this afternoon?"

"Want to wait until everyone is here and then I'll plant one on you in front of them?"

"That would be fun! Or should I plant one on you? Michael will fall off the chair thinking I'm throwing caution to the wind."

"OK, we'll go with your plan." We lay there for some time until we heard a toilet flush, and I reluctantly got out of bed, going to my room to change.

As I was about to head downstairs, I sensed Elijah behind me. "I need a kiss before we become the sterile couple again in front of Bree and Simon." I couldn't argue with that logic. His soft tongue searched my mouth shamelessly and I couldn't wait for him to work it over other areas. When he felt my smile, he drew back knowing.

It was hard keeping away from him over the course of the morning; what was left of it anyway. We had breakfast and opted to sit away from each other to avoid temptation. Bree mentioned last night, saying, "So, no discomfort with the party games last night?"

"Didn't worry me," I said, and Elijah nodded and said,

"And I'm *certainly* up for more tonight!" Simon clapped him on the back, laughing.

"You are a dog mate; lucky Ash threw you a bone!" It was not as wonderful as the bone he'd thrown at me, and also this morning…

When Michael and Glen finally arrived, it was nearly 2.00 pm. I wanted to go to Elijah and kiss him the second they walked through the door, but kept myself in check for as long as I could. Everyone ended up in the kitchen with us whilst we put their alcohol in the fridge and made room for the various food and snacks they'd brought with them. "Is that everything Babe?" he asked with a smile.

"Just about, but there's one more thing on my agenda." I walked toward him slowly and his arms came out to hold me as I leant in and kissed him deeply.

"What the hell?" Simon said. When I drew back, I smiled up at Elijah, and then laid my head against his chest, looking at them with a grin.

"When did this happen?" Bree asked, obviously shaken. "Is it what I think it is?"

"Yes," Elijah said, drawing back in to kiss me. "We're a couple." I looked at Michael and he was smiling at me, happy for my outcome, knowing it had been a long time coming.

"Because of the body shots?" Simon asked.

"Technically yes, but we'd started on our own before you got here. We were mid-way actually and just about to ignite when you started hammering on the door. I thought you'd ruined everything at the time bro," Elijah told him.

"Well, this is certainly a turn of events, but congratulations!" Bree said and came over to hug me.

"Sorry Bree, I'm not letting her go," Elijah said and pulled me to him tighter, leaning down to kiss me again. We both ignored the jibes and catcalls.

"Oh God no, not another Standish romance," Michael groaned. "I can see it now, rolling around the floor in front of us all the time…"

"He's not Lorien," I said, and Michael's face dropped.

"I'm sorry twin, I shouldn't have said that."

"It's OK Michael," Elijah said.

"No, it's not. I shouldn't have said that in mock joviality any more than if I said it in earnest. It wasn't fair or considerate and I am sorry Elijah."

"You must be if you're using my name."

"Who are you and what've you done with Michael Lennox?" I asked, unable to process this weird shift of situation for Michael.

"I'm sorry Ash, I really am." I had never seen him so apologetic. He had felt he'd truly crossed a line. I suppose considering the hard time he used to give me and Lorien, well mainly me, he was repentant that he'd used the same lewd tactics today. Neither Elijah nor I were concerned about it, but Michael sure was. "I, of all people, should've known better. I knew how you felt about Elijah and shouldn't be playing the fool now."

“So, are we never going to be at the end of your carnal comments? I was actually looking forward to them...” Elijah said, making Michael smile.

“I can make an effort I suppose,” Michael mused, and we laughed. Everything was wonderful and I felt so gloriously happy.

Lying in bed that night, guilt-free and so happy to be there together, I brought up Lorien's final words. "He'd be sitting there calling us a bunch of time-wasting fools you know," I said and smiled.

"I know," he laughed quietly. "I can't help but think though... that we wouldn't be here together if -”

"There are no ifs Elijah. We can only have the reality that's in front of us. I want you to understand that, and understand how much I love you. You're my here and now, let alone my future. We can't keep discussing what could have been and I don't want to. You're the man who makes me happy, regardless of how different our futures might have been under other circumstances." He smiled at me and leant in to kiss me.

"I love you Ash."

"And I love you Honey. As much as I hate fate, I can only thank it for what it has at least given back to me. Can you understand that?"

"Yes, I can Babe. We have to live for today and tomorrow, not yesterday."

"Exactly," I said and smiled up at him again. "My heart now belongs to you, Sweetheart."

"I'll take care of it."

"You'd better!” I warned and he laughed, tilting my face up to meet his. "Are you ready to be taken care of again?" he asked cheekily.

"Always, lover."

He Said

SIMON, BREE AND MICHAEL were coming over tonight for some tequila shots and I stopped at the pub on the way home to get the alcohol, passing by the supermarket to grab some fresh limes. It was only 4.00 pm and I knew Ash was taking Mercy to her parents for the weekend and tonight was *the* night I intended on making some form of move. I wasn't sure what at this stage, but I had to do something.

I checked my missed calls as I loaded the bags onto the island bench and nearly cried when I heard Bree. They couldn't make it after all, none of them, but she'd call again later until she got one of us. The voicemail had come through only five minutes before I got home. I felt a pang of guilt and deception as I hit the delete button. What message? I still intended to have drinks with this girl and if she didn't respond to my advances, I would pull out old reliable and blame it on the alcohol.

I threw all the makings for a quick meal into the fridge and chose what I assumed would be a suitable middle-of-the-road music selection, ready to be fired up when the time was right. I spread the dozen or so limes across the counter and lined up the two bottles of tequila. There were supposed to be five of us after all. Who knew how much citrus and liquor that would amount to? I pulled the saltshaker from the cupboard, ensuring it held an ample supply, and added it to the cavalry on the bench, my own personal arsenal. I was so excited it was shameful. I deliberated a quick shower to calm me down before she got home, but I had to be in the kitchen when she arrived, and cutting up the limes. It had to appear I had no idea about the ensuing phone call and that my hands would have to be busy, so she'd have to take it. I prayed that Bree would not ring between now and when Ash got home.

A quick glance at the clock told me I would have enough time to change. She would often stay for a visit with her folks when she dropped Mercy off, but was always home well before dinner. I bolted up the stairs and stripped off my pants and shirt, replacing them with some board-shorts and a T-Shirt. Plan A: put myself on display. *Dance monkey dance*, I thought and shook my head as I laughed, putting my clothes in the wardrobe. I didn't want her to think I was a slob if I did get her in here. If things went well, I didn't want to go to her room; it had been Mum and Dad's, it had been her and Lori's. I wanted to avoid any concerns for her in case the memories came flooding back. I tidied up a little before going back downstairs to wait for her, unable to shake that last thought from my head.

I went to the bar and took out six shot glasses, mulling this over again. I wasn't Lori. What if she only wanted me to replace him, make her feel like he was with her again? I loved her and I didn't want to be a poor substitute for my twin. I then realised that I already had myself and Ash in a relationship. I had no idea on how tonight's events would end up, and I snorted at my own stupid confidence.

As I neared the kitchen, she came through the door. As always, I went to her and gave her a kiss on the cheek, welcoming her home. I put the glasses on the bench and got straight into the job of slicing up some limes. Plan B: can't waste good food. I felt very manipulative and a little childish, but it was now or never; all I could hope for was a receptive response.

My timing was perfect – my phone rang. I had a brief moment of panic that Bree may have reached Ash on her mobile. That didn't mean *I* knew about it though. I asked Ash to get it, showing her my lime-juiced fingers, making me wonder what she truly tasted like. If my memory of the spice of her lips was anything to go by, I was seriously going to have a lot of trouble not drowning her in my own emissions. Probably best to keep away from that for a while.

She slipped her hand over mine, bringing me back from my erotic fantasies and I feigned a curious look. *Whatever could the matter be*? It said. She covered the phone and told me the bad news and I smiled, I couldn't help it, it just crept onto my face, unbidden. The face she pulled at me confused me a little. Would she still *not* want to play the fool with me? To avoid the issue, I quickly filled two of the shot glasses as she finished her conversation with Bree, confirming we were on for tomorrow night. As an outside solution, maybe I could try again then...

I questioned what the problem was when she ended the call. Dear, dear, oh my, they had to have dinner with Simon's parents. How could we pass the time now? I handed her a shot, but she wanted to get changed. As soon as her heel was all I could see on the stairs, I bundled everything outside onto the verandah table and turned on the music system. I was sitting there so cool when she returned and sat cross-legged in the chair perpendicular to me. She looked edible in a pair of bike pants and a babydoll shift and I wanted to undo the small string of buttons, which kept her luscious breasts secreted away.

I passed her the shot glass, not wanting her to forget what we were doing out here. I picked up the saltshaker, waiting on her to lick her hand. As her soft, pink tongue lightly traced over the back of it, I brought my hand up, not diverting my eyes from her, and licked my own. I sprinkled us both in salt and asked if she was ready. She didn't answer but licked, sipped and sucked. I had to laugh as she pulled a face at the bitter sensation, and I reached for the bottle to refill our glasses. She didn't look keen, so I taunted her into another round, suggesting three in total, pushing my luck to the extreme. She actually agreed to it, but I doubted she would realise the effect three quick shots would have on her. Plan C: intake plenty of fluids to avoid a hangover the next day. If my malevolent plans for this evening failed, I wanted her to be willing to play again tomorrow night.

Before she salted up for the third and final shot, I stopped her and went to get the water. We both drank it down after taking the shot, and shortly after, my bladder was ready to burst. She got up and I knew she'd be heading for the toilet. Plan D: create a chase situation, so I bolted in before she had the chance. I smiled to myself as I peed. She was banging on the door wanting me to hurry up, giving me a second thought back to Plan A again. As I opened the door to let her in, I stripped off my T-shirt. I knew she had a thing for my chest, shoulders and back. She was always an upper body man, and although Lori was hairless, she had loved to run her fingers through my chest hair when we were going out. It was worth a try. It was also a hot day, so my bases were covered. I didn't want to be *too* obvious.

She was lightning fast, and I was still standing at the bathroom door when it opened, surprising me a little. I took her hand and led her back to the verandah, not giving her a chance to do anything else but to continue with the drinking games. I refilled both glasses and opened up the door a little by licking her hand. I couldn't sway her to have another as yet, but she laughed as I licked the salt back off her. My pulse was racing; a combination of the alcohol and my hidden intentions.

She couldn't believe she was sitting here with a doctor getting drunk on tequila. Excellent, she was prepared to 'get drunk' with me. I gave her what I thought was an acceptable excuse and put Plan E into action: incorporate touching.

I pulled her to her feet and twirled her under my arm a few times before drawing her back to me. She lowered her face to watch her feet and I thought I may have overdone it, making her giddy and worried I'd let her fall. I promised her that I wouldn't, and she looked up at me and smiled, her hands shifting a little higher onto my biceps. She was quiet for a few moments and I left her to her thoughts, hopeful that they were about me in some small way at least. With her eyes averted from mine I could study her perfect mouth, full lips and marvellous symmetry. I wanted to press mine against them and taste her sweet flavour. I leant in against her and sang softly in her ear. When I saw her smile again, I asked why. She told me she'd been thinking about when she and Mercy had busted me hooning around the house, singing and sliding around on the tiles and I laughed, also recalling the day. She *had* been thinking about me, which was good.

She told me I had a beautiful voice, and I told her *she* was beautiful. I hoped that wasn't a mistake. I realised we had both stopped moving, still in the dancer's embrace. I was a coward and couldn't bring myself to lower my face to hers, although now would have been a great opportunity.

At my eighteenth, I had tried to kiss her, drunk, and all I got for my efforts was a slap to my face. And rightly so. I was way out of line.

However, if that happened again, I knew it would be the end of it, possibly for always. I pulled myself together and led her back to the table. My stomach reminded me of the food I had bought to make a quick dinner. She was aware that food would help with the alcohol consumption. Ash was no fool, and that fact alone scared me a little. This could be the biggest mistake of my life. I inwardly smiled when she reached for the bottle of tequila and our glasses, following me inside.

She didn't seem to want to make eye contact after we'd eaten and the situation felt a little flat, like eating meant the evening was over. I wasn't sure how to start the game playing again, although she had brought the tequila inside and we'd kept drinking, slower, but still going whilst we prepared dinner together. I had to reach around her at one stage, and I pressed slightly into her from behind with my chest to get to the tomatoes she'd diced, lingering only momentarily. I was sure that her back had aligned against me, but I was not certain... With untold relief, she smiled warmly at me and went back to the verandah, grabbing the glasses and bottle once more. I was right behind her...

I was getting more bravado now I had a full stomach, and the alcohol had relaxed me. I suggested body shots, and she didn't rebuke me, didn't say a word in fact. I moved closer to her and licked her cheek in what I hoped, seemed playful. She laughed, telling me it wasn't icing, and I raised an eyebrow as I tilted her head to sprinkle the salt. I didn't muck around though and licked it off in one sweep, downing the shot and sucking on the lime. I intended on making the most of this though; raising the stakes each turn and taking as many shots as she would allow.

I knew she had bike shorts on but thought a little flirting may go a long way now we were going to be licking various body parts on each other, all in innocent, good fun of course. I asked her if she had anything on under her dress. She did, of course.

A look of slight concern crossed her face when I asked her to lift it for me and I promised that her boobs were safe. I wanted her stomach, *for now*. Her skin was so hot against my tongue, and so soft. I traced a line over her slowly, drawing my tongue back into my mouth to moisten it again, wanting to keep going. I restrained myself from kissing her stomach with an open mouth. That was not part of the rules of tequila shots, so applied the salt to her and savoured what time I could against her. Had I taken too long? Was I pushing the boundaries too quickly? I sat up and smiled at her.

She called me a tequila slut, making me laugh as I licked lightly over the top of her knee, taking it back to a slightly less erotic encounter. She wanted to know how many shots I was planning to take, then asking when it was her turn. Excellent! She was keen for her go!

I told her four was a good amount and asked where she wanted my final one. I thought I was pretty crafty letting her make the decision. It would give me a fair indication on how all of this was playing out in her head. I wasn't sure I could stop now; I was so *incredibly* turned on. God, she had no idea of the power she had over me. I would be her sex-slave if that *was* all she wanted me for. Just as long as she wanted me...

She sounded nervous when answering, stammering just a little. It was my choice apparently and I quickly calculated the best option for both safety and danger. I chose her throat.

I found that what my lips wanted to do across her stomach I was now doing at her throat, nuzzling not licking, dragging my mouth over her sweet, soft skin, breathing in her vanilla-cinnamon scent. As I open-mouth kissed against her, making my way to her ear, she interrupted me, and I felt instant disappointment. This could have been the inception. She asked how much salt I intended to apply, pulling me back into line. I played my lips to her throat one last time before drawing back, hoping to make my intentions a little clearer in what I prayed was a subtle way.

I flicked a little salt over the wet trail, not really caring how much, and went back to nuzzling against her. I had no idea of what this was doing to her, but I knew what it was doing to me and I eventually drew back, knowing I had to stop. She'd made no movement to embrace this into anything passionate; she was still just playing the game. Time to move it up a notch.

She protested when I told her I had the choice of where she licked it off me, reminding her that I'd given her an option to do that as well. She did warn me, not only with her voice but in her eyes, to play nicely. *It was the alcohol, your Honour.* I had my excuse ready, just in case. I held the inside of my elbow out to her, a safe place to start from I thought. *And an excellent place to work up from.* She swept her tongue over me quickly and I told her that she wasn't putting her best effort in. She licked again, striving higher up my arm this time. I meant for her to leave her lips on me longer and didn't expect this as her reaction. Was she getting into this just the tiniest bit? Surely she wouldn't be doing this against her will, or maybe she was just pissed. Plan F: not to take advantage of her drunk. I wanted her to return my desire under her own volition, although this may not have been my initial intention. When she was done, I sat back, lacing my hands behind my head.

I knew where I wanted the next three salt lines taken from, especially the last. I traced a circle around my navel, and she followed the path; the next down between my pecs. I wanted to grab her by the shoulders and just kiss her lustily – take my chance and run with it. My final choice of area kept me in check however and after playfully musing for a few seconds, told her it was to be the nipples. She looked unsure as she leant to my left one, drawing her tongue over it quickly. I told her to try again, and she did. She didn't just lick them this time, she worked them with her lips and tongue, driving me insane. When she licked the salt from them, she lightly pressed her teeth into me, biting and suckling gently. This was the turning point.

My hand worked into her hair as I held her against me, moaning. The salt was long gone, she was now there by her own choice. I took her face in my hands and drew her gaze upwards. I had no control over my actions anymore and as she looked into my eyes, I grazed my finger across her mouth. She opened to me, and my finger sought the moistness of her inner lip before playing it across her tongue; she sucked it into her mouth. Our eyes locked, and my hands were drawn back to her face again, and I leant in to kiss her. I moved slowly. I didn't want to scare her, didn't want this trance to evaporate. My heart was beating way too rapidly, and my cock was like stone. I licked my lips in readiness and sighed out a moan in anticipation of this kiss.

In true comic fashion, a knock at the door was about to ruin my entire evening. She froze, her breathing sharp and shallow, and our eyes locked again. Yes, I did believe we were on the same page. Neither of us made a move until the knocking became a rapping. It was bloody Simon.

I smiled at her as she stood to answer the door and I quickly followed, not wanting to break the thought processes now in her head. As she reached the door, I captured her from behind and held her in my arms lightly. I knew she would be able to feel my thickness pressed against her, but I didn't care. I wanted her to know how she affected me and exactly how much.

As they entered, Bree told us we were plastered. This was not exactly true; we were pretty ripped but by no means blind. In fact, after the last five minutes, I'd never felt more sober in my life.

They joined us on the verandah, and we laughed and joked, having a great time. Simon eventually mentioned doing body shots and I looked into Ash's eyes. They blazed back at me before she dropped her face, breaking our gaze. I laughed. Bree wanted to know what the joke was, and I gave her some lame excuse, waiting for Ash to look at me again, and she did not disappoint. She seemed a little flustered and I couldn't believe what came out of her mouth next, that she was going to bed! Bree and Simon joined me in the protest for her to stay, so she settled on taking a shower instead. I could live with that. After Ash left, I said to Simon and Bree that I also needed one. I was upright immediately, going in search of her.

I wasn't sure which bathroom to check first. No lights were on in her room or shining from under the ensuite door, so I went into my room, sliding open the bathroom door. The sight that met me made me light-headed. My eyes feasted on her naked body, her arms above her head as she threaded her hair into a ponytail. She just stood there, not feeling embarrassed, not grabbing for the nearest towel to cover her nudity. Instead, she turned to me and I had her in my arms before I even realised I'd crossed the floor.

I took in the planes of her back with my hands, running them down to knead her firm cheeks, gripping into her, lifting her onto the counter. Her legs wrapped around me, locking me against her. Her fingers had been curling through the hair at the base of my neck during the heated kiss, pulling me down to her, and then they were gone. She was tugging at the tie of my board-shorts and just as I was about to help her, she had them open, sliding them down my legs with her feet. I was beyond rational thought as they hit the ground and I kicked them free. We were about to make love and I for one was more than ready. She asked me to lock Mercy's side. *Shit! Mercy!* I hadn't thought about that in our passionate urgency. Having no intention of breaking away from her, I lifted her to the other end of the counter and reached for the lock, then remembered Mercy was at Anna's. When I reminded her, the smile that played on her lips drove me to the edge.

How I wanted to sample her, throwing her ankles over my shoulders and feasting on her sweetness, slowly lapping and exploring her in a way I'd never had the chance to do before. My stomach tingled and I knew if I didn't stop thinking about that, it would be all over in about five seconds.

I lowered my hand to her instead, more than happy to enjoy the Braille version for now. She'd obviously enjoyed our sexually charged atmosphere downstairs as much as I did - her arousal obvious as she parted her legs further when she felt my gentle touch. I nuzzled into her throat as I strummed her, and she writhed against me with equal force. I could feel it building within her and I laughed quietly, revelling in the pleasure she was taking from me. As her orgasm took her, I drove into her, feeling her pulsating around me from within. I moaned, knowing I wouldn't be able to last for long.

She leant back slightly, her face a vision of ecstasy, putting her nipples prominently on display for me. She didn't have to ask twice, and I teased her intimately as my orgasm boiled through me. I pulled her off the vanity, splaying my thighs to hold her onto me as I ground against her furiously. *Oh God, Oh God, OH GOD!* repeated in my head, and I pulled her lips back to mine, ending the force with a burning matched kiss. As I slowed, I softened the kiss, taking in her fine flavour once again, savouring her tongue and lips with my own.

She dropped her feet to the ground, and I wrapped myself against her, drawing her deeply into my embrace. I'd never felt so good in my life, but I was still burning. The heat in my body wasn't ebbing and my pulse was still erratic and pounding. I reached out and turned on the shower, drawing her in to stand under the cool water with me, not breaking the kiss. Her body was throwing off matching waves of heat and finally, under that soothing running water, we found reality again.

I eventually drew back from her, moving her wet hair behind her ears. My hands formed to the sides of her face and I drew her up to kiss me again, working my lips around her throat, nuzzling lightly. I whispered to her the words I didn't think I'd say, *I love you.* My heart thudded gravely when she stammered, unable to tell me she loved me too, but I didn't want her hurting. I sighed dejectedly against her, knowing this could have been her reaction. Well at least I knew now, but had still found a moment of splendour with her that I never thought I would.

She echoed my sentiment, but stumbled over how it made her feel, and I drew back to look into her eyes, wanting the truthful answer which may not have matched what she had to say in spoken words. I knew Lori would always be in her heart, they had a love so intense, so passionate, and I was not my brother. I didn't want to be. I didn't ever want to make her feel he couldn't still be a part of her heart, but I wanted to have my own residency in there. She smiled, vanquishing my concern, and pulled me back to her. The water running over her silky skin pressed into mine was making me stir again.

I told her we had a lot to talk about, but was more interested in sealing my mouth back against her nape and she angled her head to allow me to seek the trail around her throat with ease. We didn't have time for that conversation now though, she was right about that in her murmured comment, and then she asked what I'd told Simon and Bree when I came upstairs to find her. I expected her to laugh, but a worried look was on her face. I drew her back to me for one final kiss as I turned off the shower.

She was concerned about how we were to act when back downstairs in their company. She wanted to have a clear vision of where we were going before we made this public, assuming I may not have had the same desires for her. She was so cute, and I couldn't believe her fears, her unfounded fears. But, she was worried, and I soothed as best I could, telling her it wouldn't be an issue and we would play it cool for the rest of the evening. This made her smile, and I was glad to see it aimed at me.

With her mood now lightened, I smacked my wet towel over her bum as she pulled on her pants and she threatened me. I opened my arms to her, telling her to come and get me. I had to smile when her concern rose again about being caught by a wandering Bree and Simon, coming to find out what was taking us so long. I was also a little hurt that it distressed her so much. Did it matter if they knew now?

I was disappointed when she took a seat opposite instead of beside me. I was hoping to get a little unseen rummaging action happening, realising this was probably the reason she had sat so far away. My plans this evening had all worked to my initial goal, so I threw in one more after several smouldering glances across the table, Plan G: Get someone to do the dirty work for you.

I had no idea what the conversation was that had been going on around me, but interjected, bringing Simon back to his suggestion earlier of doing body shots. He was still keen. I knew there was no way he would let me lick salt off Bree so continued on with the curiosity of how we would work it. He walked straight into my trap, telling us we would be teams and we were to copy their actions or face double shots. Excellent! I grinned at Ash, moving over to sit next to her.

Simon's first salt trail was over the tip of Bree's nose and I was more than happy to take my go. Starting from the top lip I licked, up and over her nose to the bridge. I salted her up and she wrinkled her nose. I didn't bother to lick; I sucked her into my mouth, from top lip once again to the bridge. I slyly worked my tongue into her mouth, hidden by my bottom lip.

Bree was already sizing Simon up when I drew away from her. Simon and Bree seemed oblivious to our secret stimulation and I guess they weren't expecting to see it.

Bree went in for Simon's ear and sat back when she was finished, thinking herself so smart. My clever girl brought my ear to her mouth instead of the other way around, so my face acted as a cloak to her soft lips and tongue. I slipped my arm across her back, pulling her near. Oh God, I was instantly hard again as she traced my outer ear, drawing my lobe into her mouth and nibbling it gently. I fought the desire to nudge my cheek into her as her hot mouth drove me into further arousal. Simon noticed, pointing out my closed eyes. I wasn't sure when that happened, but all I'd been focussed on was Ash's breathy exhalations.

Bree handed me the shaker and I passed it to Ash. I was ready for another intimate teasing.

When she finally pulled away, I slyly took her hand and rubbed it slowly over my cock, showing her what she'd done to me. Her eyes bulged and she pulled back quickly, but not before giving me a light squeeze. I wanted to lay her over the table and just take her. I didn't care that Bree and Simon were sitting in front row seats. I laughed quietly and settled back in my chair, knowing there was more to come, and I waited patiently.

Bree's cleavage was next on Simon's menu and I wondered how I could get to Ash's amazing nipples unseen. I threw her a pained look then smiled at her, knowing how much this tormenting was affecting both of us. All I wanted to do was launch myself at her, kissing her deeply, intensely, yet I couldn't. I taunted Ash lightly over what areas Simon's lick had covered, and she smacked me, pulling me back into line again. With great pleasure, I knelt in front of her, fumbling open the small run of buttons. She hadn't put a bra back on, which allowed me to graze my tongue slowly down and under her breasts. I went to reach for them and stopped myself in time, knowing this would betray a little more than was expected.

I moaned against her quietly and applied no salt, driving my tongue back down her frame. Her chest was rising beneath me at a rapid pace and I so desperately wanted to hold her against me, drawing a tight bud into my mouth. Later...

Bree thought she had us cornered with her next attempt and I knew exactly where she was going when she kissed Simon deeply. When she explained to a confused Ash that Simon's tongue was the next place to be licked, Bree smiled, assuming we'd be both sucking down double shots. The shots were behind me and there was only one thing I now wanted to suck down, but once again, that would have to be later...

Ash pulled a face at me and covered her mouth with her fingers. Maybe we were going to be doing double shots after all, but I would do my best to avoid that.

We'd pashed before, I reminded Bree. I sat, waiting on Ash to kiss me openly in front of our drunken friends. I was ready for some tongue and intended on making the most of it. If Bree or Simon guessed what was going on, that would be a fair call. In fact, I upped the ante, telling her to straddle over my lap as the positions we were currently sitting in would be too awkward. She would also act as a complete shield for me, from Bree and Simon.

As she tentatively climbed onto my lap I wondered if I'd pushed her too far, but no, here she was drawing toward me. I threaded my tongue into her mouth, wanting to twist my head and pull her down to me more forcefully, but I didn't want her to stop. I outlined her jaw with my finger, and she pulled away suddenly, realising I was technically overstepping the mark. It didn't matter; she still had to kiss the salt back from me.

She made light of it, ordering the salt from Bree and then telling me to stick out my tongue. Both Bree and I were happy to comply. I kissed her longer than last time, and I lowered my unseen hand between her thighs, lightly caressing at the taught material of her tights. She gasped lightly into my mouth and I kissed her deeper, but as my breathing quickened, she drew away from me again. I smiled and she moved her legs to one side of my lap, so she was sitting more comfortably, and I tucked her under my arm and kissed her forehead softly.

Bree reminded us of Michael's absence, assuming we would be glad he was not here to make the situation even more ribald. I couldn't agree with her less. If Michael *had* been here, I could imagine the intimacy Ash and I would have been put through, and I would have done so gladly, taking one for the team. I knew she would have *never* agreed to some of the suggestions that Michael would have put up on offer. Bree confirmed that he'd be here tomorrow night and we'd start from scratch. Ash and I needed to work some things out in the morning then, knowing where we stood with each other and to the rest of the world.

When Ash said she was going to bed, it was music to my ears. I hoped I was invited. I told them I wanted to be able to stomach a drink tomorrow, so was going to bed too.

I went into the kitchen and filled four glasses with water, advising Bree and Simon to drink them before going to sleep. Ash handed me two Panadol and I drank them down, finishing my water. She said goodnight as Simon and Bree crawled into bed, and I followed behind her, turning off the lamp when they were settled.

Damn it, did I knock? Did I go looking for her? Would she be waiting for me in my room? This was my preference of course, but making my way up the stairs, all of these thoughts flashed through my head, wondering why she hadn't waited for me... But she had, and was standing in the hallway, watching as I climbed the stairs.

I couldn't believe she kissed me goodnight and very formally too. What had happened between the time we left my room and coming back? I knew I'd heard her right, she loved me, but then my thoughts darkened. I knew she had *always* loved me, but not in the way I now wanted her to. What if that's what she meant, and through my stupid haze of finally getting the woman I loved, I'd over-exerted her intentions? I wasn't about to let this go. She was worried about being caught and I assured her they had never come wandering when they'd stayed here before. I also added that I didn't want to spend another night away from her, wanting to clarify right here and now what level her love was for me. She threw me a cheeky smile, and I dragged her through my open door.

We stood there and kissed for such a long time, slowly, painstakingly slowly. I tasted every area of her I could reach as I worked her clothes off, and then held her against me. I could tell she was done for the night; she was tired and fairly drunk. I eased away from her eventually, knowing we had the rest of time to make up for lost time, as it were. She leant against my chest then kissed me lightly before I went to use the bathroom. When I returned, she was already in bed and I stripped off and climbed in next to her. The touch of her was like the softest satin as she drew against me, laying over me and running her small fingers through my chest hair. It was very soothing and totally hot, but I knew that tomorrow would arrive soon enough, and we could pick up where we left off. The second she was awake actually.

I smiled to myself and ran my hand over her hair, kissing her brow. She sighed deeply, contentedly and fell asleep in my arms. I lay there for a long time finding sleep difficult, but happy to be holding my girl against me. *My girl.* Assuming all went well tomorrow, yes, she would be my girl. I would no doubt have to lay all of my thoughts out on the table for her, letting her know exactly how I felt. And if she didn't feel the same? *Great*, I thought, *now I* will *be lying here for a long time, finding sleep impossible*.

I was tired when I woke. I knew I didn't get much sleep last night; my concern for the outcomes of today outplaying the needs of my tired, drunken body. The first thing I did was slip down the stairs to see whether Bree and Simon were awake. At this time of the morning, I wasn't surprised to see they were still asleep. Good.

I closed the bedroom door behind me as I entered my room, ensuring no unexpected visitors would walk in without warning. I had more plans for us this morning, and we had to talk before we were among our friends. I *needed* to talk to her. If we were becoming a couple, I wanted to be able to freely kiss and hug her in front of them, not keeping it hidden until another chance to talk could be found. I also wanted this sorted out before Mercy came home.

The sheet was pooled around her waist and she was still lying in the same position from when I exited the bed. I could see how my shape had curled around her, slightly on her stomach. I lifted the edge of the sheet and lowered it gently, leaving her laying before me in all of her naked beauty. Her lashes lay darkly against the top of her cheekbone, a small smile playing to her pouting lips. I wanted to kiss her awake, but had other ideas as I started to stiffen. A shower first…

It was difficult to keep my hands to myself whilst showering, knowing I'd be able to last much longer if I were to expel the first round now. I wanted to make love to her in a total encompassment, not just the physical connection, and I was still wary that I wouldn't be able to control myself if I were to attempt nuzzling into her; that the party would be immediately over.

I took the chance, leaving my straining erection alone. With the towel swathed around my hips, I crept back into the bedroom as she sighed and shifted her position slightly. She was now completely on her stomach and the view from my vantage point was like seeing for the first time where once you were blind. She was radiant.

The apex of where I most wanted to kiss her was winking slightly from between her thighs, beckoning to me in an unheard whisper. I found I was lightly running my hands over my erection through the towel and stopped immediately, averting my eyes and thinking of anything to get my mind off what I had in store for her. Finally, I was flaccid again and I dropped the towel and crawled onto the bed, vertically aligning over her, laying my stomach over her pert bum.

She twitched slightly as I worked my lips across her back, it was tickling her no doubt, and I felt myself twitching too. I didn't want to wake her yet; I wanted to wake her with the strength of my love for her. I was still a little concerned that her thoughts were not going to be an echo of my own and wanted to give myself the best chance I had to keep this woman. I drew my legs apart gently, taking hers out with the movement, and unable to contain my growing erection any longer, slipped further down her body and drove in slowly, rocking her gently.

One hand sought out her flesh and it crept up and down the side of her body. I smiled when I noticed her respond breathily each time I moved past her armpit. I assume I'd found an erogenous zone and continued with the exploration.

My lips nestled into the crook of her neck, exhaling lightly, her small hands now gripping at the sheet. Was she awake or had I entered into a dream realm with her? I worked my hands in under hers, and when her fingers found my own, she interlaced them, now counterbalancing my force, meeting me halfway and returning the flow of the motion from above her. She was awake.

I drew one leg out further, allowing me to roll her toward me and I lay cheek to cheek with her for a few moments before moving in to kiss her. *Oh no!* I thought, *Oh God no!* I now prayed. I was about to end this and all too soon. Ash rolled onto her back and I reached down, hoping I could get her there first, but if all else failed, I could bring her off properly and in the way I most wanted to if I ran past the finish-line before her. Her breathing told me she was building and as she reached her peak, I guided my cock further into her to keep her going with the force of my pelvis still rasping against all of her sensitive areas. Our groans were collective, thankfully breaking that finish-line tape in a dead tie.

I lay against her for a few moments, playing her granite nipples lightly between my fingers. For having nursed Mercy, they were still wonderfully small and tight, pebble-like, insanity invoking... I smiled, ecstatic she hadn't woken and thrown me out of the bed, off her, casting missiles at me in her anger of being intruded unasked.

She then wanted to ask me something embarrassing. This would be interesting... Was she aware of the events from last night at all? Surely she must be, otherwise I wouldn't have just made love to her again.

I rolled onto my back and drew her across my chest so I could better see her reaction.

She wanted to know if we'd made love when we came to bed last night and I laughed, I couldn't help it. I told her no, and then she asked why she was naked. I reminded her there were no clothes of hers in this room and she smiled at me in recognition.

Her smile faded when she asked if I had been downstairs, and I confirmed for her that our guests were still sleeping, and we had plenty of time to talk.

We danced around, not giving each other any firm answers and then she likened our conversation to how she and Lorien had interacted.

And this is what I feared. I was *not* Lorien. I couldn't be his replacement, wouldn't be, and if this was all I *could* be for her I knew it was not enough, regardless of my drunken musings last night. I didn't want to be in his shadow for the rest of my life, knowing I was never the man she wanted me to be.

Her words assured me, bringing us both together in her explanation as those who would always share a love for him, in two different ways, but still a connected loving force for my twin. There was room in her heart to love us both and that alleviated all of my concerns. I didn't want her to forget Lori, and she was right, I would always have him in my heart, a piece of him still existing within me. That she could love me too was enough. I was used to sharing with my twin, and this bond would now continue through his widow's love for us both.

I laughed again when she said there was no other that could compare to a Standish. I just hoped I was enough for her. She and Lorien had such a passionate relationship where sex was the forte of the day, every day and at nearly thirty, there was no way I could keep up with the erotic encounters my brother had the time and ability to sustain. She was a little confused when I admitted this to her with a nervous laugh, but she cheekily reminded me of what we'd accomplished so far.

Her next question came unexpectedly, and I was surprised that she had to ask it. Did I love her, *truly* love her? I confirmed it for her, and that I had felt this way for the longest time.

I almost didn't hear her next words, so quietly spoken they were. She was scared, unbelievably scared that I didn't mean it, which I couldn't comprehend and that I'd possibly break her heart, something she was unaware I could never do. I loved her with all of *my* heart and hers was something I intended on keeping safe, treasuring it like a rare gem; and so happy that this marvellous gem would now be mine to love and treasure so solely, so completely.

Her musings took her back to the brief interlude with Damon, a subject I didn't really want to revisit. So crazy jealous I was during that time I was still ashamed of the joy I felt when it all fell apart, sadly knowing this was causing her some level of pain.

She ended this chapter of our conversation, taking me into the next with a broad smile on my face. Once she had seen me through love's eyes, she was unable to close them again and in fact she must have been lusting after me as I had over her. How much time exactly had we wasted? I wanted to know what the trigger was.

She was not going to give me anything until I opened myself to her. I knew this was probably going to be the case, thinking over it last night, unable to get to sleep. I had decided I'd be as honest and forthright as I could be when this conversation took place, and here I was, about to divulge all. It was going to be much harder on me as I'd felt this way a lot longer than she had, other than the request for a kiss from me when Lori had been off his face at the Club. I knew even then that it was not love she had for me.

She did however make me chuckle when she insisted I go first, and I stretched, causing her to move from me. I quickly rolled over to her and lay my head on her chest, allowing her to work her fingers softly through my hair. It also put me face to face with her rose-coloured bud and my hand sought it with a mind of its own. She responded to my touch instantly and as I leant forward to kiss it, she shuddered... I smiled again.

It was hard to tell her that my emotions had deceived me as far back as when Keren and I had started having problems, cementing it when Faith had stayed here when Ash was pregnant. Having someone so jealous of you makes it hard to ignore those wonderful and amazing points when it's being hammered into you. Waiting for you to deny the charges, wanting me to tell them they are the most beautiful and wonderful person in the world.

She asked why I hadn't kissed her at the club, all those years ago, when she had asked me to.

I explained our chemistry had always been there, from the very beginning when we first started going out in fact. Why wouldn't it have still been there, as it was now? I asked her when she first realised what we had now was more than she had suspected. She ducked her head in embarrassment and lay into the crook of my arm, hiding her flushed face. I prompted her again gently. She had to be able to talk to me about this, and I smiled, unknown to her, as she started to speak, not moving her face to where I could see her, staying hidden against me.

I'd always known about her thing for my muscles. Lori was well-built too but I was a little heavier set, due primarily to the surfing. She'd caught me in my gym gear, sweaty, fighting with the lawnmower. It was hard to believe it was at this instant she fell in love with me, completely and finally.

I was unsure why she had then gone out with Damon, not checking the depths of what we could have had. She was afraid, too afraid of my rebuking her and ruining the trio we had formed as a tight triangle, since Lori's passing. I could understand her hesitation. I knew this is why I'd never pressed the issue either, and I had a much longer track record of being in love with her, than she did with me. I leant down to kiss her.

Her response was immediate and passionate, wanting to make love again. It was hard to stop, I wanted it just as much, but moreso, I wanted to be able to be comfortable and real in front of our friends today, not hiding it any longer. I couldn't and I didn't want to. I reminded her we still had to talk about our new situation before we left the bedroom. She smiled up at me and blushed before turning her eyes away.

She lowered her face further, nearly nestled back into my armpit again and her fingers crept guiltily over me, slowly and so painfully. There were two things she wanted to ask, and I told her to go for it. I eased my own hand over hers and drew it to my lips, kissing her palm softly before placing it on my chest. In answer to her first question, I assured her I could go more than once, and this made her smile. I smiled back at her, waiting for her to continue, finally raising my eyebrows when she remained silent. Her asking me about going down on her, or my resistance thereof, had been a difficult question for her to raise I realised, as her blush once again played traitor to her. Because I hadn't, we hadn't so far, she wrongly assumed this fact. She had no idea.

I explained exactly how much I wanted to invade her, was what I most wanted to do to her. I would get no greater pleasure than to enjoy her flavour and the intimacy it encompassed. I was hardening again, just thinking about it, and it was now *my* traitorous body that was being problematic. She was unaware of what was currently happening south of the border. I laughed and pulled her tighter, kissing her softly on the brow. All I really wanted to do was to snake myself down her body and fill her full of my face. I shuddered a little at the thought. God, she would be the death of me…

I brought her back to the present, reminding her we still needed to work out what we were doing, and outside of the bedroom. I told her she had to go first. She didn't want to, and I realised how incredibly high her guard was, and she was so afraid that I didn't want her in the way she wanted me to. How had she ever managed to think I was such a prize and that she wouldn't be enough for me, that there could ever be anyone else I would want to love? She was unaware of her beauty, her natural grace and sense of humour. She was a complete package, well for me at least.

I then offered to go first, and she looked up at me, hope shining from her eyes. I told her I wanted to spend the rest of my life with her and that I was in love with her. She told me she felt the same way.

When she mentioned our girl Mercy and that she wanted me to adopt her, I held the powerful emotion together that wanted to burst through my very veins. No greater gift could she give to me than that of herself and her daughter... my niece. My niece who would now be my daughter.

This disclosure brought with it a myriad of other issues we needed to resolve - where we would sleep, when to tell Mercy, when to tell our parents. I was happy for it all to come at its own pace, with exception to the sleeping arrangements. I was sure she understood why I didn't want to move into her room.

And then I had to speak the words, the words to cement this for me in my own head and give me public rights to show the world how I felt about her. Were we a couple?

She confirmed this but seemed a little reluctant to go public just yet. I was wrong though, as she told me Michael and Glen already knew. How was that even possible? How could they know when I myself had only found out yesterday? And you could have blown me over; she'd approached Michael and Glen when she first had feelings for me, unsure what exactly to do about them. Some friend Michael was, why didn't he tell me? We laughed over how we would play the initial intimacy in front of them, agreeing to wait until they were all here and not just only Bree and Simon.

We lay there quietly for some time. I wished I could read her mind, or perhaps that she could read mine. I'd kept saying no, to discuss what we were doing here. But now, decision reached, I wanted to take her again and again. And she was worried about my doing it twice. I smiled to myself, knowing I could be Raging Bull if I so wished. It was my work schedule that would keep things less hectic, not my lack of desire. The toilet flushing downstairs put an end to my musings and she left my room to go and change.

I jumped out of bed and quickly made it, throwing on the first thing my hands touched in the wardrobe, a pair of cargo pants. I went to put on a T-shirt and then thought better of it. Let her be taunted. I opened her bedroom door quietly and crept in behind her, running my hands over her from behind, trickling around to her stomach. I wanted another kiss before we carried on with the charade.

I eventually drew back smiling, knowing where her thoughts lay when my tongue drilled into her mouth, creating small pants of pleasure from her. She was imagining me at other areas of her body, or so I assumed. Keeping this thought close, it did no end of good for me too.

Simon and Bree approached us a little cautiously about the frivolity we went through last night and Ash and I both fobbed it off as no big deal, ready to play again when the boys got here, which was well past 2.00 pm when they finally arrived.

As the door opened, I found myself inching a little closer to Ash and had to fight the urge to take this into my own hands, wanting to fling her onto the sofa and just invade her in front of our friends, with every digit and extension I owned. Whew! It was getting hot in here.

I kept a close distance to her, ready for whenever she believed it to be the perfect timing. It finally came whilst we were in the kitchen, our small group surrounding us as if we were the centre stage.

She bantered with me lightly, playfully in front of them, but they were unaware of what it was leading to. And as she walked toward me, my arms opened for her and she leant in. We kissed openly, deeply, intimately and deliberately. I took the smallest step back from her, enough to remove my igniting crotch from against her. It was twitching again. No, better it was secluded, so I pressed back into her, causing her to look up at me and grin. Finally, Ash laid her head against my chest, looking at them with a sultry smile.

I confirmed to Bree that this was real, then drew Ash's mouth back to mine, emphasising the point so much more clearly. Not that I'd finished with her yet; I would *never* be that.

Michael poked fun, alluding to her relationship with Lori and the change in his cheeky emotion surprised me, no, shocked me. I'd never seen Michael second-guess anything, feel uncomfortable, consider himself wrong or needing to apologise. When Ash corrected him, saying that I wasn't my twin, Michael apologised to *me*.

I told him it was OK, still unsure why his reaction to this was so repentant. Ash jibed him a little, trying to let him know that neither of us was offended, but he really felt like he'd over-stepped a line.

Lying in bed that night, we discussed Lorien's final words to me, her, us. I knew from that instant I was not solely here as his replacement; I was here because she loved me, and it made us both happy.

Through the Eyes of a Child

THE NEXT DAY I picked Mercy up from Mum and Dad's and waited on Elijah's return home so we could 'have the talk' with her, letting her know how life was going to be for all of us now that Daddy and I were officially together. Elijah ended up having to work this week after all, and I found myself daydreaming a little, staring out the kitchen window, fully revelling in the anticipation of his arrival. When I heard his key in the door, my heart started hammering. "Hey Babe," he said, putting his bag down and coming into the kitchen. "Where's Merce?"

"Out the back in the garden." He took my face in his hands and ran his thumbs slowly over my cheeks. "Did you have a good day?"

"Just the usual. How was yours?"

"Just the usual," he said and smiled at me.

"Do I get a kiss?"

"Of course." He leant down and kissed me softly, my face still in his hands. I wended my arms around him and ran them slowly over his shoulders, playing down his muscular back appreciatively. I ended up drawing back, grinning at him. "What Babe?"

"Your goatee, it tickles." He laughed,

"Want me to shave it off?"

"I'll get used to it, let's try again." He kissed me again, deeper and more intimately, his soft lips parting to run his tongue against my own.

"OK now?" He asked, running his lips out to my ear.

"Uh huh, you'll always have to kiss me like that."

"Like what?" he teased.

"To take my breath away. I don't notice then." He chuckled and drew me to him, working his hands over me tenderly.

"Daddy!" Mercy called from the bathroom door when she saw him, and her little arms enveloped our legs from the sides.

"Hi Pumpkin," he said, picking her up and bringing her to our level for a family hug. She wrapped her arms around our necks, pulling our heads to hers. "Mummy and I need to talk to you, we have some news."

"Are you boyfriend and girlfriend now?"

"Yes," he said, putting her back on the ground. We looked at each other in surprise. How on earth had she managed to work out things had changed? "Do you know what that means and how things will be different now to how Mummy and I were before?"

"I think so," she said, taking the juice from me that I'd poured and going to sit at the table. We joined her. "You'll kiss now."

"We always did that," I reminded her.

"But now you'll do it on the lips."

"Yes, that's true. I'll also be sleeping in Daddy's room with him from now on."

"Do I have to knock before I come in?"

"Yes Bump."

"Why?" I looked at Elijah and smiled shyly before answering,

"Daddy and I might be kissing." She came and sat on my knee, pushing my face into Elijah's, instigating a kiss.

"There. See, I can be around when you kiss."

"It's a different kind of kissing Merce, one that's private. You still have to knock."

"OK Dad," she said. "Are you going to get married?" This one took me a little by surprise and I let Elijah field the answer; we hadn't spoken about it. We'd only been together a few days and wasn't really a priority to our little world.

"One day," he answered simply.

"Can I be the flower girl?"

"Of course, Sweetie," I told her and gave her a kiss.

"Am I going to get a little brother or sister?"

"One day," Elijah answered again.

"That's your answer to everything Dad!" she exclaimed. Elijah laughed and kissed her too. We also hadn't seriously spoken about having children, not since our playful deal for five years down the track. We both did want more kids though, I knew that much.

"So, tell us how you feel about this Mercy?" Elijah prompted. As calm as she appeared, there must have been some questions she'd need to ask.

"It makes me happy," she answered.

"How does it make you happy?"

"My Mum and Dad are now really my Mum and Dad and we'll always be together."

"That would have been the case anyway Merce," I reminded her.

"But now there'll never be anyone else new, will there?"

"No Honey, that's right, it will always be just us now. And maybe a little brother or sister down the track for you too," Elijah said and ran his hand over her curly brown locks; so much like her father's, so much like his own.

"So now you are in love with Mum, aren't you?" she asked, reminding him of the conversation we'd had about this previously.

"Yes Merce and I have been for a long time."

"So why weren't you together before?" Elijah looked at me and we both laughed. How could you explain to a nearly six year old that we were acting less mature than she was? Our fear of rejection had been the cause of the time wastage we were now making up for.

"Things take a little more time when you're an adult," Elijah lied to her. Neither of us intended to tell her how stupid we'd been. Maybe stupid was the wrong word, but 'cautious' certainly wasn't.

"Is there anything else you want to ask Merce?" I said.

"No Mum, not at the moment."

"Well, you come to me or Dad if you have any questions. And Bump," I stopped her as she went to leave the room.

"Yes Mum?"

"If anyone has anything to say to you at school about this, you let me or Dad know OK?"

"OK Mum, but talking about your parents at school is only for babies." How silly of me, I'd forgotten! She rolled her eyes at me and took to the stairs. Elijah grinned, and then came to me, sealing the conversation with a kiss.

I felt so weird, like I was seventeen years old and about to board the train with Elijah again, for the first time. If he caught my eye watching TV, I'd blush, a kiss and cuddle in the kitchen would have me reaching for a glass of water. I just couldn't seem to turn myself off. Everything was fantastic in the bedroom though. When there, we were intimately connected, and I held no concerns whatsoever. It was out of the bedroom that was becoming an issue for me. Issue may be a little strong, but I couldn't help myself carrying on like some mid-teen half-wit. I would feel myself shaking, my palms sweating, my voice faltering. I had known this man for twelve years but the force of his chemistry reacting with mine was so strong. I could imagine it knocking me off my feet in time. Of course, he picked up on it, and quickly.

The next day he caught me coming out of his room, our room now, sweeping me into his arms. "God, I love coming home these days," he murmured, leaning down to kiss me softly. Bam - there went the old heart again. He drew back, smiling. "What have you been up to in there? I hope no one else was involved," he added with a cheeky grin. All I could do was blush and shake my head before lowering it. "What's up Babe? Your heart's palpitating." He now looked concerned, taking my hot face in his hands, peering into my eyes. This of course made my heart race faster and deepened the colour to my cheeks. "Honey?"

"It's nothing Elijah, I'm just glad to see you."

"Come with me," he said and led me back into the bedroom. He sat on the bed and drew me onto his knee, kissing me again. It was a few minutes before he spoke.

I smiled down at him and his lips found the base of my throat, coursing their softness around it, suckling lightly with his tongue. "Where's Merce?" he breathed.

"In her room."

"Too early for a little romp hey?" he asked and laughed quietly, his mouth now working into the V of my shirt.

"She knows to knock," I exhaled. He chuckled lowly before sinking us down on the bed.

"I can live with just this for now." And then he kissed me deeply and I tried to contain a groan. Oh God, what he did to me.

A few minutes later he drew back and looked into my eyes. I was panting, my body a furnace. "Honey?" he asked again.

"I'm OK," I said, sitting up.

"You don't look OK, you're burning up." Just to prove him right, another flush heated my face. This wasn't something I wanted to talk to him about though; I was embarrassed at my stupid reactions. I supposed in due time it would subside and I would re-find my footing. He placed his palm on my forehead; it was refreshingly cool. I closed my eyes.

He stole another kiss whilst I sat there like that and broke apart only when we heard Mercy in the adjoining bathroom, followed by a knock. "Come in Mercy," I called, and moved off Elijah's lap, sitting next to him on the bed.

"Hi Daddy!" she called and clambered into the space I'd just vacated.

"Hi Pumpkin, got a kiss for me?" She laid a big one on his cheek. "Thanks Bump, that's the best kiss I've had all day!" He looked at me over the top of her head and winked. I smiled and got up, wanting to leave them to it, wanting to calm myself down a little. I headed for the kitchen. Mercy came down a few minutes later.

"Where's Dad?" I asked.

"He's just changing out of his Doctor's costume." I laughed. He wore a suit to work, and because of his profession, she had no doubt put two and two together in her own head, referring to it now as his Doctor's costume. I got untold joy from our girl.

Elijah came down shortly after. He lifted the pot lids and sniffed, "That smells great Babe," and then I was folded back into his arms. "Hmmm, but this smells better... Mind if I have a taste?" He didn't wait on my answer, choosing to feast on my neck and ear lobe. Seconds later, he was drawing back again. "Seriously Ash, are you going through early menopause?" he asked cheekily. I pulled his face back to mine and kissed him lightly before going to stir the casserole. He didn't push any further.

Over dinner, he asked what our plans were for the weekend. "Nothing in particular Honey. Mercy is going to Mum and Dad's on Saturday for the night. Other than that, it's just you and me." He grinned at me and said not to make any plans, not one, none, zip. I laughed and told him OK. He obviously had something in store for Saturday night. Not that we wouldn't make love until then, but I couldn't wait. My body started to heat again, just at the thought of it.

When Saturday rolled around, Elijah took Mercy to Mum's just after lunch, telling me to get dressed whilst he was out. I still wasn't aware of his plans for this evening and asked what kind of clothes to put on. Something sexy was his response. I assumed we weren't leaving the house...

When they'd left, I ran upstairs and started ransacking Elijah's wardrobe. If he wanted something sexy, I thought I'd wear what I considered sexy... on him. I pulled out one of his clean gym shirts and the sheer black fishnet undies I'd bought him for Christmas. He would actually love this too no doubt, as the undies left nothing to the imagination and my boobs were nearly falling out the sides of his gym shirt. I was sure he'd get my point.

Not wanting to disappoint him too much though, or make it too much of a joke, I also pulled out a low-cut, short black dress and my black strappy heels. At least these would bring me closer to his height.

I didn't know what to do with myself until he got home, knowing it would be at least another fifteen to twenty minutes. I decided the fill the spa bath for later and leave it running, keeping it hot until we wanted to use it.

Elijah got home earlier than I expected and several minutes later, with the spa filled and running, I turned to see him leaning against the doorframe, a smile on his lips. I jumped slightly which made him laugh. "Well, isn't this a lovely welcome home," he said and crossed the floor to where I was still standing like a mannequin. "Not quite what I was referring to, but exquisite all the same." He looked down into my eyes as he pulled the front of the gym shirt together within his closed fist, centring it between my now bare breasts. He pressed his chest up against me and allowed the coarseness of his shirt to work against me. Within seconds, my nipples were stiff and wanting his touch. "Oh Babe," he purred and leant down to kiss me. My hands found their way into his hair and if I had pressed myself against him any further, I would have been standing behind him. He graduated down my body, ending up on his knees in front of me where he teased and tormented with his lips and mouth, my hands holding his head against me. "God, you've got great nipples Babe," he murmured, not breaking the oral ministrations for even a minor pause. His free hand snaked up my thigh and came to rest between them, grazing across their centre, drawing the rest of my body into the moment.

"Oh Honey," I exhaled, "I'll have to sit down..." My legs were starting to shake. He chuckled and looked up at me, his fingers still seeking the source of my heat. Pulling me forward he kissed me, working his tongue over and through the fishnet barrier, finally standing and holding me against him.

"What you do to me Babe," he sighed into my ear. "Were you getting in?" he then asked in reference to the filled and running spa.

"No, I put it on for later."

"I wasn't going to touch you like this until *much* later, but the sight of you when I came into the bathroom made it too much to bear." I laughed quietly, knowing the reaction he'd have to me in his clothes - if you could call them clothes... He sidled his hands in under the straps of his gym shirt and glided them slowly over my shoulders. The neck hole was so large on me he had no trouble slipping it down over my body and it pooled onto the floor. It was a green light for me, and my fingers worked at the base of his T-shirt, dragging it up his body. Neither of us broke the slow deep kiss that followed, and the T-Shirt ended up surrounding both of our faces, as it had nowhere else to go. We ended up breaking apart, laughing, and I was then able to pull it free from him. The mirth dissipated as quickly as it bubbled up and my lips found his again as we worked off each other's bottoms. I stepped into the spa and he followed, and there we stood, knee deep in the hot pulsing water for what seemed like eternity.

He took my face into his hands and the kisses slowed, with him finally drawing away and looking into my eyes. His eyes crinkled as he smiled his sunny smile at me, and he sat, drawing me in front of him. "I love you," he whispered into my ear before suckling at my nape, the blood coursing through my system now.

"I love you more," I told him.

"It's not possible Babe," he crooned.

It was with much embarrassment that he roused me at some later stage. I had managed to fall asleep on him. When I realised where I was, I turned to him and smiled shyly. "I'd have hoped the feel and sight of my naked body would have many reactions on you, but didn't expect falling asleep would be one," he teased.

"I'm at total peace Honey." He laughed and we got out of the spa.

"Let me do that," he said and took the towel from me, patting me dry from head to toe. Some areas seemed to be more carefully and dextrously dried off than others...

Back in the bedroom, he noted the dress I'd laid out and asked me what I wanted him to wear. "Are we on a date?" I asked.

"Yes, but we're having it here, at home."

"Well then, what you have on will be more than sufficient," I said and pulled the towel from around his hips, leaving him standing there naked in front of me.

"Might be a bit risky in the kitchen Babe," he laughed. I rolled my eyes at him in mock disappointment and went into his drawers to grab a pair of silk boxers.

"Will this do?" I asked.

"Won't you be overdressed?"

"Does it matter?"

"Nope." He dragged the boxers on and left me to dress.

When I came downstairs, he had put some music on in the background and was busy opening parcels in the kitchen. "I cheated," he said when I peered into the containers he was sorting through.

"Isn't it a bit early for dinner Honey?"

"I'm just getting set up for when we want to eat. Take a seat Babe; I'll only be a few minutes."

I headed for the verandah, assuming we'd be sitting and talking for much of the afternoon, and he joined me shortly after, handing me a glass of wine. I took a sip and looked at him. He was smiling at me and I found myself blushing. I felt uncomfortable actually, and couldn't place why. Possibly because I was all dolled up and it was the middle of the afternoon? Maybe because I knew what we'd be doing later, and this set my body temperature soaring. He leant in and kissed me, and I knew he could feel the reservation in my lips. "Babe?" he questioned.

"Nothing," I said and lowered my eyes before taking another sip.

"This has been going on all week Ash, what's happening in that lovely head of yours?" He stopped and his face fell a little. "You're not having second thoughts, are you?"

"Oh no Honey, nothing like that. I'm just... just... I don't know how to put it into words..."

"Try," he said and grinned at me over his glass. "Wait, hold that thought." He darted back inside and came out with a bowl of strawberries. "Let me loosen those lips first," he said and licked his own. Pulling a plump strawberry from the bowl, he placed it in between his teeth, waggling it at me. I laughed and met him halfway, biting on the fruit, which ended up being shared between us, chewing, kissing, swallowing. It was a weird but pleasant sensation.

He drew back and licked the juice from his chin, leering at me. "Great strawberries." I agreed with him. "You've got juice on your chin," he said and leant in to lick it from me, resulting in the next deep kiss.

"That there is the problem," I admitted when it ended.

"What?" he asked in true confusion, "Me kissing you?"

"Sort of. I feel like a kid again when I'm with you Elijah. When we're making love it's all fine and good, but when we're just having a kiss and a cuddle, or sitting there doing absolutely nothing, your gaze catches me and my heart races, my palms start sweating... It's embarrassing..."

"So, it's a turn-on kind of thing?"

"Most definitely," I said and lowered my eyes again, feeling the traitorous heat course through my cheeks.

"Cool," he said.

"It's not cool!" I said, laughing. "It's horrible."

"Not from where I'm sitting. I think it's great. And to think I was worried you had changed your mind."

"I'd never change my mind, Darling."

"Darling?"

"Hmmm," I agreed and moved onto his lap. He dipped me backward and kissed me in full fervour. My veins were alight with shooting energy and the kiss went on and on... His hardness became apparent beneath me and he worked me further into his lap, into his embrace, finally pulling back and gasping for air.

"Fuck Ash, God..."

"What Honey?"

"I just want you all the time and in so many ways."

"I can tell," I said, wriggling on his lap.

"A pair of boxers doesn't provide much of a barrier hey?"

"No."

He held me like that until our glasses were empty and I got up to let him inside. He came back with an ice bucket this time and I reclaimed my former position on his lap. He'd also put on a pair of jeans. "Hey?" I argued.

"I needed a bit more covering. They'll be off again later..." That they were. Tonight was to take us in new directions.

Setting the Pace

I SAT ON THE BED brushing my hair, waiting for Elijah to come out of the bathroom. I felt a little stupid having my pyjamas on, but was feeling shy all over again and my blood pressure must have been through the roof. I was doing my best to calm myself down, but it wasn't working all that well. When he walked out of the bathroom stark naked, I lowered my face. I could feel this blush rush into my cheeks like a well-poured glass of red wine. "This won't do," he tsked at me, then smiled widely when he saw my face. "Oh Babe, I love the scarlet colouring…" He took my hands and I stood, allowing him the quick task of stripping off my pyjamas. He sighed against me, taking me into his arms. "Do you know," he started, working his lips at my throat, "when you blush, it goes all the way down to your chest?" His mouth trailed down the heated path, better emphasising his point. He circled his tongue gently over one nipple and then the other, chuckling.

"Stop it!" I said and clipped him over the shoulder.

"Never," he mumbled and lowered me to the bed, his fingers tracing lightly over my eager torso. "Do you want to tell me where your erogenous zones are?"

"Wouldn't you rather find them yourself?"

"I know of one already..." He laid my arms above my head and trickled his fingers lightly across my armpit, watching my face for the ensuing reaction. "Am I right?" he asked cheekily. I opened my eyes and nodded slowly, not wanting him to stop. He nuzzled down, grazing his lips over one, purring against me. "This is good?"

"Oh yes Honey."

"You're the first woman I've known who's liked this, or has admitted it."

"Have you tried before?"

"Yes, and was stopped."

"Stupid girls." He smiled down at me and lowered his face to draw a straining nipple into his hot mouth.

“Your boobs are a lot bigger than I remember,” he said, and I laughed. “What's so funny?”

“Hearing a doctor say ‘boobs’.” He smiled down at me.

“Sorry Ma'am, these mammaries are simply outstanding.” We laughed together, and when the amusement passed, he lowered his mouth back to my outstanding mammaries. "So, what else do you like?" he mumbled.

"What you're doing right now is great," I said, and he chuckled against me, drawing me out between his lips. "They were always sensitive -"

"I remember," he interrupted.

"But since having Mercy they're out of control."

"Do you like them being bitten?"

"Not too hard."

"How's this?" he mumbled, and nibbled lightly, sending a spark right through me.

"You've had a lot of experience?" I breathed.

"No more than you have." He drew back from me, caressing his fingers over my jaw.

"So, tell me what *you* like," I asked.

"Wouldn't you rather find that out yourself?" he teased, duplicating my earlier response.

"I certainly don't have a problem with it, but I'm always open for advice."

"I have quite a few..."

"I'm listening."

"My lower back just above my bum, between my thighs, my pelvis, my nipples, the back of my sac..." I couldn't help but laugh at that one.

"Roll on your side Honey." He rolled so he was facing me, and I drew my fingers lightly across his lower back, down over his tight rear and back again. He shuddered slightly and smiled. "There?"

"Hmmm hmm," he mumbled and closed his eyes. I worked between his legs, moving in from the front so he was within easier reach as I eased my hand between his thighs, taking care of that area and the back of his sac at the same time. His erection became stone.

"I can see the results, no need to have to ask you." He opened his eyes and smiled lazily at me before looking down. "Hello Mr Winky," I said and leant down to give it a kiss.

"Shit Ash."

"What lover?" He didn't answer any further. I avoided his main areas of tumult and worked my fingers up to his pelvis, grazing them over him lightly as he rolled onto his back again. He spasmed against my tickles and grabbed my hand, stopping me.

"Don't, or it'll be all over."

"So?" He smiled in response, rolling on top of me and pinning my hands down. "Aren't I allowed to pleasure you?"

"Pleasure me?" he laughed.

"Arouse you?" I suggested. "Get you off, go down on you..." He interrupted me,

"I would never stop you."

"You just did."

"I did, didn't I?" he whispered against my ear, his breathy exhalation driving me insane. "And how do I arouse you Babe? Hmmm?" He lowered his face, so it was barely a centimetre from mine, looking directly into my eyes. I felt my heart lurch.

"You're going to give me a heart attack Elijah, stop looking at me like that..."

"I know how to resuscitate..." he said and leant down to kiss me.

His lips worked softly then parted mine with more force, claiming my mouth and breath as his own as he flicked and eased his tongue within my depths. It was a soulful, deep kiss and I got lost in it, not knowing where I was for a few moments. When he drew back eventually, I groaned in disappointment. "You liked that?"

"Kiss me again Elijah, just like that..."

He did, rolling me on top of him, locking me against him with his powerful arms. I found myself writhing lightly, unable to control my flaming lust any longer. "I want you to lick me with that magnificent tongue of yours... I don't care what happens." He smiled up at me,

"It *will* happen, I'm not kidding about that you know."

"Christ, what a turn on, just knowing that... I have an idea," I said and sidled down him, lying between his splayed thighs. "How about I take care of you first? It may relieve the pressure a little..." I took him into my mouth, running my fingers lightly over his pelvis.

"Fuck Ash," he moaned, and his fingers were in my hair, easing through the tresses. He didn't stop me this time.

It didn't take long, we were both like first-timers again, the new relationship finding its own desperate groove. "Honey..." he said, worry in his voice. I wasn't concerned about drawing back from him. I loved this man, and his fluid was something I would have in my body, regardless of which way it travelled there. "Honey... stop... Babe!" His cry became desperate and seconds later was trying to back away from me, his fingers tightening in my hair as he threw his head back, straining under his own desire not to erupt. I didn't give him a choice though. His release burnt through him in a hip-thrusting, groaning completion, pulling me up to him immediately to kiss me deeply. My face grew hot.

"How can you be blushing after what you just did to me?" he asked quietly, his mouth working around the edge of my ear before sliding his tongue in, making me moan softly. "You're a treasure Babe; I love you so much…"

"I love you too Honey."

I lay there for a few minutes in his arms. Our kisses were slow and deep - lazy in their intent. "Want me to do this to you Babe?" he purred, working his tongue into my mouth, capturing my lips wholly within his own. He circled the tip of his tongue over mine rapidly for a few moments, before drawing my lips back into his mouth, letting them go with a smacking noise. After a few repetitions of this simulated oral dance, he prompted me again. "Hmmm? You want this Babe?"

"Oh God Elijah, yes I do…" I sighed and he chuckled before graduating down my body.

He formed a perfect seal, his lips to my own, gently swiping the flat of his tongue over and through me. Opening me... readying me...

"Honey..." I soon called to him, letting him know this was nearly over for me.

"Hmmm?" The vibration of his unspoken question sent a pulse right through my body. He moved down slightly to dip into me, taking the building urge back to an erotic tease for the moment.

My fingers worked into his hair, pulling him even closer. His hands skimmed down and sensuously stroked my inner thighs, moving finally to meet his lips, holding me open before him.

I fought it, glorying in his ministrations, not wanting it to be over. And finally, I shuddered under him, each joint in my body separating and free floating in another realm before crashing back into place, rocking my very being. I felt only semi-conscious, and my world eddied around me as he slowed and soothed me, with his tongue now applying gentle caresses. I felt so alive.

He wended his way back up to me, his mouth fusing with my own. When he drew away from this blazoned kiss, he noticed I had tears on my cheeks. "Why are you crying Babe?' he asked softly. He wiped his thumbs across my face, trailing the tears out to a fine line.

"That was wonderful..." I breathed.

"Then why are you upset? I would never want to hurt you..."

"It's been a long time since I felt that good - I didn't even know I was crying. They're not sad tears; they were just keeping up with the flow from the rest of my body. I guess they got jealous and wanted their own emissions to be seen." He laughed loudly at this and took my face back into his hands.

"I love you Babe."

"I'm yours Honey. Did you manage to restrain yourself?"

"Your prior assistance did wonders. How can I ever repay you?" he asked cheekily. I rolled him onto his back and straddled him.

"This OK?" I asked and lowered myself over him, taking him in one stride.

"Oh God yes!" he groaned and held my hips, moving with me. I leant forward and kissed him, then played my tongue over his dimple, causing it to deepen. He smiled up at me and thrust with sudden solid force, taking my teasing grin back to the desirous expression to better accompany his change in pace. He held me down against him, allowing me to writhe into a fully vocal orgasm, every cell in my body beating time with my rapid heart. He sat up and folded his legs in underneath him, aligning me over his lap. One hand braced my lower back to hold me upright as the other dropped to circle against me, bringing me off again instantly, and he joined me.

With the urgency abated, he lowered me gently down and eased in and out a few more times before taking my nipple back into his mouth. I sighed and lay out-stretched, absorbing the love and intimacy I had found with this man. I didn't think it would ever be possible again at this level. "I love you Honey," I whispered, my hands trekking over his back lightly. It felt wonderful to be able to share those words with another again.

"I love you Babe, God, so much it hurts." Then the need to speak vanished as our lips drew together in a magnetic field. We feasted on each other for the longest time.

He napped for a while and I leant up on one elbow, watching his face, letting my eyes sweep down over his gorgeous frame. He had a small treasure trail of hair from beneath his navel, which grew into the line of his pubes. I leant down and licked it gently, finalising the act by lapping at his navel. He started to stir, to harden, although still not awake. I drew back and smiled down at my lover, my best friend. Mr Winky had a renewed interest, and I was curious as to how hard I could actually get him without touching it, and not waking Elijah in the process.

I eased my finger up one side of his pelvis, crossing over his flat stomach and down the other side. His pelvic muscles jumped and bunched under my gentle touch and the reaction was rewarding. It was hard to remain silent; I wanted to giggle. It then started to move under its own volition, and I sat back, startled. I looked at Elijah and he was grinning at me, now awake. "You made it do that?" I asked. He nodded and motioned back down, My Winky still moving in a slow dance. "How do you do that? Are you flexing or something?" I asked, not sure how he'd managed it.

"It *is* a muscle Babe," he said, "although it's hard to explain it to you when you don't have one of your own."

"Oh yes I do," I reminded him and took him into my mouth. Seconds later, he had me straddled over his face in a lover's knot.

Satisfied for the moment we lay there together, soft caresses and lips tendering our now calmer emotions. I eventually started to laugh. "Funny?" he asked, sitting up a little. I lay my head to his chest and toyed with the curls at my eye level, his fingers working a similar melody through my hair. He brushed it from my forehead and pressed his lips to my brow tenderly.

"I asked Lorien about that once, but he didn't answer me."

"Unusual for him!"

"Most definitely." He laughed with me.

"Can I ask you some personal questions Ash?"

"Of course, Honey."

"Did you lose your virginity the weekend you spent with Lorien at Rondo?"

"Yes."

"That was quite some time after you started going out."

"Not really, it was just after you both turned seventeen. Just a few weeks."

"If we hadn't broken up, do you think you would have been ready to have had sex with me by then?"

"I don't like talking about that Elijah. I felt so guilty for such a long time..."

"None of that matters now Honey, and I am getting to something with this."

"Oh, OK. Ahhh, I think it may have been well before your birthday. Like probably over the Christmas holidays. You really got to me that night in the pool. I was considering it even then but knew I wasn't *quite* ready."

"Bummer," he chuckled, and I waited for him to continue. "Lorien had already had sex."

"I know."

"I hadn't."

"What?" I asked, unable to believe it.

"Keren and I lost ours together." I sat up and faced him.

"Well, that explains a few things I guess."

"Like why we tried for so long to get things back on track?"

"Yes, and also why you went there again so many years later."

"They say that your first one always has a connection."

"It better not happen again!" I warned. He laughed,

"It won't. I wanted you then too, and you know that don't you?"

"I knew Keren was jealous of me but no, I didn't know that, not back then."

"You managed to capture both Standish twins' hearts with the innocent flick of your ponytail Babe." He was being playful, but this hurt.

"I feel even worse now Elijah."

"Don't Ash. I didn't mean for you to feel that way." He drew me back down to him, kissing me, dissolving all of my concerns. It worked a treat. "This is all that matters now," he whispered.

"Yes."

"Hmm, I'm hungry again," he purred and looked at me intently, his eyes flashing as he wended his way back down my body. I laughed quietly and was silenced as soon as his tongue found the small, but eager playground awaiting him.

We had found our way home again…

THE END

EPILOGUE

WE MARRIED SIX MONTHS LATER on the eighteenth of April, my wedding anniversary to Lorien. This was Elijah's idea and although I thought it strange at first, came to understand his reasoning, holding them both close to me by the choice of the date. It was also Elijah's idea to marry through a small ceremony at the office of Births, Deaths, and Marriages. Mercy was our flower girl and Bree, Simon, Michael and Glen came as our witnesses. We dressed simply, me in the same green dress I wore to Cyndi and Frankie's wedding, slightly altered, and Elijah in a dark grey suit. Our parents weren't there, but both sets were quietly acceptant, making our transition as easy as possible. They knew of the love we had for each other, regardless of it having blossomed into something more, and were of course happy for us both.

Our son was due in August and we were already referring to him as Thomas. His middle name would come as no surprise to you either; it was of course, Lorien. Thomas Lorien Standish's arrival was eagerly anticipated by his big sister, nearing seven. The 'talk' was then taken care of by her doctor-father without going into too much detail. She didn't ask any further and we were happy for another year or two to pass before the final questions were answered as to how exactly Thomas had been put in my stomach.

We planned on having more children, many more in fact, and I made my choice to be wife and mother, finally handing in my resignation at Sommersett High. They were going to keep me on as a casual, relieving when staff were sick or wanted to take their annual leave. It was a great arrangement and I fell into the routine gladly.

We weren't the only ones expecting. Bree was due to give birth in July, a fact that had all four of them ecstatic. Both Glen and Michael had donated their sperm, so without a DNA test there was no telling who the father was. Neither of them wanted to know, nor did Simon and Bree. Mum and Dad would raise the little girl with Michael and Glen being her uncles. It had worked out wonderfully and there was talk of more children down the road. Elijah and I were so happy for them, not to mention Mercy getting what she referred to as her cousin, not that they shared a bloodline.

It was my last day of school and I picked Mercy up and walked her home. Today's method of transport was to skip. "Today was your last day of school?" she asked, slowing to my pace and taking my hand as we crossed the road.

"Yes Bump."

"Lucky!" she said and made a face.

"I thought you liked school?"

"I do, but you're still a big lucky." I smiled down at her. "Am I going to Grandma and Grandpa's this afternoon?"

"Yes, as soon as you change."

"We're going to the dinosaur park this weekend." She meant the Australian Reptile Park at Somersby on the Central Coast. "Are you and Dad coming?"

"No Merce, it's a special trip just for you, Grandma and Grandpa." She grinned at me, a few spaces in her mouth just sprouting the newest of her teeth.

Mum and Dad usually had Mercy two weekends of the month, which was something all of them enjoyed. They loved to spoil her and she in turn loved to be spoilt. On the weekends we had her at home we usually went to Michael's, or all of them would come over. However, on the weekends we didn't have Mercy, Saturday night was always date night and we looked forward to it all week.

It was my turn to cook this Saturday and I was pulling the veal from the freezer to defrost when Elijah came home. "What's on the menu for tomorrow night?" he asked, taking me into his arms and kissing me deeply, not allowing me time to answer.

"Veal," I managed to get out eventually.

"Not tongue?" he asked, running his out to my ear, his fingers working at the buttons on my shirt.

"No, let's have that tonight," I breathed. He chuckled against me, unzipping my skirt at the rear, letting it fall to the ground.

"How was your last day?" he mumbled, unhooking my bra as I worked off his pants. We were the only two people I knew who could have a normal conversation during the onset to foreplay.

"Fine," I said, drawing his shirt down over his shoulders, adding it to the pile of clothing at our feet.

"Is Mercy at your parents?" I nodded and he smiled at me in a way to make my knees a little weak. "Are you going to put the nurse outfit on for me?"

"You've only just undressed me Honey," I laughed. His eyes roamed over my body hungrily before meeting mine again.

"Later…" he said and lowered me to the carpet. We made love right there on the dining room floor, for the first time that evening anyway.

* This is also dedicated to Dean, my Elijah - my first tentative steps to re-join the world of love became a stride, then a skip, a run, and now I fly. I thank you for shaking the dirt from my broken wings and giving me reason to soar above the plains again.

GLOSSARY OF AUSSIE SLANG

- Beating around the bush: to talk about non-important things, to avoid discussing the actual point.
- Blind: see 'write yourself off'. I was blind!
- Bloody: completely, entirely, truly, very, purely, damn. An adverbial mild expletive used to emphasise the word following it. Bloody brilliant! Bloody thief. Bloody good! Bloody bad! Bloody angry!
- Bludger: an idle or lazy person.
- Boardies: abbreviation of board-shorts. Knee length quick drying swim shorts, worn by all sexes, but predominantly males.
- Bolted: took off, moved with great speed.
- Busted: caught in the act, guilty.
- Chuck a sickie: to report into work as sick, when you are not, just to have the day off.
- Cop a ribbing: get teased.
- Curry favour: to try to make someone like you or notice you in order to get something that you want – used to show disapproval.
- Dog: rogue, rascal, scoundrel.
- Dolled up: to make an effort in your appearance, to dress up.
- Eyeing / Eyeing off / Eyeballing: checking out, considering, reviewing, estimating, sizing up.
- Factory outlet: a shop in which goods, especially surplus stock, are sold directly by the manufacturers at a discount.
- Footy: football. In NSW footy refers to NRL – rugby league.
- Full on: intense.

- Getting right into it/stuck into it: going hard, full fervour. Can also be to show any kind of enthusiasm.
- Go for it / for your life / for broke: an expression of encouragement. Can be also used with sarcastic undertones.
- Good on you: well done, congratulations. Can also be used in a derogatory/sarcastic sense, 'You broke the last plate? Good on you!'.
- Grog: alcohol.
- Half-arsed: not to a very high attempt or standard.
- Have a go: (at someone) to attack or criticise, or be verbally playful with.
- Hoon/ing: In Australia, traditionally a 'hoon' is a person who deliberately drives a vehicle in a reckless or dangerous manner. In the book instance, it plays on this scenario, and shows Elijah's wild side, being out of control in his private space.
- HSC: higher school certificate. The final exams taken by senior school students, before graduating high school.
- Hundreds and thousands: candy sprinkles.
- In the buff: naked.
- Kindy: Kindergarten. The first year of school in Australia, and follows pre-school.
- King Brown: King Brown snake. A very deadly species of snake in Australia.
- Knock yourself out: go for it, enjoy yourself, make great effort.
- Knocked back: refused. You can also knock back a beer, as in to drink.
- Lollies: candy.

- Mate: friend, buddy, pal. You can refer to anyone as 'mate', from your best friend to a complete stranger. However, 'a' mate, or 'my' mate, is someone you know and like.
- Mozzie: mosquito.
- Muck around: waste your time, fail to achieve anything.
- Off the hook: to escape from a difficult situation.
- Perving: checking someone out in an erotic way without their knowledge. Not considered overly crass or depraved, but girlfriends don't like to catch their boyfriends doing it, and vice versa.
- Pissed: see 'write yourself off'.
- Plastered: see 'write yourself off'.
- Plumber's crack: Derived from when a tradesperson, ie a plumber, is called out and when bending, their pants ride down at the back to reveal a portion of their crack above their beltline. It is not a flattering comment as a rule.
- Pretty much: just about.
- Quad: quadrangle. A rectangle-shaped outdoor courtyard, and in this instance, the school buildings occupy three of its sides.
- Quickeze: a chewable antacid tablet with the same properties as Pepto Bismal.
- Raw: to be naked. 'I stripped down to the raw'.
- Rear its ugly head: a problem of difficult situation arising.
- Schooner: 375 ml glass, usually containing beer.
- Sec: second. Not necessarily a literal meaning of one second. Hang on a sec could refer to as long as it takes, and definitely not only one second.
- Shush: quiet. Rhymes with push.

- Smart-arse: see dickhead. Smart-arsed (as in grin): a very wide grin, usually showing smugness, self-satisfaction, or inner humour.
- Smashed: see 'write yourself off'.
- Smidge: abbreviation of smidgen. A very small part.
- Stewing: to ponder or brood over something over a period of time.
- Sunnies: sunglasses.
- Take-away: take-out. Place where you buy a variety of ready-made meals such as hamburgers, fish and chips, chips (aka fries), plus an assortment of other deep-fried food. Carries ice creams and soft drinks (soda), chips (crisps) and often lollies (candy), milk, bread, etc. In the USA this would be a 7-11 or an AM/PM.
- Too (very) right: absolutely!
- Trackies: track suit pants. Sweatpants.
- Try-hard: persistent without hope of success.
- Wanker: see dickhead.
- Wet one: a juicy kiss.
- Write yourself off: get really drunk, also 'smashed', 'paro' (as in paralytic), 'wasted', 'maggoted', 'hammered', 'pissed', 'plastered', ' blind'.
- Wuss: weak, cowardly or timid.

This glossary of Australian slang was developed to assist non-Aussies with any terms they find confusing in the novel. This could range from another country having a different understanding of the same word or phrase, to not understanding the term whatsoever.

The glossary outlines the reference to how the slang is used in the novel and is not all encompassing of every use of the word or phrase in Australia. Slang can also vary from state to state, which is why immigrants who have lived here for decades still look at we born and bred Aussies in total confusion when we speak. Who can blame them! ☺

A special thank you to my dear friend Jennifer D McLaughlin, my USA mate and pen-pal since we were 13 years old. Her input into this glossary from an American perspective has been immeasurable. Thanks Jen!

About the author

Cassandra Ann Frew (nee Souter) was born on a July winter's night in Hornsby NSW. At the age of three, the family moved to a dairy farm outside Lismore NSW where she spent the majority of her childhood. At ten years old, the family moved to Lake Macquarie NSW.

Cassie found her love of romance writing during her high school years, and her first several 'novels' were hand-written exercise books, passed around for her friends to read.

Her career in business and administration has led her into further self-education including web design, IT, professional proofreading and editing, creative writing and industrial psychology. She is also a Justice of the Peace and a Civil Celebrant.

Her most rewarding achievement to date is what she has in common with the residents of the Standish household – their love of music, playing an instrument and the 80s. What a decade!

These stories belong to my readers, and to Ashlyn and the Standish family. This is how love should be, can be, is.

www.ingramcontent.com/pod-product-compliance
Lightning Source LLC
Chambersburg PA
CBHW031112030726
47496CB00002BA/507
9780648863588